Red ALERT
LYNNE CONNOLLY

ELLORA'S CAVE
ROMANTICA PUBLISHING

An Ellora's Cave Publication

www.ellorascave.com

Red Alert

ISBN 9781419963292
ALL RIGHTS RESERVED.
Red Alert Copyright © 2009 Lynne Connolly
Edited by Briana St. James.
Cover art by Syneca.

Electronic book publication March 2009
Trade paperback publication 2011

With the exception of quotes used in reviews, this book may not be reproduced or used in whole or in part by any means existing without written permission from the publisher, Ellora's Cave Publishing, Inc.® 1056 Home Avenue, Akron OH 44310-3502.

Warning: The unauthorized reproduction or distribution of this copyrighted work is illegal. Criminal copyright infringement, including infringement without monetary gain, is investigated by the FBI and is punishable by up to 5 years in federal prison and a fine of $250,000.
(http://www.fbi.gov/ipr/)

This book is a work of fiction and any resemblance to persons, living or dead, or places, events or locales is purely coincidental. The characters are productions of the author's imagination and used fictitiously.

RED ALERT
☙☙

Best wishes

Lynne Connolly

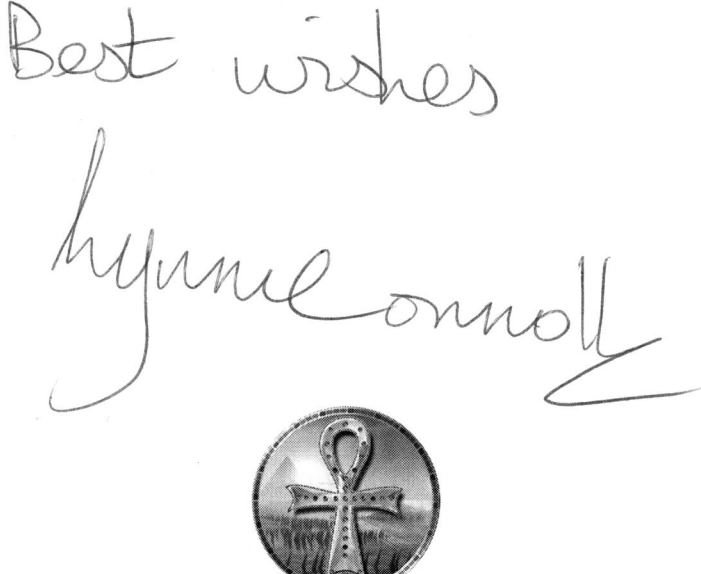

Dedication

To Chris and Elspeth, with thanks for much laughter and support.

Trademarks Acknowledgement

The author acknowledges the trademarked status and trademark owners of the following wordmarks mentioned in this work of fiction:

CNN News: Cable News Network, LP Turner Broadcasting System, Inc.

Lamborghini Gallardo Spyder: Automobili Lamborghini Holding S.p.A.

Chapter One

Tomorrow...

Megan stood when the nurse called her name, steeling herself for the ordeal ahead. The entrance doors to the unit opened with a click and cool air touched her cheek. She paused to look around, glad of any distraction.

A man entered the hospital ward. The breeze ruffled his dark hair and he turned back to close the door, unconsciously displaying the strength of his powerful body in the stacked muscle rippling the t-shirt under his worn leather jacket. Just how she liked her men, tall and strong.

Normally, that was. Today, all she could think about was sleep and getting some — soon. Even the results of today's test gave way to that desperate need. She hadn't slept the night through for weeks. She was about to hear that she was in for long bouts of painful treatment with a death sentence at the end — the fate she'd been dreading for weeks, but in her current state of exhaustion even that took second place to sleep. She dismissed the sexy stranger with a weary shrug and turned her attention to the nurse.

The nurse led her past a line of curtained cubicles into a private room. "The doctor will be with you in a moment," she snapped before exiting briskly.

What was her problem? Megan couldn't help her busy day. For her information, Megan's day would be much worse and she hadn't snapped at anybody. Yet.

The quiet in the room assaulted her senses after the bustle of the ward. Humanity in all its shuffling, smelly reality lay out there but here Megan felt sequestered, almost as if the room was soundproofed. Anxiety tightened her throat and she looked around for a distraction. Worry wouldn't help her now. She'd taken the tests, and once she had her results, she'd know what would happen next.

But here, in a room with a steel hospital bed, reality hit with sickening impact. They must have brought her here because they wanted her to stay, not just give her the results and tell her to come back later. That meant whatever was wrong with her was urgent, needing immediate treatment.

She said the words "brain tumor" aloud a few times, trying to get used to the idea. It still sent a shudder through her every time.

Biting her lip, Megan glanced up at the TV bolted to the wall above her head. Pictures flashed across the screen, an internal hospital channel showing reminders to eat your five portions of vegetables a day, images of a well-manicured hand slicing carrots into sticks, then green peppers into appetizing slices. She watched the silent images then glanced away. Food was the last thing on her mind.

Usually a patient was stuck with the hospital information channel but not here. A remote lay on the windowsill. Megan picked it up, flicked off the mute and turned to the next channel. CNN News.

"Can New York take this new pressure on its infrastructure?" the commentator said. "How long will it be before there's a collision in the sky and a bloody mess in the street?"

The camera switched to a view of a dragon in full flight. The creature must have a twenty-foot wingspan. Its great blue-green body gleamed in the weak spring sunshine, the hue shining iridescently as it beat its wings against the wind currents. So beautiful. So impossible, until yesterday.

Damn but she wished she could see one. The existence of people calling themselves Talents had blasted shock waves around the world. She'd seen the footage of the dragon in flight a dozen times since yesterday, when it was the central part of a documentary devoted to the subject. An amateur cameraman—if there was such a thing in New York where everybody seemed to be selling their private photos to one agency or another—shot the dragon in flight over Central Park. Other corroborative film and evidence followed, with the strong suggestion that these "creatures" were urban terrorists and spies.

So far, Talents hadn't spoken, although a spokesman said they would break their long silence later today. That kind of confirmed it. One solitary documentary couldn't persuade the world but when they came out and said they existed and they'd prove it, that would send the networks into orgasms of delight.

If Megan hadn't been dreaming about a particular dragon for the past couple of months, it might have come as more of a shock to her but she had her own concerns now, and they overshadowed everything else. The commentator continued. "A representative from STORM will be speaking to the public later today. The Society of Talented Officers Resisting Mistreatment has been with us for some time but until recently nobody knew the specific definition of Talents. It means dragons, vampires and other creatures who have lived among us for centuries. Little is yet known of these Talented beings although they have promised to reveal more in the interest of public awareness."

Megan slumped bonelessly to the bed, remote in hand.

She blinked and sat up when the door opened and a short, bespectacled doctor strode in, followed closely by two assistants, or maybe they were students. One big, red-haired man whose muscles bulged in a white jacket two sizes too small for him and an even bigger African-American, his head shaved.

My, they make students big these days. A note of alarm sounded in her head. Something was wrong here, though in her current state she couldn't begin to imagine what it was.

The doctor carried a brown folder that he handed off to one of his assistants without taking his attention away from her. "Miss Armstrong," he said, his professional smile revealing gleaming white teeth. "I'm Dr. Jones."

She didn't like his smile. Unctuous, she'd call it. Smarmy described it even better. His hair looked as if he hadn't spared the wet-look gel and his chiseled, handsome face didn't dispel her initial repulsion. "I understand you've been having bad dreams, Miss Armstrong."

"A bit more than that." She glanced up at the TV and remembered she held the remote in her hand. She muted it. "Sorry."

The doctor glanced at the screen. "Seeing if any more dragons have appeared?"

"I guess so." She shrugged. "Seen any in the ER?"

"Not that I know about." The doctor flashed her another smile, a wintry one this time. He placed his cool fingers on her temples. "Hmm. You feel a little warm." He reached over her head for the in-ear thermometer. "We've had the results of your CT scan and we're concerned about some abnormalities."

Here it came. Megan braced herself.

"You have a shadow at the back of your brain, Miss Armstrong." That explained the presence of the students. *An interesting case,* he would tell them. *Very unusual, worth studying.* They could cut her up afterward to examine what killed her. At least she wouldn't be there to see the blood. She'd never liked blood.

Shock flooded her body, tightening her throat and limbs. She fought it down. She needed information, a clear picture of what was happening inside her body. She fought out the word while she still could. "C-cancer?"

The doctor gave her a smile. God, she hated his smiles. She wanted to slap that smug grin off his face. "Not necessarily. Many of these abnormalities are benign. But it's pressing against your brain and probably causing the sleep difficulties. You're having nightmares, aren't you?"

"Vivid ones. Always the same."

"Tell me. There might be some clues there."

Megan opened her mind to the memories, allowed herself to see the picture that haunted her every night. "Tell me about your dreams."

"More dragons, I'm afraid." She flashed him an uncertain smile. "My dreams are always the same. A dragon shape-shifter, or that's what he says he is. He's restrained, tied down to a bed in a room with no windows. It's full of instruments. He's been tortured. Once I saw him with his arm laid open, the blood throbbing through his veins. He told me not to worry, he'd mend. But they did horrible things to him. He said for me to get in touch with his brother but it's a dream, so I knew that must be wrong."

"What was his brother's name?"

She hesitated, a warning note sounding in her head. *Don't tell them.* The voice sounded velvety, rough. Her imagination. It had to be. Sleep deprivation did some weird things. "You think it could be a reflection of my life? Wishful thinking? Only it isn't, is it?" She waved a hand at the TV screen. "I've been having these dreams for a long time, long before the news of STORM and the shape-shifters broke. Now I'm beginning to wonder. Is it real, or is it me? They're normal except for one thing, so this Ricardo could be telling the truth."

Dr. Jones' eyes opened wide and glanced at the African-American student. "Ricardo. That's his name?"

She mentally chastised herself for letting it slip. "Yes. He says he's a dragon but I never saw him change or shape-shift or whatever they call it. He says he can't."

Dr. Jones tsked. "They appear perfectly human until they change, then they become perfectly dragon, or whatever shape they have. It's disgusting when you see them shape-shift." He paused and glanced at one of the students, who moved a little farther away from him to stand in front of the door. "Mutants, you could call them."

She wouldn't call them "mutants". Different, yes but "mutant" made them sound perverted and she didn't think they were. A new minority, sure, but no more "mutant" than any other minority.

Didn't this doctor know a little too much about creatures who'd only revealed themselves in public yesterday? Her spine prickled in warning. There was definitely something wrong here. She wanted out of this quiet little room. She blinked and glanced at the door, past the beefy student who blocked her way.

"What's wrong?"

"N-nothing. I just got a weird feeling—you know, like somebody's walked over my grave."

Dr. Jones shot a glance over his shoulder and the student nearest the door, the red-haired one, left the room, closing the door carefully behind him.

Something crawled over her senses, making the hairs on the back of her neck prickle. This whole situation didn't feel right. "Why is it so important? If there's something in my brain causing these dreams, Ricardo doesn't exist, does he?" She should be glad. If the swelling in her brain caused the dreams, a shape-shifting dragon called Ricardo Gianetti wasn't lying on a table somewhere, tortured and suffering.

He exists.

She looked around for the source of the deep, night-dark voice, sure she didn't imagine it this time. "I'm sorry, did you say something?"

"No." Dr. Jones fixed her with a bland stare. "But I will now. We need you to stay in the hospital for a while. We'll do another scan and operate as soon as possible, then we'll know more."

"What will you do?"

"We'll schedule you for exploratory surgery, probably tomorrow." He checked his watch. "It's eleven a.m. now, which means we can operate any time from eleven tonight onward, after we've starved you and done the blood tests. I'll make sure you're on the list as a priority." He looked back up at her, blue eyes assessing, professional smile firmly in place. "It's too early to jump to conclusions, so try not to worry."

"Like you try not to think about elephants, once somebody's put the idea in your head?" What a stupid thing to say. Of course she'd worry. "And although I'm British, my work permits and health insurance are in order. In case you were wondering." Most medics would, once they realized she wasn't an American citizen but Dr. Jones hadn't even asked. Nor had the nurse who'd brought her here.

The doctor's smile didn't waver, neither did it broaden or become more natural. That was about as fake a smile as she'd ever seen. "Get some rest and take your mind off things. Think about dragons." With a jerk of his head he indicated the TV screen. It still flashed out pictures of that damn dragon flying across the screen.

"Would it be possible for me to make a phone call?" She'd switched her cell phone off, as instructed on her visit to the CT room. "Just to a friend to say where I am and ask him to bring some things in for me."

For the first time since he'd entered the room, the African-American spoke. "We'd rather you didn't use a cell phone. We'll arrange for a phone to be brought to you."

Her hackles rose a little more. Something was wrong here. All her instincts told her so. The doctor had been interested in her dream, which should be a symptom, a figment of her tumor-induced imagination, and he knew more about shape-shifters than he could have picked up from one sensation-seeking documentary.

You want out?

That voice again, in her head. No one could hear it but her. She was looking right at Dr. Jones and no trace of awareness crossed his face. *Who are you?*

A Talent. I know Ricardo. Don't listen to them. I can get you out of here.

He knew Ricardo? Ricardo wasn't a figment of her tortured imagination? *I don't understand.*

Choose. Now. Them or me?

Her skin, now prickling in goose bumps despite the stuffy heat in this room, told her the danger lay here, not with him. *You.*

Get out of the room. I'm just outside.

She slid off the bed, measuring the distance between her and the door. "Listen, the sleep clinic at the university only sent me here for a CT scan. How about I go back and show them the results and see what *they* think?"

"There's no need for that. Time is of the essence here, Miss Armstrong. You should rest."

The med student took a step toward her and she saw the syringe in his hand, its tip glinting wickedly in the weak sunlight filtering through the blinds.

Her goose bumps and prickling hairs became all-out terror. The two men who came in with Dr. Jones weren't students at all. They were muscle.

A scuffle outside the door made Dr. Jones turn his head toward the sound. Megan took the opportunity and lashed out with her foot. It struck with a satisfyingly solid *whump*, right in his solar plexus.

Dr. Jones doubled up, gasping for air. Well, the first step to getting out had been easy. But facing the "student" standing between her and the door, Megan knew he wouldn't be such a pushover. He stood, feet planted wide apart, knees slightly bent in a position she recognized from her weekly karate class.

Fuck.

She had to hurry, before Jones regained his breath. When she kicked up toward the guy's balls, intending the kick to be a feint for an upward hand jab, the bastard grabbed her ankle and threw her to the hard floor. The *very* hard floor. Her head hit the ground with a solidity Megan felt in every bone of her body, intensifying her ever-present headache, and she kicked back with her free foot, only to find it caught in the same meaty fist.

Pressure on the side of her pants alerted her to the syringe pressing into her flesh.

The door burst open, propelled by the heavy body of the red-haired "student". He fell next to her, already unconscious, his big body completely relaxed. One massive arm dropped over her body, dislodging the needle's trajectory.

A whirlwind followed the student, or what seemed like one to Megan. Dark, unruly hair was the only feature she was absolutely sure of topping a tall, powerful body with excellent reactions, because the intruder spun around on his heel, his arm already whipping out to take her attacker full across his face.

The open-handed slap knocked the African-American aside but he came back, one blow too superficial to cause any real damage. Just in time to receive the jackhammer punch under his chin that knocked his head back with a crunch that sounded fatal.

The student fell back against the room's only chair, collapsing it with the sound of breaking wood and the fleshier crunch of breaking bone.

It was the man she'd glimpsed earlier entering the main ward. Closer up he was even more lethally sexy. Arousal, totally unexpected, purred through her veins. "There are more outside, so the only way we're going to get out of here is through that window." He swept the room with an appraising glance and picked up the metal bedside table as if it weighed nothing at all, ignoring the clatter as the drawer fell out. "Close your eyes if you're scared of heights and hold on tight."

Lifting the table over his head, he swung it at the window. The sound of shattering glass rewarded him and he stepped forward to knock out the remaining jagged shards and drag the wrecked blind aside.

Was that a hand or a claw? A claw, she realized, as fingernails lengthened into talons and blue-green scales clustered over his hand and arm.

She gasped in shock. "Holy fuck!"

He turned to face her, scales gathering on his neck, his voice throaty and raw. "Climb up and hold on. Or stay here and face them."

Feet pounded up the hallway outside and at the same time, her rescuer completed his transformation into a man-sized dragon. Clothes ripped and tore, falling from his body, and she felt a sense of irritation in her mind that came from him. Irritation?

Yeah, I liked that jacket. Grab the pieces and let's go. Pick up your stuff too. Then put your arms around my neck. Or stay here and let them kill you.

His neck was much longer and greener than it had been a minute ago. When she heard the shout "In here!" from outside the room she knew this was decision time.

She grabbed her purse, pausing to sling it over her head so the strap crossed her body, and picked up the remains of the leather jacket, only remembering the folder containing her scan results at the last minute, then she obeyed him—it—and put her arms around his—its—neck.

When we're through the window, I'm going full size. Be prepared to hang on 'cuz we ain't coming down for a while.

I must be mad.

If you are, I am too. Ready?

As I'll ever be.

Her feet lifted off the ground just as she was beginning to wonder how the hell she could talk to somebody mind to mind. She closed her eyes and hung on.

Chapter Two

A blast of bright light made Megan open her eyes.

The dragon soared up toward the higher buildings before straightening out his flight. Then it grew larger, just as it said it would. She found herself sitting between the great wings of a beast that until a few months ago was supposed to be only a legend. Well here it was. A real live dragon.

It was maybe ten feet from head to tail, covered in blue-green scales, dry and warm, not slimy as she'd imagined when she'd seen one on the TV. Its broad back gave her good purchase, if she lowered her body so she lay on her bag, the remnants of his jacket and the manila envelope holding her scan results. Wind whipped past them and she spread her hands over the thick neck, clutching the folds of skin she found there. "Holy shit!"

Hold on tight. We're not going far.

"Yeah."

And by the way, dragon or man, I'm always masculine. Never an "it". Amusement rather than irritation colored his inner voice. Dark, smoky, sexy. And yes, very masculine.

That's better.

Can you tell everything I'm thinking?

No. Only your outer thoughts. I could go deeper but it would hurt you. We try not to pry.

My, you are civilized.

You have no idea, was his bitingly sarcastic reply.

This was a hell of a way to find out she wasn't afraid of heights.

They were higher now. He kept to about thirtieth-floor level, as far as she could guess. He headed for the heart of Manhattan. The oasis of Central Park sprawled below them, the lush green punctuated by sharp flashes as people took photos. Despite her fatigue, a sense of elation rose in her, purely from the flight. "We'll be on the news. Will they be able to make out my face?"

Try to speak telepathically. I can hear you better like that when we're airborne. No they won't make out your face, my body should obscure it. I'll just make sure.

A warm, soft feeling enveloped them, enclosing her in an unseen envelope, like atmospheric pressure around a plane. "What did you do?"

Fuzzed. Put a mental shield around us, so people see what they expect to see, not what's really here. How do you think we kept ourselves secret for so long?

New York looked different from the air but it was still the city Megan had fallen in love with the minute she stepped off the shuttle bus from the airport. Today was a cold, fresh spring day with a crisp blue sky, one of the best.

Where are you taking me?

To a parking garage. Then home.

My home?

Mine.

He descended so smoothly she hardly noticed until the flat, car-strewn rooftop loomed up under his great clawed feet. He extended them and landed as gently as an experienced pilot. Smoother.

She stayed on his back. The roof appeared to waver, and only then did vertigo hit. Closing her eyes, Megan willed her stomach to behave until she felt the movement cease.

You can get off me now.

Megan opened her eyes and found the ground a mere three feet away. After grabbing the jacket, bag and folder, she extended her legs down one side of the scaly body and slid down to the blessedly solid ground. She closed her eyes and took a few deep breaths, sheer relief pouring through her.

"You did well."

The deep, masculine voice sounded just like the one in her head. And a little like the one that cried out to her in her dreams. Shivering a little, she opened her eyes and confronted a tall, strong man. A tall, strong, completely nude man with a ripped body.

Although she tried really hard not to look down for, oh, perhaps a whole second, she couldn't resist any longer than that. Her gaze traveled down the broad chest, liberally sprinkled with curly black hair, the join-the-dots line from navel down to — oh yes.

Long, strong and semi-erect. Semi-erect? Startled, she jerked her attention up to his face, blinking.

He gave her a devastatingly wicked smile and took the two steps that separated them. "I can't lie to you when I'm naked, can I?"

"What, the violence turns you on? Or is it the transformation?" she managed, weak but still fighting. She badly wanted to go to him and just be held, be told it was all right, this was all a dream. But it wasn't.

"No, it was the lush brunette who's just spent the last twenty minutes snuggled against my back." He smiled wryly, a warm, genuine smile, so very different from the ones Dr. Jones had flashed at her a short time before. "I felt your body against my back, the way your breasts pressed against me and your crotch pushed me. That'll do it every time."

"You don't even know my name. It's Megan. Megan Armstrong."

"Well, Megan Armstrong, let me claim my reward for rescuing you."

Before she could step back, his arms went around her, pressing her close, and his mouth settled on hers.

Oh but he tasted delicious. Of warmth and strength and pure, rampant male. She relaxed and let him support her weight. She hadn't allowed herself any weaknesses for years but at the end of her rope, it felt so good to be held. This man took what he wanted and what he wanted, she gave.

His erection rose hard between them and he pushed into her stomach, letting her feel his hot, hard length against her and she moaned a little into their kiss. His mouth ravaged hers, and what started as a gentle kiss of greeting turned into something else when she parted her lips for him and gave him tacit control. His tongue plunged into her, sweeping her mouth in a taking that gave her no doubt of what he wanted from her. And at the moment, too tired to resist, too turned-on to care, she'd let him. He could push her down against the hood of the nearest car, drag her panties off her and help himself. Some human contact after days of being impersonally pushed and pulled around by doctors. Someone who saw her as more than a case to be studied.

He pulled back, just enough to kiss her softly, lips meeting in a tender introduction, watching her from under half-closed lids. Then took her mouth again, his groan vibrating the back of her throat and lower down. He finished with a brief, hard kiss before he pulled back and met her bemused stare, his dark eyes burning with lust.

She stared at him, more awake than she'd been in days. "Who are you?"

"Alessandro Gianetti."

His teeth flashed in a quick grin when he saw her shock. "Yes, Megan. I'm Alessandro Gianetti, the brother of the man you've been dreaming about. Call me Sandro."

"But that means—"

"It means none of this is your imagination. It means you're telepathic." His grin disappeared. "It means you're in danger."

"But—"

"Come on. If we stay here much longer, I'll be arrested for indecent exposure." He bent and swept up the remains of his jacket and the file containing her medical records.

Totally unconcerned about his nudity, he led the way to a flashy, bright yellow sports car. She followed a few paces behind, enjoying the view. A powerful back gave way to the sinfully curved ass. She still hummed with arousal, her panties damp with it for the first time in weeks. Months.

He squatted by the car and fumbled under it before pulling out a key. Instead of opening a door, he opened the trunk and dragged out a pair of jeans. He climbed into them and a shadow of regret crossed Megan's mind. Turning his head, he gave her a devilish grin. "We're going to have to work on teaching you to keep your thoughts private. Not that I don't enjoy hearing them." He grabbed a t-shirt and dragged it over his head, shaking out his shaggy mane of hair afterward.

He walked around to the front of the car and opened it, glancing back at her. "Let's get going."

"Where?"

"My place on the Upper East Side. I'll call some people from there."

"Who?"

"I'm a member of STORM."

Megan swallowed. The agency set up for Talents, previously covert, now splashed all over the news.

She must have hesitated too long, because he walked back to her and took her hands. "Megan, I promise I won't hurt you. What you've been dreaming about is real. Ricardo exists. It's likely the only thing causing your sleeplessness is the dreams."

The thought dawned slowly. "Could that really be true? The doctors said they'd found abnormalities. I thought it was all dreams."

"I think it is. But if you're dreaming about Ricardo, they'll want you."

"Who?"

"The IRDC."

"What?"

"The International Research and Development Clinic."

She frowned. "Don't they search for cures for rare diseases?"

He frowned, the dark brows harsh over his eyes. "They say they do. The rare diseases are usually Talents, and for cures, try extraction by extreme force. Someone from the IRDC kidnapped Ricardo and now they're using him as a human guinea-pig. They believe Talents are diseased or infected in some way and if they study them and extract the essence of their Talent, they can gift mankind. They are doomed to failure but it doesn't stop them trying. Bastards."

Sorrow pierced her. Ricardo existed, which meant he really was suffering.

Sandro's mouth tightened. "Yeah. They must be jamming the usual psi channels. But you've managed to get in touch with him, God knows how, and it's possible we could find him through you."

"How did you know where to find me?"

"I've been hunting Ricardo for weeks and I got a trace of him one day in a coffee-shop downtown. It came from you. Do you remember?" She shook her head. Her fatigue had destroyed everything except her determination to carry on, find out what was wrong with her and get better. "Now I want to get you home. Safe."

Safe sounded good.

Sometimes you just had to trust people and go with the flow. This was one of those times.

She turned to the car door Sandro was holding open for her but before she could move, pinwheels spun in her head and her sight turned black at the edges.

When Megan swayed, Sandro's instinct was to catch her in his arms and take her somewhere she could rest for a good long time. When he entered her mind, he felt the bone-deep fatigue that must have been with her for months. She had more stamina than she imagined. He knew strong men in their prime who would have caved in long before now.

He moved toward her but she blinked, shook her head, then grabbed the car door to swing herself inside the vehicle. He needed to get her away from here and into bed. She desperately needed rest. He'd do his best to ensure she got it.

He got in the driver's side and reached for the ignition. She didn't look up for a moment. He guessed she was making sure she masked her fatigue and his admiration for her went up a notch. When he gunned the engine she glared at him, the throaty sound of the vehicle jerking her out of her reverie.

"You don't like performance cars?"

She fidgeted in the bucket seat. "I'm not really a car person."

He'd guessed that already, otherwise the Gallardo Spyder would have impressed the fuck out of her.

Unfortunately, they hit rush hour on the streets. Fortunately, they hadn't far to go. He grabbed his cell phone off the dashboard and punched the speed dial button.

"STORM, how may I help you?"

Fuck, that was going to take some getting used to. No coded messages, just straight there. "It's Gianetti. Get me Kozak, will you?"

"Kozak." The vampire's deadpan tones didn't fool him for a minute. Too many vamps had suffered from the IRDC kidnappings for him to be as cold as he sounded.

"I got her. Only just in time. The IRDC were moving in. Arrange for damage control at the hospital and get the team to my apartment, will you?"

"When?"

"Now."

He cut off and glanced at Megan, nodding in her seat. Maybe a nap now would do her good but as he watched, she gasped and pulled herself awake. How many times had she done that over the last few weeks? Too many, he guessed. He swung out of the garage into a steady stream of traffic.

He revved the engine. Fucking traffic. His lips tightened. Spyders weren't designed to go at a five-mile-an-hour crawl. "Maybe we should have flown but I live discreetly. Nobody knows I'm a Talent at my apartment building and I want to keep it that way for now."

He drummed his fingers on the wheel, the thudding distracting him just enough to keep his concentration sharp.

"You don't like waiting, do you?" She sat back, eyes still wide. He knew she was forcing them open, just to stay awake.

"Nope." He drummed some more. "Never have." The traffic moved and he released the handbrake only to reapply it when they gained all of twenty yards. "Not in all my many years have I learned patience."

"Am I allowed to ask how old you are?"

He grinned. "Four hundred and fifty-two."

His age impressed her more than the Spyder. She blinked and stared at him with definite interest. Good. "Wow. Really? Did you see the French Revolution?"

"Closer than I wanted to." He glanced at her, to see her eyes sparkling and a broad smile wreathing her face. "You're a history buff? You want me as your project?" He wouldn't object to that. He inched forward some more, growling when the lights changed back to red.

She met his gaze unguardedly and he felt a tingle from the contact. An entirely pleasurable one. "If you don't mind. You're going to ask me tons of questions, so it's only fair, isn't it?"

Tons. He loved that. He hadn't heard an English accent for a while outside the TV and he'd forgotten how sexy it could be. "You don't seem so tired now. Does history do that to you?"

"Amongst other things. I'm an archivist, a librarian, and it's the archivist's dream to find something nobody was aware of before, something that's been lurking on a shelf just waiting to be discovered. A new Mozart concerto or a Leonardo drawing."

He laughed at that. "I'm not in their league, *cara*. I'm just a humble witness."

"Humble? You?" Her banter delighted him. Very few people did that with him these days. He was too old, too high-ranking for people to imagine he had a sense of humor.

"Yeah, sure." At last the lights changed and he could move on. He gunned the engine from sheer frustration when the car in front of him stalled.

"Is this a *very* powerful car?"

He glanced at her to see if she was joking. Her guileless expression told him she really didn't know. "It's a Lamborghini Gallardo Spyder." No glimmer of recognition crossed her face and he sighed. He still found her sexy, despite her complete lack of knowledge of decent transport. He was a sad man. "This car is an animal. It's not subtle but the raw power is awesome."

"Oh. A substitute phallus."

He gave a sharp bark of laughter. What could he say to that? Anything would be superfluous or flippant or stupid. He didn't need a substitute phallus. What he needed was a woman. This woman. From the moment he'd felt her soft body against his back he wanted her.

"So how come you're bigger as a dragon?"

"How come water expands when it becomes ice?"

"Oh." It was a bit more complicated than that but it served as an explanation. His body mass spread when he became a dragon, and over the years he'd learned how to expand and contract within the limits his body allowed.

He turned into the stream of traffic filtering into his side of the park. From there at least they kept moving until they reached his building, where he swung into an underground car lot. He'd have to take the Spyder out to the country soon. Driving it from one car lot to another was no way to treat a car like this.

After doing his usual mental scan, second nature to him, he exited the car. Megan swayed as she got out but only for a second or two. Her jaw clenched and she lifted her chin. "Which way?"

He wanted to pick her up and carry her. But she wouldn't accept his help, not her. Too gutsy to appear needy. So he moved toward the elevators, walking slower than usual and trying to make the pace seem normal for him. Difficult but not impossible.

He let her precede him into the elevator then got out his keycard. At her quizzical look he explained, "I live in the penthouse."

"The penthouse?" She smiled, true warmth entering her eyes. "Well something good has come out of today. I got a dragon ride and I get to see a penthouse." Her look turned pensive. "And both the good things came from you."

He grinned at her. "So they did." They traveled in silence until the elevator came smoothly to a halt and the doors slid open.

He enjoyed her wide-eyed stare after he opened his apartment door and let her inside. His place had a large living area, with floor-to-ceiling windows at one end. He liked the long, unimpeded space.

"Your apartment is lovely." She smoothed her hand over the top of the chaise-lounge. "This looks like a real antique."

"It is a real antique. Just like me," he reminded her. "No, I didn't buy it new, I got it a few years ago when I bought this apartment. Take a seat. I'll get some coffee and see what I have to eat."

"I'm not hungry."

"I haven't seen you eat since I met you. How about an omelet?"

His kitchen was open to the rest of the lower area, a breakfast bar separating it from the main area. Stainless steel gleamed at him in the light of the afternoon sun. It had taken far too long to get here. He glanced at the clock and switched on the kitchen TV. "My boss will be making the official announcement about us soon. Wanna see?"

"Sure."

She sounded too tired to care but the TV distracted her enough to keep her awake.

His boss, Ann Reynolds, appeared onscreen. He'd already missed some of the broadcast. "Vampires, shape-shifters and other beings all exist. They always have although they remained secret until the recent revelations. Now we have to cope with them together, as a nation."

All the usual stuff. He'd heard it before, though not in public. He wondered how the great American public would take it. But take it or not, they had to accept it now that Ann was busy giving them the proof.

She answered the questions with far more patience than she gave anyone in the office. "STORM has existed for around fifty years now. We've worked with high-level government agencies, although very few people knew about us before."

"Why would you want to have an agency like that?"

Ann grimaced, not bothering to hide her distaste. "Because as long as Talents have existed, which we presume is as long as mankind has been in existence, people have sought to destroy them. Any minority has people who want to destroy it, people who are afraid of the unknown, who want to smash it instead of live with it." She paused and Sandro knew she was about to reveal more of their secrets. He hated this part. Like every other Talent, they'd spent their lives hiding, so had their ancestors and it went against the grain to let their secrets go. But they had to, all but a few they'd decided to keep secret for now. Gradual revealing of what they were and what they could do would be less shocking. As if anything could ameliorate the film of dragons in flight. "Some Talents live longer than the average human being, though not all do. Vampires and shape-shifters have significantly longer life spans than m—human beings." Sandro growled. New, more politically correct terminology went with the openness. Ann continued smoothly, well into her stride now. The perfect figurehead, a smartly dressed middle-aged woman who could connect with the people out there. More so because she was mortal—a human being. "Before today, they had to conceal that fact, so the government agencies helped them to find new identities, so they could live their lives out of the spotlight."

"What is the 'mistreatment' referred to in the STORM acronym?"

"Not all ordinary people are ignorant of us. They have persecuted Talents for generations in many different ways. We needed to defend ourselves."

The interviewer's voice hardened. "So you had a secret organization of soldiers and agents fighting ordinary human beings?"

"No more than the CIA or MI5 do. Senior government officials know about us, in every country we operate in, and not all our operations are for or include Talents. We have worked alongside accredited government agents for at least the past thirty years."

Let them choke on that, Sandro thought.

More snatches of film followed, facts and information about the beings who'd lived among humans all this time, how they'd hidden, used government agencies to gain new identities. A popular politician appeared on the screen and Megan caught her breath. Sandro hid his smile. "You trust me," he said, "and whatever form I take I'm still a good American first. I was born here and I'll always choose to live here. I'm a citizen and I will fight for the rights of Talents just as I've fought for the rights of underprivileged classes for years."

Snatching ingredients out of his fridge, Sandro whisked eggs, grated cheese and made a fast omelet, afraid she'd fall asleep before she'd eaten it, despite the revelations on the TV. Instead of taking her into the dining room, he set it up on the breakfast bar where he could watch her eat. He whisked up more eggs and dumped the mixture in the pan.

She murmured her thanks and shook out her napkin. "This looks good."

"Why do I get the feeling it could be cardboard and you'd say that?"

She chuckled. "No, really. I know I need to eat but I'm not hungry. This is just right."

Grabbing the pan off the stove, he shook his omelet onto a plate and joined her, sitting opposite her at the table instead of next to her, as he wanted to do. She didn't need that kind of intimacy now although he sure as hell did. He had no idea that close proximity to this woman he needed to help him find his missing brother would send his sexual responses off the scale. Watching her eat, making sure she finished it, he was hardly aware of eating his own food.

"What are you smiling at?"

"A memory of a woman I used to know. You remind me of her, a bit."

She put her fork down on her empty plate. "In what way?"

"She was brave and clever. She wouldn't back down for anyone and she didn't care who she upset in search of the truth." He toyed with his last bite. "She died a long time ago, June fifteenth, 1854, to be exact. The fifty years I spent with her were the best I ever had."

"Oh." Her eyes sparkled when he looked up from his empty plate, her interest unfeigned.

He smiled. "Yes, 'Oh.' Shall I show you her picture?" He flicked off the TV and led the way to the living area, where he opened his desk and found Jane's miniature. "This is the one object I've kept with me since it was made. Other things come and go but not this."

She touched the frame, took the little painting. He knew it so well, the blue dress and the slightly amused look. "She was lovely."

"Yes she was."

"What was her name?"

"Jane. Jane McBride. Before she married me, that is. I was using the name McDonald then, so she became Jane McDonald." The name took his memories right back to the glen where he'd asked her to marry him and the look of amazement she'd given him. She'd really had no idea he was going to ask her.

"Scottish?"

"We both were."

She gazed up at him. "You're Scottish?"

He chuckled. "No, I'm Italian, like Ricardo. We were just posing as Scots for that lifetime. Her death tore me up, and I wanted a fresh start so I came to the States. Ricardo joined me soon after that."

She handed him the picture back. "You miss her."

Not so much anymore. He caressed Jane's face with the tip of his finger before putting the miniature back in its case and closing the lid.

She swallowed, and when she didn't lift her head to look at him he knew she must be blinking tears away. "Your one true love."

"I wouldn't say that." He put his finger under her chin and urged her to look at him. "Fifty years isn't bad. Many Talents have stories like that and we learn to cope. I don't think love is dead for me, just dormant.

"Megan, let me read you. I can tell if there's any truth in what the hospital told you."

"You can do a mental scan for a tumor?"

He saw the hope flare in her eyes. "Pretty much."

She swallowed. "Okay."

It only took a few minutes. A few minutes of intensely personal contact, which sorely tested his ability to keep his hands off her. He wanted to drag her close and take her but he wasn't a monster. She desperately needed her sleep and some reassurance. "Megan, there's no tumor. If those scans show one, then they're faked or they used somebody else's scans to fool the system."

"You're sure?"

"I'm positive, baby. When I take you in to STORM you can have it confirmed by one of our medics if you like. You've managed to contact Ricardo where none of us could. I suspect it's because he can only connect at a level we can't reach. A bit like those high-pitched sounds only teenagers and dogs can pick up. And because he's real and in trouble, you also picked up his distress and it's been stopping you sleeping."

"They said it wasn't real. They said the dreams were a symptom of the illness. Until yesterday I had no idea dragons existed."

"You know now."

Pure relief swept through her veins. She wasn't dying. *She wasn't dying.* She wanted to jump in the air, take a drink, celebrate.

But not here, not now. *Play it cool, Megan.* She took a steadying breath and tried for flippancy. "We're all dying."

Her answer elicited a chuckle. "So we are. But not just yet."

His eyes burned into hers, filling her with a need to touch him. She leaned forward and his arms went around her. He touched his lips to hers before the buzz from the intercom sounded loudly into the quiet apartment.

Sandro grimaced and released her with some reluctance before he crossed the room to hit the button. A disembodied voice came from the speaker. "As ordered, boss."

He hit the sequence of numbers that gave them ingress.

Several more people entered before the door had time to close. Megan regarded them suspiciously and inched closer to Sandro.

"My team." He didn't move away from her but indicated a dark-eyed man with razor-sharp cheekbones and long hair drawn into a tight ponytail behind his head. "Johann Kozak, vampire."

Vampire? Jesus, yesterday morning vampires were confined to *Dracula* and *Buffy*. Today, they existed. She forced herself to stay focused. Not pass out, not say anything stupid.

Before Sandro could introduce her, the woman spoke. "Carilla Toledo Vargas, jaguar shape-shifter." Her dark-haired, exotic features proclaimed her South American heritage. Megan managed a nod.

The blond-haired man smiled at her. He had a dazzling smile. His suit was expensive, his hair carefully styled but for all that, he wore a dangerous don't-touch-me air she sensed was natural for him. "Chase Maynord, Sorcerer." His presence touched her mind. This was creepy. She wasn't sure she liked it.

"This is a mortal, she's not used to our ways," Sandro snapped.

"Okay. Sorry." The presence withdrew. More than ever she became aware of her singular presence here. A mortal amongst Talents.

"Sorcerer?"

The blond in the dazzlingly well-cut suit gave her an equally dazzling smile. "I'm a mortal with very strong psi gifts."

"Oh." Of course, she thought sardonically, why hadn't she guessed?

The vampire walked toward the window. The late afternoon sun slanted through the blinds but he didn't burn, no smoke fizzled up when he walked across a beam of light. As if she'd spoken her thoughts aloud, he said, "We can tolerate sunlight but we're only in control of our powers between sunset and sunrise, except for telepathy, which everyone has to some degree. I won't disappear in a puff of smoke unless somebody uses a flamethrower on me." He turned his head and pinned her with a sexy grin. "And I don't sleep in the ground either. Otherwise Central Park could sell sleeping pits." He smiled at her. No fangs either. "So I take it we're protecting Megan?"

"That's our priority. Ann's busy doing interviews, introducing the world to the idea of Talents, so she's too busy to take much interest. Steve Murchison's team is on the hospital."

"Better Ann than me," grunted Johann, his black hair gleaming in the sunlight.

"And you've lived among us all this time?" Megan still found it hard to believe.

"All this time." The blond man—Chase—smiled at her.

"Megan, you only trust the people in this room and Ann Reynolds, who I'll introduce you to another time." Sandro's sharp tones, so unlike the honey he'd used earlier, alerted her to the importance of what he was saying. This man was a leader. "Chase, Carilla, Johann and me. No one else unless I say so. A Talent betrayed us to the media and Talents work for the IRDC so you can't trust anyone else, Talent or mortal."

"And Jack," she added.

Chase quirked an eyebrow. "Jack?"

"My roomie."

Briefly, Sandro bared his teeth in an animalistic gesture of challenge, one that sent frissons through her. "Jack Hargreaves," he growled.

She stared at him in surprise. Chase asked, "Your roomie's male?"

She kept her attention on Sandro. "Yes. Jack came over to Oxford University on a scholarship and we've been friends ever since." She tried to force the reminder of the one night Jack and she had spent together before they agreed that they were better friends than lovers out of her mind but she heard Sandro's low growl when the memory flickered across her consciousness.

She couldn't mistake his tone now. Sandro didn't like that her best friend and apartment sharer was male. Well he could just suck it up. Jack was part of her life and always would be.

"How did you know about Jack?" There was only one way Sandro could know, so she guessed before he told her. "And why didn't you just ask me about Ricardo?"

He put his hand over hers and led her to a large, comfortable-looking leather sofa, sitting down next to her. He didn't let go of her hand and squeezed it gently. She pulled her hand away.

He sighed. "I've been following you since I picked up that trace of Ricardo from you." Sandro ran his fingers through his hair, rousing his unruly waves into new heights of untidiness. "I wasn't sure whose side you were on, and if I moved before I knew, I might destroy the only lead we had. I couldn't read you clearly and I was on the verge of taking you to Chase so he could read you. Only today, when they made a move on you, was I completely sure you weren't involved with the IRDC."

Megan swallowed her initial anger. Okay, so he'd followed her. But he was looking for his only brother, his only relative by the sound of it. She swallowed down her resentment, knowing she'd probably do the same in his situation.

"Tell us about your dreams, Megan." He sounded totally in control but she sensed an uneasiness in him. One she was about to confirm.

"I dream about Ricardo a lot. I can't sleep." She paused, taking a minute to steel herself against what she had to tell Ricardo's brother. "Sometimes he's tied down to his bed. He's being tortured. Sometimes I come in when they're hurting him. They don't care if he cries or not, they're intent on cutting him up, as if he's an experiment." She paused, forcing the vivid images out of her head. If she let them in, she'd never finish her story.

Sandro reached for her hand, gripping it hard and this time she didn't pull away. "Ricardo's hurting. Nobody knows I'm there but him, as if I'm standing behind one of those one-way mirrors."

Sandro's breath stopped before resuming a little heavier than before. "Oh God." His hand clenched into a fist so tight she began to lose the feeling in her fingers. She flinched and immediately his grip slackened and he pulled his hand away. She didn't want to see his expression—she didn't think she dared look.

A heavy silence fell. Megan thought of Ricardo, an artist and a poet, a man with a strong body that his captors methodically and dispassionately sliced apart every day. She didn't want to imagine what this was doing to his brother.

"You brought us hope, Megan, and a clue. Ricardo's contacting you telepathically and telepathy doesn't work long-distance. He's close."

"So what do you want to do?"

"They want to kill you because you're a security risk. You could lead us to them and you've given us the important lead we needed. They'll want to stop you. So we'll take care of you until—until we've concluded this case." She didn't know if the others noticed his slight hesitation. "And you're a weapon too. We could use you as bait to draw them out."

This was her way out. End the torture of watching someone she now knew was real and free both of them. She didn't have a choice. "Yes, I'll do it."

"Thank you." Abruptly, he turned away, toward his grim-faced team. "We can work a switch. Carilla, you're about the same height. With a wig and a bit of fuzzing, you could fool enough people."

Carilla assessed Megan with a cool gaze. "Yes, I could do that."

"So we show Megan off in public but we do a switch and you go to her apartment at night. Draw them out, try to capture them."

"And where do I go?" she asked.

"You come back here. With me."

Chapter Three

"I'll show you your room. You look beat."

"Well thank you." Megan's acid tones made Sandro smile. "It's great to know I'm holding up."

"I think you're holding up very well."

The penthouse was on two levels, the second floor leading off a mezzanine. He took her up the stairs, past his bed on the open space. When he opened the door, he watched her face. He already knew what the room looked like.

Pleasure warmed her mind and filtered into his. "This is a lovely room."

"Not too plain for you?"

She shook her head. "Frankly, I could sleep in the middle of Grand Central Station right now." Basically furnished with a large bed and vanity, the closets behind sliding doors painted to match the pale blue color scheme, serenity predominated in here.

"I have another bedroom. This is the one Ricardo uses when he stays over, so if you have any problems with that, you can use the other room. Did your doctor give you anything to help you sleep without dreaming?"

She swallowed, and when he saw the movement he had the urge to kiss her throat and soothe her troubles away. But he couldn't do that. At least, not yet. "Yes, I have some pills. But I don't use them very often."

"*Do* they stop the dreams?"

She turned away slightly but he felt the pain in her mind. "No, they just stop me waking up. I still dream." She turned back to him so suddenly he wasn't sure if she'd seen his grief,

grief he couldn't afford to show because once the dam burst, he wasn't sure he could seal it up again, and he had a job to do. He wanted to talk to his brother again so much but he couldn't put her through the agony of seeing him in that place. Sandro had seen labs before—he had a very good idea what she saw. Chase would examine her later after she'd had some sleep. Maybe the relief of knowing she didn't have cancer would help her now.

They'd try it without the pills first.

"There's a bathroom through there," he gestured to the door at the far end, "and I can find you something to wear tonight if you want. Will a t-shirt do?"

She smiled and nodded, so he left the room, returning with a t-shirt baggy and soft with washing. It would cover her nicely. Very nicely.

Megan stood by the window, staring out at the buildings opposite. "Do I get any of my clothes soon?"

"Sure. Carilla will bring them for you tomorrow."

She crossed the room and took the t-shirt out of his hands. "Thanks." When she absently smoothed her hands over the fabric, he felt the gesture on his own skin. He wanted her to touch him like that. Shit, the first time he'd seen her he wanted her and the feeling was even stronger since she flew on his back this afternoon. "Jack will worry. If he thinks I'm in danger he won't accept what he's told."

"If Carilla tells him he mustn't try to find out where you're staying, do you think that would help?"

"Maybe. What happens now?"

Her questions, straightforward and honest, deserved straightforward answers. Megan was part of his team now. "You'll sleep, and when you do I'll stay with you, in your mind. If Ricardo contacts you I'll be there." Tempting and intimate, he wanted her with him, in his bed but if she felt more comfortable keeping him at a distance, that would be the way he'd play it. For now. "Tomorrow, you'll go into work as usual, only you'll have a new boyfriend. Me. We'll keep it simple, say we met in a wine bar. We'll watch you at work, you'll never be alone."

"But I'll tell Jack the truth."

"Jack will know. Carilla will tell him." He allowed himself a brief touch, stroking one finger over her palm. "Get some rest. Take a long, hot bath, and relax."

It nearly killed him to leave the room when he wanted nothing more than to hold her and help her get some rest but he managed it.

Sandro spent the rest of the evening going over the events of the day, trying to slot them in to the rest of his knowledge about the IRDC and Ricardo's capture. His brother was close by, somewhere in the environs of New York. That gave Sandro more hope than he'd had for a long time.

Eventually, realizing he was too tired to do anything else, he turned off the desk light and his laptop and went to bed. In deference to his visitor, he donned a pair of black silk pajama bottoms. He had the habit of wandering around his apartment nude in the mornings, getting a coffee then showering and wandering around until he needed to dress for work. He couldn't do that for a while. He climbed into bed and fell instantly asleep.

Only for a scream to wake him, seemingly five minutes later.

* * * * *

Sandro flung back the comforter and leaped out of bed, noting the time from the digital clock glowing on the shelf as he passed. It was two a.m. and he'd been asleep for all of two hours.

The scream came again when he put his hand on her door. As he shoved at the door, a bolt of psychic lightning struck him, forcing his inner eye open.

He stood in a different room. A gray metal bed dominated it, placed against one wall, surrounded by beeping machinery, drips and other paraphernalia. At first he couldn't see the man in the bed, then he wished he hadn't. "Ricardo!"

One arm was heavily bandaged, the other strapped down, a multitude of needles stuck into it, each leading to its own container. In and out. A vein lay open, raw to the atmosphere, so slow to heal it meant Ricardo must be dangerously weak. They'd catheterized him. Sandro saw the container with what must be days' worth of urine. He felt his brother's pain and humiliation, ached for him. Straps bound Ricardo around his upper and lower arms, his legs and his waist. At first he must have fought against them, as the marks of healed scrapes stood livid against his too-pale skin.

They would use the drug Cephalox to prevent any shape-shifting. Sandro clenched his fist. This was his brother. The gentle, artistic man who reminded him why he was alive, why he fought for his people.

Ricardo turned his head and saw him. His eyes were full of despair, no spark of the liveliness Sandro loved in him remaining. "Aren't you looking for me?" were the first words from him Sandro had heard in months.

"God, of course we are, Ricardo."

"Yeah, right." The sneer was so unlike anything he'd seen in his brother before Sandro hardly recognized him. Ricardo looked away.

"Where are you, Ricardo? Where are they keeping you?"

Ricardo turned his head again, the only part of his body he could move freely. Sandro couldn't see Megan. He must be locked in her body, a psychic entity sharing her vision.

"I don't know where I am. They knocked me out." Sandro tried to take a step forward, pushed all his energy into his legs but he couldn't move a muscle, except to breathe and speak. Ricardo coughed, a scary, rattling sound deep in his throat. "I didn't see the exterior of this place. The room is soundproofed,

I think. I can't hear anything outside." He coughed again. "I don't think I'm getting out of this, Sandro, so let me say this and don't interrupt. You always interrupt." A faint smile crossed his lips and Sandro's heart broke. "I love you. You brought me up after our parents died, you fought for me, you told me to be what I wanted to be. Sandro, don't waste time blaming yourself. I know you've done your best. Just find these bastards and kill them for me, will you?"

Sandro licked his dry lips. "Who are they? Any names?"

"Don't know. They only use first names, John, Fred, Bill. I don't even know if they're the real names. They don't talk to me much. That's not what they want. They want the elixir of life, the reason we live so long. Well, they're about to find out we're not immortal." His grin widened a little. "It's been good to see you and I'm glad you found Megan. She's helped me. I didn't think she was real for the longest time but if she brought you, she must be. Be good to her."

Sandro felt Ricardo going away from him, slipping into unconsciousness, the drugs pumping into him overcoming his fight to stay with them. He tried so hard to push himself, to stay, to lock his mind with Ricardo's but nothing worked and the room grew dark as his brother's consciousness ebbed away.

"I'll be back, *fratello mio*," he whispered. He opened his eyes to the dim bedroom at his apartment.

He felt a hand slip into his and didn't have to look to know it was Megan.

* * * * *

Back in her own body in the tranquil bedroom, Megan came around first. Sandro stood, one hand on the doorknob, and she opened her eyes to see him sag. She made it across to him and grasped his free hand. If he fell she wouldn't have a chance of stopping him dropping heavily to the floor.

Megan tugged Sandro to the bed and made him sit down. "Sandro. Sandro, come back."

Tears poured down his face, although he didn't make a sound. Not until he turned into her arms and fell against her so strongly they fell onto the bed together, Megan squashed under his heavy body.

But then he sobbed, a single, heart-wrenching reverberation from the depths of his soul, and she forgot not breathing, forgot she'd only met him that morning. She just wanted to hold him, soothe him. Despite his size, he felt helpless in her arms.

He shuddered and took a deep breath. "No," she whispered, her mouth next to his ear. "Let it out. Let go, Sandro."

He opened up, opened his mind to her and she gasped with shock. Sandro's warmth, his essence flowed into her. Ricardo was the last of his family, his only relative and his loneliness swamped her, anguish searing his soul. If they killed his brother, nothing would stop Sandro destroying his captors when he found them.

If they killed his brother, nothing would stop Sandro destroying his captors when he found them. He touched her wet cheek tenderly and their eyes met in the dim light of dawn filtering around the edges of the window blind. "Don't cry, Megan."

He got to his feet and picked her up. When she struggled, his grip tightened so she wouldn't fall and he dropped a kiss on her forehead. "Come and share my bed for a while."

Her instant acceptance surprised her. She'd met him for the first time the previous day and already she was ready to share his bed? He shouldn't feel so good, carrying her the few steps to the open area where he slept. His heat warmed her right through and instinctively she moved closer to him. So why not? He was ripped, sexy as hell and he obviously didn't want to be alone tonight.

She momentarily forgot her concerns when he laid her in his bed and joined her there, cuddling her close after drawing the comforter over them. "Sleep," he murmured. "You're still tired, and we have to get you to work tomorrow."

But she'd woken up again. "What's the time?"

"Just after four."

He lifted up, resting on one elbow to look down on her face. Somewhere on the floor below them a lamp glowed, and another light, dimmed to soft radiance, stood on a small table by the bed. "Anything I can do to help you sleep?" His smile was anything but innocent.

"Well—" Looking at him, his rugged, handsome face, the dark hair curling around his forehead, the bare chest liberally sprinkled with curling hair, she didn't want to resist. Perhaps something good would happen tonight after all.

She wanted this man. Whether from loneliness, desperation, the deep sharing she'd experienced earlier, or just because he was the sexiest man she'd seen since—ever—her libido glowed into life, like the sun peeping over the horizon at dawn.

His smile changed into a welcome, knowing grin and he bent to kiss her.

They resumed where they'd left off on the rooftop, his mouth caressing hers, then opening, encouraging her to open for him. Not that she needed much encouragement.

When his tongue swept into her mouth, she lifted her arms and felt his warm, hard body come down onto hers. His chest caressed her breasts through the thin t-shirt, stimulating her nipples to tingling awareness. He nestled his legs inside hers, and without thought, she lifted her knees to hug his hips in an intimate caress. The silk of his pajama bottoms stroked her sensitive inner thighs into anticipatory awareness. His tongue invaded, stroked and seduced. Warmth invaded her, and with his big body surrounding hers, she felt deliciously possessed. He finished the kiss slowly, lingeringly and dropped small kisses on her mouth and face.

She wriggled to feel more of him and he lifted his head, smiling at her. "You should sleep but you feel so fucking good." He stroked her waist, the heat of his body warming her. "I wanted you the first minute I saw you but you only met me today. Tell me to stop."

She gazed up at him and chose to ignore his last remark. "It seems longer. Did you do something else while you were in my mind?"

He gave a one-sided smile. "No. But Talents often link close and fast because they enter each others' minds. It's usual for me but not for you. I should leave you alone." His gaze grew heated and it dropped to her breasts before rising to her face once more. "If you tell me now I can do it. Just."

He pulled away only for her to urge him back. "I don't care. I didn't realize until just now how long it's been since I've shared like this with anyone."

"You want this? You want me to make love to you?"

"I think we both need it." She gave a shaky laugh. "No, that's just an excuse and we're grownups, aren't we?" She took a deep breath and told him the truth. "I think you're incredibly hot. The whole dragon thing is amazing, wonderful," she swept her hand up his chest and around his neck, "your body is beautiful, your eyes say you want me and that's more important to me than this." She wriggled under him, emphasizing his cock that had become harder, more insistent since she began speaking. "I want this."

He closed his eyes and she felt his mind caress hers, a gentle touch against her pleasure center. She shuddered in response. He could just do that and she'd probably come. He lifted up to his knees. His eager arousal ridged the smooth black silk of his pants, making her mouth water. "You're sure?" She nodded. "Then let's get naked, sweetheart."

His low, purring tones added to her need but when she reached for the hem of her t-shirt, he put his hands over hers, and nudged them aside. "No. Let me." He slowly drew up the fabric until it caught under her body, then with a low growl he slid one arm under her shoulders and lifted her so he could pull the garment up some more. When the t-shirt bunched under her arms, he stared, openly examining what he'd just revealed.

Megan heated under his gaze. No one had never looked at her so frankly before, with a thoroughness she wasn't used to. She wanted the protection of covers again but as she turned to grab them, he caught her, one big hand on either side of her waist, and his gaze moved to her face. "I'm looking because you're lovely and because I'm enjoying the sight of you."

"I'm not model-thin."

"I don't like model-thin. Not many men do, if you ask them." He slid one hand slowly up her body to cup one full breast. "These are a man's wet dream. Beautiful, lush, and look at that nipple. It's peaking all by itself. Although I bet it could do with some help." He swooped with the suddenness of a bird of prey, hungrily sucking her nipple into his mouth. Arching to meet him, propelled by the shock that swept through her at his touch, she became aware of the t-shirt, still bunched up. She ripped it over her head and tossed it away.

Sandro kissed across to her other breast, pulling hard at her nipple, and lifted his hand to caress the one he'd just left. Her half-suppressed cry when he pinched it made him increase his efforts, stroking and nipping, touching his teeth to her skin and making her shudder as every nerve ending came alive and begged for his touch. The soft suction increased and when he lifted his head, the sudden chill made her nipple peak even more.

She wanted this, needed it, deserved it.

Lying back, she watched him and lifted her hand to thread her fingers through his curls, enjoying the feeling of silky hair and hot male. She released her breath in one long sigh, ending in a giggle when one of his curls tickled the sensitive spot under her arm.

Sandro lifted his head and smiled at her over the dark, hard tips of her breasts. He smoothed his hands over her eager body, learning every curve and dip. "Your skin feels so silky, so soft." One hand crept down farther, spreading over her mound in a possessive gesture she loved. "And wet," he purred, pushing one finger into the cleft, sliding it around, collecting her essence before he opened her with finger and thumb and groaned. "God, you're lovely!"

Sliding down the bed, he gave her pussy a full, open-mouthed kiss, swirling his tongue into her heat, pushing it deeper until he entered her, then drew it out and lapped, his tongue softly moving, stimulating and arousing.

What was he doing that felt so wonderful, so much better than any lover before? Her body arched toward him of its own accord and his lapping became more purposeful, concentrating on her clit. When he sucked the peak of flesh into his mouth, she gripped the sheet in an effort to stop moving, stop wriggling because this felt too damn good to miss. He pushed a finger into her pussy, then another, working them inside her, then fucked her with them, deeply in and out. She remembered how big his hands were, how long his fingers and she moaned.

A gasp, then another, then she shattered, every part of her exploding in sync. Cool air hit her skin. She heard something tear, paper or foil, and she reached for him, needing his warmth.

While her senses were still scattered in the aftermath of her orgasm, he slid up the bed and entered her and her body tightened around him. Her eyes shot open. He smiled down at her.

"Yes, I'm wearing a condom," he said. "Keep your eyes open. I want you to watch me while I fuck you." He bent and gave her a soft kiss, leaving a breath of her essence on her lips. "Ready?"

She nodded, still regaining some of her senses. But he didn't let her. Instead, he thrust deep inside, watching her closely. "That isn't quite right, is it?" he murmured, and adjusted his position a little, trying again. This time he hit the spot dead-on. When she caught her breath and twisted under him, he smiled. "That's better."

His sure, slow strokes made her glow and reach for him, needing something to hold on to. Every time he hit her sweet spot, caressed with his cock head and retreated, slowly building the anticipation for his next stroke.

His next thrust made her arch, and he slipped his hand under her, holding her tightly against him. "Sandro!"

"Oh yes, I like that, baby. Say my name again."

She obliged a great many times over the next few minutes as his invasion of her body became surer, as he learned what she liked and she learned how he felt. Long and hard, he filled her over and over again.

When she thought she'd crest any minute, he moved, so he wasn't stroking her at the right angle anymore. Inwardly sighing, she opened her eyes. When had she closed them?

"That's better," he said, pushing again, finding that spot again. "Keep your eyes open, sweetheart, and I'll do what you want."

He stroked her again, sliding his hand from under her to support his upper body above her, then lifted, and she screamed when he drove even deeper inside her. She forced her eyes open, watched his big body, sweat trickling down his chest in rivulets, flattening the curls of body hair, then he threw back his head and roared.

And his roar was her name.

When Megan awoke—in Sandro's bed—he'd risen before her, dressed and made breakfast. Megan didn't normally eat a cooked breakfast but her appetite revived after the longest rest she'd had for months and she ate everything he cooked for her. She had a late start this morning. Just as well, considering the night they'd had. But she felt more refreshed than she had in months.

He drove her to work. Unfortunately only a few students were about to see her grand entrance from the bright yellow Spyder. He didn't get out but leaned over to kiss her, touching her chin with two fingers. "Our agents will contact you telepathically so you'll know who they are. Let them watch you. And don't leave tonight. I'll pick you up."

Now she felt like a heroine in a James Bond film. Thrown into danger, seduced and driven around in a performance car, it couldn't get much closer. Except that James Bond wasn't a shape-shifting dragon.

The John McIver Medical University was privately endowed, small and prestigious. As well as the world-famous sleep clinic, pioneering work took place there, the doctors developing cures for the diseases that cropped up as fast as they dealt with one. The AIDS clinic brought the university fame in the early nineties, one of the first to keep patients with full-blown AIDS alive, and now the income helped to fund the less lucrative departments.

The library stood in the oldest part of the university. Megan climbed the stone steps and entered, letting the atmosphere wash over her, the faint smell of old books and ink lingering in the air.

She stowed her purse in the staff lockers before she headed for the main counter. Jack watched in silence as she draped her jacket over a chair back. After nodding to Sheryl, who'd redone her hair an even more aggressive shade of golden blonde than last week, Megan checked the rota. She was on the counter most of the morning, and later on the information desk. Like most qualified librarians, she had to take what jobs were offered and this one was for a library assistant rather than a librarian.

Frowning, she tried to recall yesterday's rota. She could have sworn she had a stint in the office today, processing new books. Then she smiled wryly. STORM would have arranged it differently, wanting her under their eyes, though she hadn't any idea how they could have done it.

I applied some gentle persuasion to one of your colleagues. I'm at the table to your left. No, don't look around for me. The voice was feminine, not one she remembered from yesterday.

Jack's very real voice intruded on the telepathic conversation. "What's going on?"

"Didn't they tell you?"

Jack looked around, just like a spy in an old-fashioned movie. "I'll meet you in the psychology stack in ten minutes."

"Okay."

She got on with her work, wondering how things could change so much in a day. One day.

She opened her mind again to her bodyguard. *I have to go to the bathroom soon.*

Okay but I'll stay in your mind while you're gone.

What does that mean? Can you hear what I'm doing there?

A chuckle, as if she'd made a joke. *Not if you don't want me to. I'll be discreet and close my eyes and ears, though I'll know if you get into trouble.*

How will you do that?

I'll monitor your emotions.

Wow, this was a new world. Brave or not remained to be seen.

Ten minutes later, she'd made it to the psychology stack. Situated in a small extension, it was approached by a couple of wooden stairs that creaked whenever anyone trod on them so it was a good place for a private conversation.

Jack waited for her, his fingers drumming impatiently on a nearby bookcase. "So are you going to tell me what the *fuck* is going on?" he demanded, keeping his voice low.

"You've met Carilla then?" she said cautiously.

His face relaxed a smidgeon and a reluctant grin flashed across his features. "Oh yeah. If you could have chosen your substitute, she'd be my choice. But she wouldn't tell me where you were, Megan, and I worried about you. She came up with some crock of shit about witness protection. Jesus, you didn't call me after you went to the hospital and I know you'd have done that if you could. So tell me."

A band around her heart relaxed. She'd been stupid to think she was alone in New York. She had Jack. While their romance, such as it was, had fizzled and died, their friendship was still going strong. "Okay but keep it to yourself."

"Sure." Jack looked over her head, and then back at her. Tall, with muscles he enjoyed developing in the gym and running around the park, Jack was the antithesis of the typical librarian—he was well dressed, with a penchant for ridiculous ties, dark hair cut in an over-one-eye style. "Be quick. There's a woman sitting by the front desk I don't remember seeing before."

"That's okay, she's there for me. She's my minder." At his quizzical look, she explained. "Britspeak for a bodyguard." She put her hand on his shirt front, the cream silk warming under her hand. "First, I'm not dying. No tumor, nothing."

He sighed in relief and then his perceptive gaze sharpened once more. "So where does the dreamy Ricardo come in?"

She shook her head. "He's real, Jack. Not a figment and the dreams are so vivid they keep waking me up. Hence the sleep problems. They attacked me at the hospital. So a Talent broke me out."

"A Talent? One of those—" He made flapping gestures with his hands, imitating wings.

She grinned. "Yes, one of those. His name's Sandro and Ricardo is his brother."

Jack's dark eyebrows shot up and one disappeared under his heavy fall of hair. "Fuck."

"Ricardo's been missing almost as long as I've been having the dreams. He's contacting me but he can't contact anybody else. They don't know why. So Carilla didn't lie to you, I am in protection, sort of because they're using me as bait. The bad guys, the ones who have Ricardo, want me dead."

Jack's brows came together in a forbidding frown. "Bait? Did they ask or did you volunteer?"

"I volunteered."

A movement on the stairs made her spin around.

Her minder, a woman with natural-looking ash blonde hair, climbed the stairs, met her gaze briefly and stood before the shelves by the exit.

"I don't like this," Jack said. "I think you should go home to England. You're due some leave — take it."

"I'm safer here. They'll come after me." She glanced at the woman. "It's okay, Jack, I'm in a safe house and they won't let me out of their sight until they catch these people and get Ricardo back. But Ricardo is real, Jack, really captive, really suffering. I've got to do what I can to help."

Jack frowned. "So Carilla is bait as well?"

"Don't worry about her. She's a Talent."

"Christ!" Impatiently, Jack shoved his hair behind his ears. "You're meeting legends!"

She chuckled. "I suppose I am."

"So where are you?"

She told him without hesitation. "In an apartment on the Upper East Side."

He pursed his lips but didn't whistle. "Living the good life."

"Sure am. You should see this apartment. I always thought we were lucky to get ours but this beats it hollow. Jack, you don't have to be in this. You could take leave and go visit your parents or something. They don't want you, they want me."

He made a rude noise between his lips, too loud, and then glanced around. "Now look what you're doing to me. I'm not leaving. If you're in danger, I want to be around to take care of you. And—" He looked away, his cheeks reddening.

"Carilla's hot," she finished for him. "Come on, Jack, admit it. You like her."

"Weeeeell...yeah." He smiled at her. "But hot or not, if anything happens to you, I'll take her down. And her friends."

"I offered, Jack. I'm their only lead. Now that I know Ricardo's real, I can't leave him to suffer, can I?"

"I guess not," he said reluctantly. "I'm going to miss you. Come back soon, Megan, and be safe."

She made to leave, then turned back, remembering what she hadn't told him. "The cover story is that I've met a man last night in a wine bar. I'm staying at his apartment and that's why I'm in the same clothes as I was yesterday. We want it to be obvious that I didn't go home last night."

"Clean underwear, I hope."

"Commando," she said briefly and left to the sound of his low chuckle.

On her way out, the woman stopped her. "Could you tell me where I could find the complete works of Freud?"

Megan grinned. "That shelf, and that one, and that one too," she said, gesturing to the biggest bookcase.

The woman lowered her voice. "Who was that? I can't sense any panic in you but you were gone longer than you said."

"That's my best friend, Jack. We share an apartment."

She lowered her lashes to study Jack. "So that's Jack Hargreaves. Nice. Sandro's out of luck, is he?"

Megan lifted her chin. "That's for me to know." Sweeping past, she had to catch herself when she nearly stumbled down the stairs. Fuck, this whole business was getting to her. Although she did feel better. A few more nights like that and she'd—she stopped, her hand on the stair rail. What was she thinking? Last night should never have happened, never. At the end of her rope, exhausted, frightened and faced with the hottest hottie on the planet, she didn't have a chance. Tonight it would be different. Maybe.

At noon she received a text from Sandro on her cell phone. *Can't meet you for lunch, go with Chase or stay where you are.* Typical of him not to use text abbreviations. A man from another century coming to terms with modern technology but not quite accepting it. Still, looking at Chase waiting for her by the desk, she had to admit Talents made fine-looking men. Damn fine.

* * * * *

Sandro had slept with dozens of women since Jane died but none had affected him as much before now. Somehow Megan had gotten under his skin, and all he could think of was her body, her smile and her kiss.

"Gianetti!"

"Ann." He looked up and smiled automatically, having learned a very long time ago that a smile often made the unpalatable bearable. She didn't look pleased.

"You don't fool me with that shit-eating grin. I want a full report—and I mean full. I've left this operation up to you while I dealt with this coming out crap. Now I need you to brief me, and fast." She scowled. "Bloody press, one of them even followed me to the bathroom yesterday."

Ann Reynolds sat in the Barcelona chair set opposite his desk. Its lower stature to the chair he sat in didn't abash her in the least. Neither did it make Sandro feel any more superior.

His middle-aged, smartly dressed, human boss scowled at him. "You're too emotional where your brother is concerned, Sandro. But remember, we need information, not just dead bodies. The IRDC won't go away just because we're out in the open. Dead bodies are a complication, Gianetti. We need to stay above the law, especially now. Any deviation and the IRDC will label us terrorists, aliens, any name they can get hold of, and it'll be war. Some members of society already want us dead and gone." Her mouth settled into a grim line. "They want to have Talents legally classified as animals."

Shocked to the core, Sandro saw the implications at once. "Dear God, Ann!"

Her already thin mouth thinned even more. "Our next big fight is going to be in Congress. They're pushing through a law, using the IRDC sponsored congressmen and senators."

"Don't we have Talents there?"

"Sure but it'll be a close-run thing. Today, the Talented congressmen and senators are making declarations. They have to show they're good Americans as well as Talents, and they have to win Congress over to their side. Fast. It's going to get nasty, Sandro, so I'm going to be even busier. This has to be yours, this operation to find Ricardo. Don't fuck it up."

Sandro sighed and twiddled his pen a bit more, concentrating on turning it from knuckle to knuckle. "Whose idea was it to start this? Wouldn't we have been better hidden, as we've always been?"

"Too late now. It's done, and we have to go forward, not look back."

Sandro shook his head. "I don't know if I want all this."

"Sandro, I need you. You're experienced, you don't lose your head in a crisis. But Ricardo's kidnapping caught you on the wrong foot. You're far too involved. If I had time to study the options, I'd pull you off the case and give it to someone else." Sandro concentrated harder, sped his movements up, watched the plastic flash in the weak spring sunlight. "If I thought you would stay out of it, I'd have put you on leave until we closed down the lab that has him. Now you have our one clue in your possession. And you've seduced her, or you're on the way to it. Haven't you?"

Sandro looked up, deliberately keeping his expression bland. He might have known Ann would go straight for the jugular. "She's very sexy."

"Tcha!" Ann wasn't given to dramatic gestures but sometimes her hands did the talking and this time was no exception. They clenched into tight fists. "You fuck her, you get control and you get to the lab first." Sandro wouldn't have allowed anyone but Ann to say that. He didn't need to seduce Megan to get her to help them. That wasn't part of his job.

Ann got to her feet and her hands uncurled so she could plant them firmly on his desk. "Do not—I repeat, *do not* go renegade on me, Sandro. I will give you up as a sacrifice to the media and the politicians if you screw this up. You will be at their mercy, and however powerful shape-shifters are, they can't prevail against the media. I'll call you an outlaw, a maverick, and I'll have you hunted down."

Sandro shrugged. "It might be worth it to get Ricardo back." Slowly, he lifted his head and met her fiery glare without flinching. "Ann, I am old. I've lived a long time. Give me up and I'll fly into the sky and self-combust after I destroy the lab and everyone in it. You ever seen that? Sure as hell nobody living in New York today has ever seen it. Spectacular and shocking. You threaten me with martyrdom and I'll show you what martyrdom really means."

For the space of a minute they glared at each other, neither giving way. Ann had made her lack of psi abilities her strength. Nobody could penetrate her powerful psychic shield. What she thought she kept to herself. But this time she let him see her fury, and under that, her ice-cold determination to retain control of this new world.

Eventually, she drew back and straightened the already straight seams of her boxy jacket. "I can live with that," she said, and without looking back, left the office, her final words floating behind her. "I can even use it."

Sandro's chuckle turned into a full-blown laugh. Nobody bested Ann Reynolds. Every day he gave thanks she was on his side, because sure as hell, he'd hate to have her as an enemy.

Chapter Four

The watchers were so discreet, Jack told Megan he wouldn't have noticed them if she hadn't pointed them out to him. Her watcher left the library at five minutes to eight and she felt another presence.

Sandro nudged aside the last minder and took possession as if he had a right to be there. *Stay where you are, I'll pick you up. I'm on my way.*

The assumption she'd just do as he told her irked Megan. When this was over, she'd teach him a few things about consideration.

No she wouldn't. When this was over, she'd probably never see him again. Right now she'd settle for getting Ricardo out alive.

The day of extra awareness about her mental processes had taught Megan a few things. When Sandro had told her about "layers" in her mind, she hadn't known what he meant. Now she had a much clearer idea. Her mind wasn't just conscious and subconscious. It was more like the layers of an onion, many layers over a single core. Her minders only stayed in her outer layer, the one that processed her day-to-day activities. It was enough to spot instantly if anything happened to disturb her day. They could have gone lower, and when she heard Sandro's voice, it seemed to come from deeper inside her.

She shivered when she remembered the physical connection, last night's lovemaking. Could she risk more of that?

I want as much as you'll let me take.

She tried going deeper.

You're learning fast, baby.

She found her jacket and left the library with fellow worker Sheryl, standing on the shallow steps where Sandro had left her that morning. Sheryl chattered happily, patting her freshly dyed golden locks into place. "I got a new date last night. He's picking me up tonight. A real cutie, with money too. Here he is."

With a deep rumble a smart red sports car pulled up to the curb before a man leaped out and strode toward them. "I could introduce you to his brother, if you want," Sheryl offered with all the condescension of a successful dating queen toward one of the unfortunate Undated. "I met him last night too. He's not quite as good-looking as Alan but he'd probably suit you better. He's quieter." She fluffed her hair again.

Alan was good-looking, carefully groomed and dressed to kill in a city suit. He smelled good too, Megan noticed when he came closer, if a little strong. He glanced over their heads and she realized he was checking his appearance in the reflective glass window behind them.

Jack exited the building, spoiling Alan's view of himself, and ran down the steps to stand at her other side. "I'll wait with you until your friend comes. Besides, I want to meet him."

"Ms. Armstrong."

Megan jumped. She hadn't heard his approach. "Dr. Bennett!"

The man who'd taken her case, the man she'd told everything about her dreams and the man who'd sent her to the hospital. Her anxiety spiked.

Jack moved closer to her. Dr. Bennett was sixtyish and what hair he had left was gray but he was still a strong, healthy man. He smiled easily. "I meant to call on you earlier but I clean forgot. Seeing you outside reminded me." He glanced at Jack. "Evening, Hargreaves. May I have a few minutes alone with my patient?"

Before Jack could give him a forcible answer, Megan gave him a gentler one. "There's no need, Dr. Bennett. Jack's my friend. He knows everything about my condition." It wasn't Dr. Bennett's fault that her sleeplessness didn't have a physiological cause, or even a psychological one. How could he have known?

"So how did you get on at the hospital?"

She never liked the doctor's crooked front teeth when he smiled but she'd never seen him as threatening before. So why did his lanky height suddenly seem intimidating?

Her imagination. After all this shape-shifter, espionage stuff, her exhaustion from lack of sleep, her mind was playing tricks on her, making her paranoid.

"Fine." She watched him closely, aware of Jack's tense body by her side, waiting, as she was, for any antagonistic move. "They gave me some pills."

The doctor's mouth turned down at the corners. "That's disappointing. I could have done that. I wanted them to study you and give a second opinion, not send you away with more sleeping pills. And I haven't received the results of the scan yet."

She feigned ignorance. "Really? They said it didn't show anything. They didn't give them to me. I presumed they'd contact you with the results."

His eyes narrowed and he concentrated on her face. "You look better. More color in your face. What pills did they give you?"

Since they hadn't given her any, she faltered before managing, "The ones you gave me last time. I haven't taken any."

"You must have taken something. You've slept, haven't you?"

A subdued roar came from the direction of the road, louder as the car approached. The Spyder. Everyone looked in the direction of the as yet unseen but not unheard vehicle.

Sheryl lifted her chin. "What's that?"

Megan ignored her. Alan reached them and paused. "A sports car. Like mine."

She glanced at Alan's car. "Not quite. His is yellow."

That became blatantly obvious in the next minute as the Spyder growled its way to the front of the library. When both doors opened, Megan wondered if perhaps her lead had been enough and they'd rescued Ricardo and her heart lifted. At least, that was what she told herself was the reason for her sudden lift of spirits.

Sandro got out one side and Carilla the other. Carilla wore a suit remarkably similar to the one Megan had on. Sheryl's mouth dropped open at the sight of the tall, broad-shouldered Sandro then snapped shut again at the sight of the sultry Carilla. Sandro and Carilla looked good together. A natural couple.

But Sandro didn't look at anyone but Megan. His smoldering gaze took her in from head to foot and back again before he quickened his step and took her in his arms. Before she could protest, almost before she could breathe, he covered her mouth with his in a passionate kiss. His tongue entered her mouth in a quick foray, touching and caressing, a lover's handshake.

He drew back to smile down at her. "I missed you. Sorry I'm late, Carilla needed a ride." *Who are these people?*

A work colleague and her date. Out of the loop. And Jack. And Dr. Bennett, the doctor from the sleep clinic.

Sandro eyed Bennett warily but Jack spoke first. "You should get a room."

Megan stepped back, coloring up. "Sorry."

"I'm not." Catching her hand in his, Sandro took his time looking away from her to the other people. His chin went up. For the first time she noticed that he was handsome, his aquiline nose and heavy-lidded, dark eyes giving him an air of aristocratic hauteur.

Carilla gave Jack her best sultry smile and slid her arm through his before deciding to notice Sheryl and Alan. "Hi. Friends of Jack?" She smiled at Megan. "Sorry I made Sandro late."

Sandro glanced at Carilla and seemingly saw the other couple for the first time. "Hi, I'm Sandro. This is Carilla. We work together, like Megan and Jack."

Jack, never slow on the uptake, gave Carilla a gentle kiss, which she seemed to enjoy as much as Megan had enjoyed Sandro's passionate greeting.

It would have been better if it had been for real but at the very least she'd shocked the man-hungry Sheryl. "We met last night and hit it off."

"We could be sisters," Carilla remarked, smiling at Megan's outfit. "So useful, these black pantsuits, aren't they?"

"Almost a uniform," Megan agreed from the shelter of Sandro's arm. She felt absurdly safe here. As if she could be safe from a predator like him!

Dr. Bennett stared at Sandro with fascination. He stepped back, eyeing him like a lab specimen, dispassionately and curiously, his eyes narrowing with speculation. "Do you sleep well?" Megan knew that look.

Sandro smiled easily, as if he hadn't noticed the doctor's attitude. "I sleep very well, Dr. Bennett."

He sighed. "Pity. I need people for a new study." He brightened. "How about being part of the control group?"

Sandro's mouth tightened. "No."

"Under any circumstances?" He wasn't giving in easily.

Sandro nodded to Bennett and turned away, addressing Jack. After one last lingering look at him, the doctor nodded to them all and moved away.

"Shall we go?" Carilla asked.

"Yeah, sure. My car's just over here."

Alan watched Carilla get into Jack's Golf, completely ignoring Sheryl. "That girl has a particularly slinky way of getting into a car."

Not surprising, considering her other form's a cat. Megan looked up, surprised by the new acidic tone in his voice. But Sandro only smiled. "Dinner?"

"Th-that sounds great. But I'm not dressed for anywhere fancy."

"You look gorgeous to me, baby."

Now she badly wanted to hit him. *That is such a cheesy thing to say.*

I bet lover boy there has used that line more than once.

Now she wanted to laugh. Alan did look like the kind of man who'd say something as patronizing as that and expect it to be taken as a compliment.

She nodded to the couple and Sandro walked her to the car, standing over her protectively until she'd climbed inside and strapped herself in. Only then did he walk around to his side.

He got into the car and started the engine, continuing the conversation verbally. "He's the kind to last about three dates."

"Will you stop doing that?"

"Doing what?" He waited, the engine idling, until Jack swept past them, then turned the car around to follow them out.

"Talking both ways as if there's no difference."

He flashed her a grin. "Not now that I know it brings a sparkle to your eyes." The grin vanished. He paused at the turnoff onto the main road. "But I do need to teach you how to keep all your thoughts at a more intimate level. You're going to have to let me in, sweetheart, so I can show you."

The endearment seemed so natural, she wondered if he used it with everyone.

"No I don't." He swung the car into traffic, then shot her an apologetic glance. "Sorry. I hear outer thoughts just like conversation. By the time I've realized they're not actual words, I've answered it. I haven't been able to correct that in over four hundred years."

The reminder of his age chilled Megan, a reminder of just how different they were. "What's it like to see all those changes in your lifetime? Horses to cars? Farmers to factory owners?"

"Exciting." His smile revealed his zest for life. "It scares some people but I love to watch it and see just how ingenious humans can be."

She settled back into the admittedly comfortable bucket seat. "How come you Talents don't rule the world?"

His laugh came, full-throated and glorious. "Good question. We used to. Tried it, didn't like it. We learned, or our ancestors did, that there's no pleasure in turning anyone into an unthinking slave. We disappeared from sight about a thousand years ago. People worshipped and reviled us in turn, and eventually our forefathers decided to live amongst men but to keep ourselves hidden. That's what we did, until two days ago."

"What did you do before you joined STORM?"

"Me?" He shifted up a gear. "CIA." She caught her breath. His hand moved to touch hers. "Working for Talents from the inside but also for my country. Ann Reynolds recruited me from there."

He drove to a small side street near the Metropolitan Opera House and into a small car lot. This area looked alarmingly exclusive.

Megan panicked. Nothing like a dress emergency to get her adrenaline running. "I can't go and eat like this! I've been in these clothes for two days now and I'm not—"

"Wearing underwear," he finished meditatively, reading her thought. She read his, a heated flash of desire, instantly banked down. "It makes this meal all the sweeter." He paused while he parked the car, edging it carefully between two others. By the time she got out of the vehicle, her blushes had subsided to a manageable level. She had no defense against him. Everything she thought, he heard.

"I don't understand any of this," she whispered.

He cradled her cheek in his hand and she couldn't stop herself rubbing against it. "Don't try. Some things are deeper than reason."

For an instant, she saw open, naked vulnerability in his face and it moved her as nothing else he could have done.

He gave her a quick, heated kiss. "We'll find Ricardo and the proof we need. Now that we're in public, the rules will change and we'll have to work within the system a lot more. We need to have the labs outlawed before they can claim they're doing essential research and try to get the FDA on their side. Then we need to get legislation passed. At the moment, Talents aren't even classed as people, did you know that?"

She shook her head. "That's ridiculous."

"There are extremists who want to keep it that way. They've already started a law to class us as animals and you can bet there'll be some court cases soon. Sometimes the extremists win." His mouth compressed into a thin line.

Gripping her hand, he walked toward the restaurant. "But not this time."

Despite her nervousness, the meal went well. He'd chosen an unassuming Italian place where the lights were low and the food well cooked and delicious. Two hours flew by in gentle laughter and get-to-know-you talk. A date. Their first.

Night had fallen by the time they left the restaurant and the air had freshened.

They're here. Startled, she almost looked around to see who spoke, a different voice in her mind, clearer and brighter than Sandro's intimate connections.

Okay. We'll take a stroll up the street and back, let them come. You're here in force?

Yeah.

She didn't know who growled until Sandro replied. *Thanks, Johann. Stay close but out of sight.*

The glow from the street lights illuminated the scene. They stood in a quiet area, leading on to a road where traffic flowed in a never-ending stream in both directions. But here, it seemed almost peaceful. They strolled toward the traffic but she felt Sandro's tension through their clasped hands. *I've partially shifted,* he said, his voice deeper inside her now. *I have extra strength. Johann and Chase are behind us. I'm taking no chances with you, sweetheart.*

She swallowed away her nerves. Two distinct presences filtered in to her head, two very masculine, very powerful entities but neither did anything but rest there.

Only the sudden absence of Chase gave her any warning at all, then out of the alley they were just crossing erupted three figures, one in the air, feet extended, coming straight at her in a flying leap.

Her karate training came to her aid and she went into a crouch, rolling out of the way. Out of the corner of her eye, she saw the flash of white shirtsleeve as Sandro extended his arm to catch the foot and twist, turning their assailant in mid-air to fall heavily to the ground.

I – have – three, came from Johann, his voice staccato as he fought off his own attackers.

Megan took a second to assess the situation. Sandro was fending off two men and Johann three. Neither felt under duress in her mind but as she came to her feet she headed for the wall, so she could feel stone against her back, and someone else leaped on her from behind, dragging her to the ground. This attacker was heavier than Megan, so she couldn't shake him off or prevent a heavy fall so she turned as she fell, as much as she could. She took the brunt of the impact on one shoulder and let the pain drive a cry out of her. A cry that she took and honed into determination.

Her sideways fall enabled her to roll. A man should never take a woman down onto her back if she knows anything about self-defense. It brought her feet and legs into play, stronger than her arms and with their own weapons—the substantial shoes she used for work.

Wishing she was wearing stilettos with those oh-so-useful heels, Megan lashed up with one foot and the man swerved to one side. Trained in martial arts then, not just a thug. A pity. He effortlessly regained his balance.

A dark-skinned man but definitely Caucasian, with a knitted cap pulled low down over his brows, wearing black clothing—jeans and a long-sleeved t-shirt.

All this she noted in the instant before he came back at her. He fell forward and grasped her hands, trying to subdue her with his bigger body, but she'd already brought one knee up, and as he fell, she shoved, using her knee to dig into his stomach to try to get enough purchase to kick him in the groin. But he was too close and she couldn't manage more than a nudge, which would turn him on more than it would hurt him. Worse, she'd given notice of her intentions.

He grasped her hands in one of his and brought the other down, aiming a killing strike at her temple. She ducked, just enough so he missed the right spot. Still, he caught the side of her head.

Light exploded behind her eyes. She held on and didn't pass out, forcing herself to stay conscious. She let her head fall to one side in a fake faint and closed her eyes, peeking through her lashes, ready for any vulnerable movement.

When her attacker lifted off her, she was ready. This time she didn't make any mistakes, and before he realized she was conscious she'd kicked up as hard as she could and caught him in the tender area between balls and ass.

Her attacker howled in pain and she followed up her advantage, coming to her feet in one swift movement, knees bent, legs spread for balance. Bloodlust filled her body, adrenaline pounding through every vein. These people were part of the organization that had taken Ricardo and used him like a lab animal, caused him unimaginable pain. The least she could do was give some back.

Megan went after her attacker with a kick to the side of his body, then she rained blows, hands and feet, on all the tender parts of him before going in for the kill.

As she raised her hand to deliver the chop across the throat that would mean one less torturer in the world, someone caught it from behind and pulled her close.

In her present state, everyone was her enemy, no one was leaving this street alive. She jerked back, using her elbows and shifting her stance to try to get him off balance so she could throw him.

"Easy, easy," came a familiar voice in her ear. "We need them alive."

The fight went out of her and she slumped against Sandro, aware that she'd broken the first law her masters had taught her. "Never lose your temper," Master Chu had said. "They will always win if they can make you do that."

She sighed, staring up at the black sky just visible above the tall buildings around them. "Sorry. I've never been in a real-life combat situation before."

"That's okay. It gets easier, though I hope to God we don't have to face many of these."

A chuckle alerted them to Johan's presence. "How's Chase? I felt him go down," Sandro asked him.

"He's fine. They knocked him out cold but there were only three. I killed one and saved two. One I want to feed from before we take them in. I'm hungry." He touched his lips with his tongue and Megan caught sight of two long, white teeth. Fangs. She shuddered.

"Hey," Sandro murmured. "He won't kill the guy. Vampires never kill their prey."

"We can't, not by feeding from them," Johan said, catching the words. "It'd kill us."

"You don't suck them dry?"

Johann raised a brow. "I don't *suck* anything. And we only take a little blood. There's more disinformation about vampires than about any other Talent. Maybe," he added with a dark chuckle, "because we spread a lot of it ourselves."

"You should try being a dragon," Sandro said dryly. He looked around at the unconscious bodies. "I want them questioned." He fixed Johann with a piercing stare. "Rigorously."

"It'll be a pleasure." Johann's smile had nothing humorous about it. Only wicked anticipation. "Help me get them close together and I'll call for transport to take us to STORM."

Sandro moved away from Megan after one gentle touch on her shoulder and picked up one of the men he'd taken, slinging the inert body over one shoulder as if he weighed nothing at all. They stacked the bodies close together on the sidewalk and left the dead man where he was. Now that the fight was over, people came running.

Johann stepped in front of them and drew out a badge. "NYPD. Step back please. I've radioed for help." He indicated Chase. "That's my partner. We've been looking for these bozos all evening. Maybe now I can get off shift."

She caught Sandro's brief mental exchange with the vampire. *You're enjoying this a bit too much, Johann.*

Sandro touched her elbow. "Let's get you out of here."

"Aren't we waiting for the transport?"

"Johann can handle it from here. Let's go. Now."

He tugged her arm until she got the message and began to walk swiftly away from the scene.

A flash, bright in the dark alley, made her blink. "Do you want people to take pictures?"

He bared his teeth in a feral grin. "Oh yeah. We want the message to get back to them loud and clear. That you're protected. And we know what they want."

When they turned the corner on to the busy street, it seemed as if the scene behind them was a world away. People rushed to get somewhere, anywhere other than where they were now.

He shook his head. "You never said you could fight like that. I was prepared to take him down but you coped better than I imagined."

"I do karate and a bit of kung-fu. Mainly for exercise. Gyms bore me silly. I started the karate at school, so I'm not so bad at it. But this is the first time I used it in anger."

His mouth settled in the grim line that showed her he was displeased. "And the last, if I have anything to do with it. There were more of them than we expected and they were more highly trained. They must want you real bad."

Could this gentle, considerate man be the same one who'd beaten their attackers without mercy earlier?

Megan pondered the dichotomy that was Sandro Gianetti on their return to his apartment. Excusing himself in the politest way possible, he returned five minutes later toting a variety of bags and cases, some of which she recognized.

"My clothes!"

He smiled and dropped the bags on the floor. "Where do you want these?"

When she saw his look, she knew he wasn't asking that at all. "Wherever you think best," she told him, and watched his expression lighten. Glad she could bring that to him, she followed him up the stairs with some of the bags and dropped them in the room where she'd spent the first part of the previous night.

"Shall I leave you to it?" Again, the slight hangdog look, quickly shaded by his long lashes.

"No. Let me see what Carilla has brought me for work though. I positively refuse to wear this suit again. I doubt I'll *ever* wear it again."

"I'll make some coffee. Unless you'd like something else?"

Busy snapping open the largest case, she glanced at him. "No, no thanks, coffee would be great." Then she saw him hesitate, his hand on the doorknob.

She winked at him. "Commando."

He groaned. "Oh God, it drove me mad all through dinner."

She straightened up and faced him. "It's not as if we could do anything."

"That's what you think." He walked back to her, slowly, hot eyes raking up her body and down again, lingering on one spot. "I could have fuzzed. Taken you on the table, in front of everybody."

"Could you?"

He took her elbows and drew her close. "Probably not. But knowing there's only one piece of cloth between me and heaven turns me on so much, I can't begin to tell you what's in my mind."

She glanced down. "You don't have to. I think you're showing me only too well."

She went fully into his arms as if she belonged there and his mouth came down on hers, taking possession with an insistence she couldn't ignore.

The crash when he shoved the case aside and took her down to the bed made her flinch but he murmured, his lips touching hers, "Forget it. Just concentrate on this. On us."

She was only too glad to comply. He stretched out on her body, covering her with heat and need, kissing her with a thoroughness she'd never known before. His hand covered her crotch, pressing wickedly, his fingers probed through the fabric of her pants to find her and tease her and she forgot everything except getting him inside her. She felt the dampness come and wriggled, the seam of her pants adding extra friction to his fingers. She rocked against him, moaning. When he unzipped her she waited impatiently for his flesh to touch hers but he moved away, undoing his slacks.

Impatient probing at her bare skin, the hot, hard demands of a man so turned on he wasn't thinking straight made her grip his upper arms tight, feeling the muscles bunch and flex as he bent to kiss her.

When he pushed inside her open pants, sliding over her, she melted, her juices flooding out to welcome him. So hot, so needy, she couldn't bear to stop, even to push her pants down farther than her upper thighs. The restriction made her writhe and when he entered her, the rounded cock head sliding just inside her body, she moaned and arched. Nothing else mattered now. She wanted this man so badly her mind turned into mush and became one screaming demand.

He slid inside and she gasped, pushing up to meet him. He groaned again and reached down to shove her pants farther down her legs so she could lift her knees, giving him deeper access to her body, only her ankles manacled by her clothes now. He filled her completely, his hard cock the perfect instrument of pleasure, fitting her so perfectly she went completely mindless in the drive toward her peak.

Her skin tingled, her hands seized and grasped, dragging him into her. She couldn't bear it if he left her now needing him so much, so passionately she hardly recognized herself in the creature that twisted and cried out under him, urging him to take her higher, faster, go deeper.

Rocking into her, Sandro kissed her. His tongue invaded her mouth to touch her, caress and thrust.

Then she felt him in her mind. He entered without words, touching her, smoothing her, as if he stroked her as he was stroking her below, stimulating and encouraging her response.

This was so out of control, she wasn't sure where her orgasm started, in her mind or her body. It burned, burst into heat and consumed her.

Megan had never screamed during sex before but Sandro drew back, one hand cupping her head, the other bracing his weight off her upper body. "Oh yes, baby, come for me, keep coming, never stop!"

Losing control completely, she gave herself up to him, the stresses of the evening adding to her desire to give him all she was, all she had. The explosion rocked them both and he cried out too, his voice mingling with hers as their essences mingled in her body.

The realization brought her down to earth so suddenly, she flinched as if she'd received a shot of static electricity. "Sandro! What have we done?"

She shoved him hard, catching him off balance, and he left her body, rolling off her to land on his back before he grabbed her waist and levered himself up again.

She thrashed under him. "Let me go! I have to go and wash—or something!"

"No, wait." He planted one leg over hers to stop her struggles. "Listen to me."

"Sandro, we did this with no protection, no nothing!"

He leaned on one elbow and she saw and felt the rush of relief in his mind. "It's the fourth day."

"I don't understand."

He traced her chin with one finger. "Sweetheart, shape-shifters are only fertile for three days a month. The three days of the full moon, when we're compelled to shift. Yesterday was the last day. I'm not fertile today, so I can't make you pregnant. And shifting into another form means that I'm immune to most human diseases."

She caught her breath. "I really missed something when I didn't watch every news program, didn't I?" She stopped struggling, taking in what he was telling her.

"No, you didn't. We haven't told anyone outside the community yet. No doubt someone will say something before long but nobody has, not yet."

"So you can't make me pregnant and you can't give me any diseases?"

"I can only make you pregnant during three days of every month and I can't give you diseases." He watched her, dark eyes alert, waiting for her response. "I'm sorry. I should have told you before but I wanted you so much, I couldn't stop. The last thing I want to do is cause you distress." He bit his lip. "I have, haven't I?"

"No."

Suddenly she felt vulnerable and foolish. She lay on the bed, a damp patch forming under her, her pants pushed down her legs and with a man she'd met for the first time yesterday. What was wrong with her? Why couldn't she keep away? Tonight, catching his exuberance, she'd been completely unable to resist. Falling onto the bed with him like a lovestruck girl. This man was older and more experienced than she could imagine, and she threw herself at him, allowed him to do whatever he wanted to her?

Where was her dignity, her pride?

"I'm sorry."

"What for?" He leaned over her and undid the first button on her now severely rumpled shirt.

"You must be used to something a bit more subtle than me. The commando thing, I mean—"

He stopped unbuttoning to press a finger over her lips. "You are irresistible, Megan Armstrong. If anybody should be apologizing, it's me, for my lack of finesse. All I did was make sure you were ready. And I didn't even stop to ask you if you wanted unprotected sex. I just wanted to get inside you five minutes before I did and I thought you were going to send me away. After all, why shouldn't you?"

She bit her lip. "There's a reason why I fell into your arms. And you deserve to know."

She told him ten minutes later when they were naked and ensconced in a steaming bathtub. Sitting between his legs, held against his body, she leaned on his shoulder. "I don't fall into bed with every man who asks, Sandro. Honestly. But I wanted you in the worse way."

"I'm glad you did. Because I wanted you. In the best way." He kissed her, caressing her mouth with the tenderness that had been absent fifteen minutes before.

In his arms, she felt cherished and wanted. "But you'd been watching me for a while. You investigated me. One thing you might not have discovered."

"We were pretty thorough," he admitted.

"Didn't you wonder why I left England?"

"You wanted a change. That's what you said on your job application to the John McIver University and to people we spoke to after we identified you."

Her mouth dropped open.

He closed her mouth with one finger under her chin. "STORM isn't a national organization. It's international." He dropped a gentle kiss on her lips. "So tell me. Why did you leave England? What did we miss?"

"Something nobody was supposed to know. I fell in love with the wrong man."

His hold on her slackened and she felt a new chill in her mind. "My professor. I was doing a part-time postgraduate course in research technology."

"Yes, I know that."

She knew he must be racking his brain for the details, what he'd missed. She was glad they'd hidden their tracks so well. "We ignored it as long as we could. But months of discussions, the occasional social meeting, and we knew we'd got it bad." She remembered the day she and Paul admitted their love. Lots of tears and so much worry tearing them both into tiny pieces. "He wanted me to earn my qualification, said I could do it, so we made a plan. We'd wait. What was two years in the scheme of things? We wouldn't take our feelings any further. Not yet. But after the final exams, when the papers went to an external marker, we'd give in to it. We committed, made a promise. All without touching each other. Except for one time." Once. One incredible hour when they kissed and finally admitted how they felt about each other. "We never slept together. We planned that after the exams, we'd go out to dinner together and begin our relationship properly. He wasn't married or involved, my course was the only thing keeping us apart." She bit her lip, remembering his dear face, the thrill he brought to her with his touch. "He died on the day of my last exam."

The shock arced through them both. She didn't know if Sandro had initiated it or her but they stiffened and she lifted off him slightly, leaning forward. She felt his hands on her arms, then he placed them on the sides of the bath and sat perfectly still.

"What happened?"

"A car accident. A motorcyclist came out of a side road at full speed and hit Paul's car. Neither of them survived." Tears welled up. She thought she'd cried them all out but it appeared not. "Only Jack knows. He was and is my best friend, and so he was the only person I told. He was worried while the affair was going on but he finally accepted we were behaving ourselves and wished us all the best. After Paul died, I couldn't think straight. I went home, refused to see anybody or answer the phone. Jack flew across the ocean and came straight to me. He looked after me until I was well enough to cope. I couldn't shake off my depression. I needed a complete change. Jack found me this job at the university, hunted down an apartment large enough for us to share. I owe him my sanity."

"He's been a good friend to you." His mind withdrew from hers and she wasn't sure what he was thinking anymore.

"Yes he was. But we're not romantically involved, Jack and me. It just didn't happen for us. So don't think that."

When she leaned forward to push herself up and out of the bath, Sandro moved, locking his arms around her waist. "Don't go. You feel too tense." He pulled her against him and he felt so good. Megan just wanted to let everything go and relax, as she hadn't done for a long time now. "I don't want you to be alone, I can feel your pain and I can't bear it."

She swallowed back the worst of her tears. "I decided after Paul that if I ever felt that way about anyone again, I wouldn't wait. I would take what opportunities life put my way. I could have left that course or found another supervisor but we decided we had plenty of time. As it turned out, we had no time at all."

Sandro lifted his hand to brush away the wetness on her cheek. She hadn't even been aware that her tears had spilled over. "So you haven't felt like that about anybody else?"

"Not before you." Too late, she realized she'd let too much slip. Did Sandro think she'd fallen in love with him? Not possible, not after two days.

He echoed her thoughts. "No, not after two days." He kissed her forehead, his lips lingering warmly on her temple. "We have a strong physical connection, you and me but I don't think we should confuse it with anything else. Not yet. This is driven by adrenaline and tension, not emotions."

For all that, he held her tenderly and she felt nothing in his mind except warmth and care. They fitted together so well, mentally and physically, and she'd never felt this deeply for another man, not since Paul.

Tiredness swept over her like a wave and she didn't want to argue anymore. She just wanted the warmth and security of being in his arms.

Then she realized her tiredness came from outside her, not just the events of the day. But in his arms she felt safer slipping into sleep.

*****

Ricardo lay in his bed in that room. No one else was with him. Sandro blinked. The transition was so sudden, he'd had no time to prepare.

"Ricardo."

Immediately his brother turned his head. Sandro blinked back his tears. This time he was aware of Megan, although they seemed to be occupying the same space. He was channeling through her, using her ability to contact with him.

Ricardo was rake-thin, hair shorn roughly around his head, dark eyes bloodshot and the expression in them was more than Sandro could bear. "Sandro." His voice sounded thready, barely reaching above a whisper.

Can you talk to me this way?

Yes.

Even his mental voice sounded faint. Sandro concentrated on finding the connection. Telepathy had no direction, it couldn't be tracked like GPS but there had to be a way. *Had* to.

He couldn't bear to hear the hope in Ricardo's voice. *Is there a way we can maintain this contact all the time?*

No. I tried.

A high-pitched whining sound irritated him.

That's the sonic field. I hear it all the time. Megan must have an unusually high range, because she's the only person I've been able to contact, in or out of this place.

Have you thought it might be because she's your bondmate? He hated the thought but he had to ask. If Ricardo said yes, Sandro would step aside.

Ricardo's pale brow creased in a frown. *I don't know. It could be that, I guess. Look after her, Sandro. Is she beautiful?*

Oh yes.

Megan had remained silent until now, but he felt her shock at his statement. *You must be thinking of someone else.*

No. He kept his mind steadily concentrated on Ricardo. Both his brother's arms were bandaged this time. That awful open, pulsing wound was hidden today.

They're leaving me to heal, they say. They won't let me shift, they keep me pumped up with Cephalox. I'm probably addicted to it by now. Somehow I don't think I'll need to worry about that. So it'll be several days, maybe weeks before I'm better. Amusement colored his voice. *I used the old trick of holding my breath until I turned blue. I didn't much care if it killed me or not but it scared them. They've taken a lot from me, I thought at one point I'd be going out of here in pieces. So now I have to rest, and eat the tasteless shit they bring me until I'm well enough for them to fuck me around again. I've bought some time.*

Sandro made a small moan of relief. *Ricardo, hang in there. We're coming, I swear.*

How? I don't know where I am.

We're using telepathy, bro. That means you're close. Telepathy ain't long distance.

A telling pause followed, before Ricardo's favorite expression. *Doh!*

Sandro wanted to laugh and he wanted to cry at the same time but he didn't have time. He felt Ricardo's weakness, knew his brother needed to rest. But he didn't want to leave him. To see and not to touch, to hear and not be able to *do* anything.

Do what you can to slow them down. Be as ill as you can.

Ricardo laughed, a cracked, weak sound instead of the full, rich belly laugh Sandro remembered. *I won't have much trouble with that.*

Sleep. Call Megan when you need me. I'll never be far away.

As he felt Ricardo drifting away, he heard her voice. *I'm always here for you, Ricardo. I'm sorry I didn't believe in you before.*

* * * * *

Sandro awoke in a rapidly cooling bath. He dragged out the plug and lifted a groggy Megan while reaching for two of the large bath towels hanging on the heated rail. By the time she came around, he was rubbing her, stimulating her to warmth.

She smiled up at him. "He's clever, isn't he?"

"Uh-huh." He concentrated on warming her, then threw a towel around his shoulders to cover them both. "He's buying time." Her face mirrored his relief and he found himself stupidly smiling at her. "We have a chance."

"What's Cephalox?"

He carried on rubbing warmth into her body. "A drug developed by our scientists to stop shape-shifters shifting form at awkward times, like when they're on the operating table. But it's dangerous and addictive. The shape-shifter's morphine."

"Oh. While you were talking to Ricardo I listened and took a good look around." She glanced away from him. "Nothing. The room's well soundproofed and those window blinds are impenetrable."

"I channel through you," he told her. "I have no form when we're there." He grinned. "I've seen it work before and if you saw it, it might creep you out. You look real to him and I'm a shadow around you."

"Like a ghost?"

"Just like that." He gave her back one last rub and dropped the towel to the tiled floor, satisfied that it was wetter than she was. "We've been mistaken for ghosts sometimes."

She blinked up at him. "Is that all ghosts are?"

"No. I think they're all kinds of things, our channeling included."

"Have you ever seen one?"

"Maybe." He grinned when she lifted an eyebrow. "I'm not sure if I saw one or not. A shadow in a great house one time when I was a houseguest. It couldn't have been caused by natural factors, like the movement of sunlight or a reflection. I don't know what it was."

She moved away from him and he caught his breath on a groan when he saw her smooth, supple back curving into a bottom he wanted to grasp in both hands. "Do you believe in life after death?" she asked, her voice almost a whisper.

She deserved a real answer, nothing flippant or unconsidered. "I think something goes on after we die. I don't know what." He took his time, bracing his arms against the towel rail when he bent to pick up the discarded towels and dump them in the laundry bag by the door.

Before she could wonder what had become of him, he followed her into the bedroom, watching her fling a robe over her shoulders. He knew it was wrong to take her. She was too vulnerable. He'd taken on the task of watching her himself because no one else got even a trace of Ricardo's presence. But he would have followed her anyway.

This time would be brief, so he'd fill it and then move on without regrets. What he couldn't have borne was never knowing her at all.

He tracked her, breathing in her scent, filling his senses with her presence, catching up with her just as she reached the bed.

Convenient. Very convenient.

Chapter Five

A week later, Sandro took a calming breath outside Ann's office, ready for the task that might be the most difficult he'd ever undertaken. A shocked glance in the mirror this morning had been confirmed by the doctor here at STORM headquarters and he had to face facts now. His dream was effectively over. At the back of his mind he'd known it was too good to be true.

At her sharp, "Come!" he fixed a smile in place and went in.

She was sitting on her couch, a full pot of coffee on the table before her, two cups already poured. Both black, as they both liked it.

Ann wasn't good at personal order. Her office, although luxurious, was the untidiest in the building. However hard her assistant Claud worked to keep her in order, Ann was always ahead of him, scattering papers, destroying Claud's carefully organized filing cabinets, spilling coffee all over her notes. But her mind was razor-sharp, her person always immaculate, close-cropped brown hair growing over the years into gray, a succession of power suits her invariable office wear. But the eyes were the same as the ones Sandro had met all those years ago, blue, perceptive and utterly beautiful in their clarity. And she never forgot how Sandro liked his coffee.

As usual, she got to her feet and embraced him before they both sat on the wide, black leather sofa. Although she never showed her personal feelings for anyone in public, Ann and Sandro had been through a lot together. Old colleagues, old friends, old adversaries once or twice but today would be different.

He waited for her to lead and she didn't disappoint. "Give me a run-down about the case. Not what's in the reports. I want to know what you think."

"Something I learned about only last night. We investigated Megan's background but we didn't find out that she had a secret love." Ann raised a cynical eyebrow but said nothing. "She fell in love with her professor but they decided to wait until after her finals, when it wouldn't be unethical for them to be together. He was killed the day of her last exam, the day they'd planned to make love for the first time."

"Straight out of the movies," Ann commented.

"Yep. It seems a bit slick to me too. I was running a check on him when you called for me. Paul Johnstone, professor at London University, where Megan was doing a one-year part-time postgraduate course. Forty-four, divorced, two teenage children. Cordial relations with his ex-wife, who had remarried. He died in a road accident on the date she said. The other guy died too, so if it was a setup, it was to kill both of them."

He paused. "Here's the interesting part. Her roomie, Jack Hargreaves, flew across to console her. It seems she'd told him. He brought her back here to New York, found her the job at the university and found an apartment for them to share. And they're not romantically involved." He picked up his coffee and took a sip of the steaming brew.

Ann saw the possibilities, as he'd known she would. "Interesting. So Hargreaves could have staged the accident, or he could have just used the situation to take her over. The IRDC is international, has laboratories everywhere, so he could be an agent, ordered to use her."

"Why would they do that? She didn't have the dreams about Ricardo until a few months ago."

Ann leaned forward, her mind ticking over the possibilities. "Just one possibility to bear in mind. Find out if there's anything they might have wanted her for. Maybe they discovered her telepathic abilities, the way she can pierce the usual sonic jamming devices. Maybe Hargreaves is telepathic. Find out." She drank the rest of her coffee. "Is that why you slept with her? To contact Ricardo?"

He smiled, knowing Ann too well to rise to her lure. He'd half expected the rapid change of subject, meant to take him off-guard. "No. I have more than one bedroom and I don't have to sleep with her to enter her mind."

"So what have you found out from her?"

"Ricardo's somewhere close. No more than ten miles from here in any direction. The link, when he connects, is strong. I spoke to him last night. He's buying time. They think he's close to death, so they're letting him heal." He bit his lower lip, letting the nip of pain bring him back to reality. "Ann, if he dies, I'm going in on my own. Nothing will stop me from finding them and killing them, every one. And I won't be going in fuzzed or hidden."

Ann stared at him, blue eyes flashing. "Not while you work here you won't. That is the very last thing I want. I want that lab intact, so we can extract the records and find links to the next one. And I want the scientists alive, so I can question them. Some of them might wish they'd died, if they resist."

"Not good enough," he snapped back. "Not this time."

Her eyes lost some of their fire and she frowned. He watched her formidable intelligence come into play, enjoying, despite his determination, her sharp mind working. "It's not the first time you've had friends or family in danger. You're always in control, Sandro, I've never known you to lose your cool."

"I'll play it your way for a while but not forever. I'm giving you fair warning, Ann. I owe you that, as a friend."

She stared at him for a full minute before she reached for the pot and poured two more coffees. Cradling her cup in her hands, she turned to face him full-on, studying his face closely. "Tell me I'm wrong, Sandro."

He smiled gently. "You're wrong." He took a sip of the coffee, savoring the tart flavor. From now on every taste, every breath was doubly important to him. "Except you're not."

He'd never seen sorrow in her eyes before but he saw it now. Without warning, she leaned over and snapped on a reading light, bending the flexible stem to angle it up at his face to put him in a spotlight.

He waited for her to finish her examination. "Oh God. I never imagined this would happen. When, Sandro?" Her voice softened, her mouth turned down and she seemed like a different woman. Softer, gentler, kinder.

"I visited the doctor here this morning and she confirmed it." He kept his voice steady. "I'm dying, Ann. I have maybe a year, maybe two. This has to be my last operation with STORM." He paused to take another sip. "I want some time to myself after that."

"So that's why you slept with Megan."

He swallowed. "I didn't know then. I've been ignoring the symptoms for weeks now, telling myself the extra lines around my eyes were from overwork, the odd gray hair was just coincidental. I'd hoped the subtle signs of aging were something else. The first lines appeared on my face a couple of months ago. Sometimes they do deepen when I've been in the sun, and I'd just come back from that job in Mexico. But they haven't faded. They're a little deeper. And I feel it inside. I'm not as strong as I was, and my stamina isn't the same. Only a small amount but it's there. This morning I took a good, hard look at myself and I went to Dr. Yasmin for the tests."

He finished his drink, savoring every mouthful, taking his time because he so needed it. "I've fallen in love with Megan. I want a taste of heaven before I give her up. I'll keep her until I can give her over to Ricardo's care. He'll look after her. Perhaps he'll fall in love with her too."

"What if we don't find him in time?"

"Then I take my revenge and let them do what they want. Short of taking me alive." He'd decided what he must do. What he wanted to do.

"When did you notice?"

"What, that I loved her?"

Ann's laugh sounded decidedly shaky. "That of course but are you sure you're dying?"

He shook his head, staring at the glossy surface of the tabletop. The highly polished mahogany reflected a cloudy image of his face but after his close scrutiny this morning he knew exactly what it looked like. "I can feel it as well as see it. In six months, I'll look like a sixty-year-old human. I want to go somewhere quiet. I want to go home, Ann, to Tuscany, to the place I was born. On my own."

"You think she'll let you?"

He lifted his eyes and met hers again, the blue brilliant with unshed tears. "Megan? She doesn't know how I feel. Not about her and not about this. I don't plan to tell her."

"Does your team know?"

"Not yet. I'll tell them all when this operation is over." He blinked hard, stifling his tears. They wouldn't do him any good now. "I don't want Megan to see me old and feeble. I want her to remember this, not what I'll become." He took Ann's hand in his, warming her chilly tremble. He couldn't meet her shocked gaze. Not yet. "Four hundred and fifty-two years is a good life, Ann. I'm not sorry. Just sorry I didn't meet Megan earlier, that's all. Please, don't tell her. She doesn't know enough about my kind to spot the signs on her own. I don't want her to know until I've gone." He smiled. "The last few weeks have been wonderful in a strange kind of way. Keeping tracks on her, learning her warmth and her strength. I hadn't even realized she was so tired until I made direct contact. You don't find that kind of courage every day, Talent or human, she has it and she thinks nothing of it. The last two days have been incredible. She's everything I thought she was and more. Ricardo can't convert her but perhaps someone else can." A thought dawned on him. "Hell, *I* can."

"You didn't give your Gift to anyone else?"

He shook his head.

"Why did you never convert Jane?" Ann asked abruptly. "I never asked you before because I didn't want to pry but with today's news, I don't care anymore. I want to know. I've always wondered. If you'd fallen for me, and I for you, instead of becoming friends, you'd have offered and I'd have accepted. Wasn't she compatible?"

He let his mind go back to one of the most painful days of his life. "She refused. It made her afraid. She was never comfortable with my dragon form, never accepted the dragon as she did the man." He avoided looking at her but he knew Ann had caught the brevity of his statement.

"How did you manage? You have to shape-shift during the three days of every month when the moon is full. How did you cope with that?"

He shrugged. "I did it when she wasn't around, and I didn't stay as the dragon for long." It was much more than that. Part of him had died when Jane refused to accept his other half. He was as much dragon as he was man, and she rejected that part of him. "If Megan wants my Gift, it would be my privilege to give it to her. Ricardo gave his Gift to his best friend's woman a few years ago, so he can't convert her. Maybe I can. Until this morning, I thought we could share a life."

When he felt Ann's hand on his, he turned it so they sat with clasped hands, at ease with their friendship. He felt Ann's pain but knew she could cope with it. "I'll keep your secret, Sandro, even help you. However, I have a few conditions."

"Name them."

"First, that you tell Megan the truth before you leave. Whichever way you leave. She deserves to know. She's not a shy Jane, she revels in your dragon form."

"How can you possibly know that?" Ann constantly surprised him, her simple observation of body language and behavior often surpassing his telepathic readings of people.

"The way you talk about her."

He grinned. "She likes me being a dragon. When we flew home from the hospital I felt her soften. God, I wanted her so badly then!"

"Take her for another flight before you have to leave."

He thought about it. Yes, he'd like that. Just for fun. And he knew she would. "So what are your other conditions?"

"You haven't said yes to that one yet." She reached for the coffee pot again. He refused another by putting his hand over his cup. Ann shrugged and refilled hers.

"I won't until I hear the rest."

She eyed him over the rim of her cup. "I want some of the members of that lab alive, Sandro. We need them, and the computers they'll have, so going in there all guns blazing might be a good way for you but it doesn't work for me."

He gave her a curt nod of understanding, not of agreement.

"And I want to stay with you for a while."

This one rocked him. He'd never been anything but friends with Ann. Had she wanted him all this time?

She chuckled, perceptive as always. Ann didn't need telepathy to read people. "No, not like that. As a friend. I've always wanted to go to Tuscany, so I'll come with you." She paused and sipped, then gave him a grave, considering look. "Here's the truth. We've been friends for longer than I care to remember. Thirty years, forty? I've known you nearly all my life, Sandro, longer than I've known George. Being the daughter of a Talent but not a Talent myself gives me an extra insight. And I don't think you should die alone."

"Have you ever been with a Talent who died?"

She shook her head. "Not of natural causes. I was with my mother when she died. She was mortal. Would it be any different?"

"No." His hand still twined with hers, their fingers locked together. "I'm going to die of old age. But I'll age rapidly. Toward the end, it might be possible to watch it. I won't crumble into dust or anything dramatic like that. I'll reach decrepitude and in all likelihood I'll just die in my sleep. If I don't die taking the lab down."

"Then I'll come with you. I can do it, and if you don't want Ricardo or Megan there, then it will have to be me." She gently freed her hand from his and leaned back so she could watch him full-face. "I'll help you conceal your destination, although it'll be hard to hide it from Ricardo. Wasn't he born in the same place?"

Sandro shook his head. "He was born in Venice, in another life. He doesn't know about the farmhouse in Tuscany. I'll leave it to him when I die, then he'll know but not until then. There are nearly three hundred years between Ricardo and me, Ann. I lived several lifetimes before he came along."

"Okay, either I tell Ricardo so he can go with you, or I come. Which is it to be?"

He sighed. Interfering woman! "You know it has to be you. I want Ricardo to look after Megan. And she can't be there when I die. No, I know what you're going to say." He held up a hand, smiling. "I know she's strong enough." He dropped his hand and admitted something to her he wouldn't have told another living soul. "But I'm not, Ann. I can't bear her watching me in pity, taking care of me as if I were her grandfather. Don't ask me to do it."

Ann put her coffee cup down in its saucer, the slight tinkle of china the only sound in the room. "Then it's me. I won't have you dying alone, Sandro, that's all there is to it."

With a shocking suddenness, her face creased and she covered it with her hands. He heard her take a few deep breaths.

"All right, damn you." He couldn't watch her cry, he had to do something fast. "I agree to your conditions. If I need to go in and destroy everything to get Ricardo out, I will. If I don't have to, I won't. Otherwise I'll play it your way." She gave a terse nod. "I'll tell Megan I'm dying but only when I have to. I get to choose the time." Another nod. "And yes, after this case I'll go, and you can come with me as long as you don't tell anyone else. Except George, of course," he added with a smile.

"Can nothing be done?" It was the first echo of weakness he'd heard from Ann Reynolds. Ever.

"No, Ann, my time has come. Some shifters get seven hundred years, some get five hundred. It seems I'm getting four hundred and fifty and a few. I'm not complaining." Except he couldn't consider more than a short time with Megan. And he couldn't tell her he loved her.

With any luck, she didn't love him and she'd leave him for Ricardo when they found him without regrets. He'd do her best not to give her any.

Taking Megan home from work that night, Sandro barely remembered how he got back but habit aided him more than usual. Driving into his usual place, his mind elsewhere, he made sure he had his keys and got out of the car.

Scan! His senses reminded him. Fuck, he could have put the whole operation in peril. What if someone was lurking in this parking garage to make absolutely certain he was alone?

He scanned quickly, and was more than relieved to find no one there. Not a soul, apart from the one person he wanted more than anyone else in the world right at this moment. Megan.

When he opened the car door, she scrambled out, and when she stumbled, her legs cramped from crouching on the floor, he lifted her into his arms and headed for the elevators. When she protested, he stopped her mouth with a kiss. "We have to get out of here fast. Don't want anyone driving in." He grinned down at her. "Besides, you feel good in my arms, and I want you here."

She chuckled and relaxed against his chest. Sandro allowed himself the illusion of forever in the time it took the elevator to get down to their floor. It was a great dream, one he'd revisit in a few months' time when she wasn't a part of his life anymore. But for now it was him, and her, and a bed a mere elevator ride away.

The elevator pinged its arrival and Sandro wasn't too far gone to scan it before the doors opened. Empty. He managed to push his keycard into its slot and left it there for the ride up, having better things to do than watch the floors pass by.

He took her lips, feeling her open willingly for him, welcoming him in. Too far gone for finesse, he plunged his tongue inside her mouth and shuddered when she stroked it with hers, retreating and advancing in teasing forays against him. Her body heated against his, and she pressed closer to him, forcing his cock to leap to attention.

She made him behave like a randy schoolboy. Perhaps that was one reason he'd fallen in love with her.

No, he couldn't think like that, not now. They were so attuned, she could probably read him at will and he didn't want that, or she might start thinking their affair was something more permanent. Something it could never be.

Still kissing her, he opened his eyes when the elevator glided to a halt to make sure they were headed in the right direction. After grabbing his card, he took the few strides to his front door and disengaged while he unlocked the door. "I have a little plan for us tonight."

"And that would be?" She lifted a hand to stroke his jaw.

"Wait and see." He whispered the words close to her lips so his breath heated them. He watched, fascinated as they flushed and opened for him.

He climbed the stairs and took her mouth again at the top for a long, luxurious time, before lowering her gently to the bed. Now he could roll over her, covering her as his body was howling for him to do. He lifted his mouth away from hers and completed the roll. "You wait right here."

When he returned, she was lying on the bed propped up on one elbow, her hair gloriously tousled, half down from its daytime up-do, her lipstick almost gone, revealing the lusciousness underneath.

Her eyes widened when she saw what he carried. He propped the full-length mirror against the rails between the platform his bed rested on and the drop to the floor below. Grabbing the pile of books by his bed, he used them to secure the mirror. Reading would be the last thing on his mind tonight.

Megan watched him with a speculative expression in her lovely blue eyes. Blue, the color of innocence—and, he was learning, the color of passion.

He could attack her like an animal, rut with her for both their pleasures, or he could make love to her. Tonight, he would love her and commit everything to memory. He would treasure every moment until the day he died.

"What are you thinking about?" Her voice had lowered, darkened with passion.

He smiled. "You. Just you."

He stripped, not once taking his eyes from her face, and she watched him. Dropping his clothes at his feet, he felt a flood of heat when she opened her arms to him.

He went to her then, sliding up the bed to where she lay before glancing down to check the mirror was in place. Perfect. The glow of the gentle light he left on most of the time was enough to illuminate them but not cast a spotlight on them.

Enough to relax and see by. The dimmer switch was just by his hand, on the wall.

Megan. Tonight he could allow himself to believe she was his destiny. Badly timed but destiny could be like that.

She touched him and he turned to her. "Are you sure this is a good idea?"

"Oh yes, I'm sure." He lifted his hand and framed her face, savoring her cool, soft skin. "It's time you saw how lovely you are."

Her smile showed him her uncertainty and a trust in him that took his breath away. "Open to me, *carissima*. Body and soul. Open."

He felt her mind release and when he entered, gazing deep into her eyes, she gave way softly, and it felt like he was sliding into a pool of warm, soothing gel.

When he reciprocated, he made sure a few nuggets were tucked well away behind barriers at the back of his mind. "Tonight," he whispered, "I want you to see yourself as you are. I want to help you to control your mind, set up barriers no one can enter."

"Except you."

"No, not even me. Your mind should be your private fortress." He watched her, feeling her mind swirl around him as she assessed what he was telling her. It felt delicious. He'd entered her before but never this deeply, this intimately and he found it addictive. If Megan had a color it was the palest shell-pink, nurturing and life-affirming, delicate but holding an inner strength that could never be broken. "Tonight, we'll make your mind as strong as it can be. And I'll make sure you enjoy every moment of it."

He began to weave a pattern in her, and at the same time took her mouth in a deep, loving kiss. His love for her he hid away with his secrets. Deep affection and caring remained, to surround her and worship her.

She opened her mouth as she'd opened her mind—trustingly, with a wholehearted giving. He rolled her onto her back and slid his hand up to her breasts, caressing and teasing through the thin fabric of the high-necked sweater she wore.

But not for long. Lifting away from the kiss, watching her in the gentle light, he drew the sweater over her head. He made short work of her bra.

Pink, full nipples tempted him to taste and tease them into hard buds. He didn't resist their silent invitation and bent to lick. Her indrawn breath and flinch, making her breast quiver under his lips, told him of her tense response, just as the color of her mind deepened and warmed.

Delicious. Sandro closed his eyes, savoring her warm, soft skin. He curled his tongue around her nipple, making a sheath for it to harden in, protecting it before nipping and licking once more. A small yelp and a sigh rewarded him. When she curled one hand around his head, threading her fingers into his hair, he purred like a cat.

He kissed his way to her other breast and turned it into a facsimile of the first, lapping at it instead of sucking to obtain the same result. When he lifted, with a long sucking, releasing it only at the peak, he watched it settle back, hard and aching for him. Smiling, he looked up at her face. "Good?"

"You know it," she breathed. But when she made to come to him, he pushed her back against the soft coverlet. "No. Let me. I want to explore you, show you what you can be—what you are."

"Only with you."

That annoyed him. "No, you're lovely, whoever you're with."

She smiled. "Most men would get awfully territorial if I even mentioned someone else." She drew a finger along his forearm. "I like that you don't come over all Neanderthal."

If she only knew! He gritted his teeth in an effort not to show her, tell her that she was his and his alone. Because it wasn't true, the practical part of his mind reminded him. It couldn't be true.

"Something wrong?"

"No." His answer was too short but he couldn't help that now. He bent his head to her, reminding the breast under his mouth what they were doing here. He was loving her. Her gasp told him his reminder had the right effect.

Down farther, to stroke and tease her navel, evoking a wriggle, and then to the still-dressed half. He slid her skirt down her legs, hooking his fingers under her panties to bring them down too. She didn't need them any more.

That left her in a pair of sheer black stockings, clinging to her legs as lovingly as he wanted to. He left them on for now, intrigued by the different textures and colors. When he stroked his hands down her legs he decided that, delicious though the sensation was, he preferred her bare skin, warm, responsive and silkier than the most expensive hosiery.

He paused to savor the unique perfume of Megan, so unlike any other woman he'd lain with, before touching the tip of his tongue to her, pushing through the dark curls to the secrets within.

She groaned and arched up, her involuntary movement bringing her closer to his mouth, an invitation he took with delight. He delved his tongue into her, curling it to reach her sensitive inner tissues. Her moans and cries were his reward, more than ample. He would have been perfectly happy with her response but his own body had begun an insistent throb, demanding its turn with her.

The perfect kind of beneficent control, he thought, lifting out of her to tickle her clit with the tip of his tongue, inciting and inflaming her so much he had to rest his hands on her hips to stop her wrenching her body away from his control. "Sandro! Please!"

He wanted to give her the greatest, the best orgasm she'd ever had without having a man's body inside hers. Something for her to remember, a part of him left behind forever in her.

He tasted every crease, every fold, greedily lapping at the juices she gave him, a reward well-earned. She tasted like no other woman, a mixture of tart apples and rich cream, delicious and addictive. He took his time, savoring every fraction of her soft, hot skin.

Sandro played her to a near-climax, then backed off for the scant few seconds it took her to cool down a little before starting again. He learned what worked fastest, what brought a thrill of delight to her, by sensing the responses of her body and her mind, working in tandem to the same end. When he lapped the very tip of her clit she went crazy, her arousal heating up but never quite reaching her peak. The longer he kept her going, the better her climax would be. This was such fun he never wanted to stop, despite her wordless moans and cries.

When she was incoherent, blind to everything but him, he took her clit into his mouth and sucked hard, the pulses echoing the thrust of two fingers into her wet pussy.

Her scream came loud and long, and he briefly wondered if anyone heard and decided he didn't care. He wanted her screaming—as long as it was in ecstasy.

Oh baby, you are so very beautiful like this.

As he whispered the words into her mind, he scooted up the bed, over and behind her. Just as he felt her wondering, unarticulated query, he lifted her, urging her on to her knees.

Unable to wait any longer, he pushed into her, holding her around the waist. He was so fast, he caught the last pulses of her orgasm with his cock.

He nearly came. He'd been concentrating so hard on Megan, he hadn't realized just how close he was. Yelping, he threw his head back, drawing in a deep breath. "Please, not yet!"

Her gasping chuckle brought him down just enough to regain control and he lowered his head to the most beautiful sight of his life.

In the gentle glow of the background lighting, he saw Megan reflected in the mirror, knees apart on the rumpled bedsheets, a dark figure behind her, surrounding her. Him. Instead of using the dimmer switch, he used his mind to raise the light, enough so he could see his cock embedded in her vagina, the image still shadowy but clearer now.

"Look at that, Megan. Me in you, you receiving me so sweetly, so perfectly." Before he could betray himself he bent his head and kissed the side of her neck, licking away some of the saltiness caused by their exertions. "Now watch, and tell me that's not a beautiful sight." He slid his hands over her waist. "That seductive curve, inviting me to touch—here." He cupped her breasts in his hands, taking their fullness before tracing the hard, peaked nipples with his thumbs. Spreading his hands wide, he cupped them completely, allowing the nipples to slide through the gaps between his two middle fingers. Warm satin under his hands, living, breathing woman. His woman.

He pushed and watched his cock slide deeper inside her. The sight, combined with the sensation and the giving feeling in her mind, made him hold on to the single mental thread he had left, the only thing between him and coming. He didn't need it long this time but then he saw the expression on her face.

"I hadn't realized."

"Realized what, *mia inamorata*?"

"How—how intoxicating it is to see this."

"Yes." He lifted his gaze from her breasts to the mirror in front of them. "Oh yes!"

Gripping her waist, he thrust hard, withdrew and thrust again, his glistening cock moving in and out of her with an inevitability both accepted and welcomed. He slid his hand down to her stomach and spread it over the soft skin before pushing hard. He shuddered. "Oh God!"

The gentle pressure caused her to shiver against him, the skin of her back delicately quivering against his front.

"Put your hand over mine."

She lifted one trembling hand and did as he bade her. He spread his fingers so she could place hers between them. "Feel what I feel, Megan. Me in you."

He thrust hard and let it happen, the small miracle every shape-shifter could perform but rarely did, because it marked them out as different. He gave her another inch.

His cock grew inside her and he remained still while it happened. "You feel that?"

Her lovely eyes widened, the slumberous, sexy expression changing to one of surprise. "How did you do that?"

"It goes with being a shape-shifter, sweetheart. But I haven't used this skill in a long, long time. I wanted to do it with you."

"Why?" She kept completely still, only bracing her body to accept him, which recommenced on a regular, thrusting rhythm, even as they spoke.

"I don't need it to come, and I can satisfy a woman without it." He kissed her neck again, tasted her as if he needed it like breathing. "It's a very intimate act."

She sighed and leaned against him, her hand holding his in place, her vagina quivering around him as he brought her closer to orgasm. He kissed his way up her neck to her ear, taking that delectable morsel into his mouth to nibble it softly before releasing it to glance in the mirror once again.

Her body arched back against his, their linked hands pressing her stomach to move closer to where he moved in and out of her, slowly stimulating her with a regular rhythm. She turned her head toward him and he gave up the reflection to kiss her, plunging his tongue into her mouth to take her hard.

Without warning, he tore his mouth away and shoved her forward with his free hand. She fell on to her hands, onto all fours, and as she did he increased his tempo, pounding into her, dragging her back against him to open her even more and take her completely.

Her temperature increased. His mind locked in hers, and he monitored her spiral of pleasure, took her up further, and when he leaned back a little, sighed with delight when small mental detonations, like sparks from a firework, told him he'd found the center of her sensitivity.

It was also his. This position stroked his cock at just the right angle, her wet, hot tissues rubbing the head, her tight channel clenching him with every thrust.

He gave himself up to pure sensation, locking his mind with hers so his pleasure was hers, hers was his and there seemed no end.

Sparks exploded around them, and his cries mingled with hers in a futuristic symphony until the spiral reached its apex and she screamed, taking him with her up and up still more, higher than he'd ever flown.

He gave her everything he had, his body erupting within hers as she bucked wildly against him.

Only then did weariness take him and he fell across her, rolling her under him and then to one side. "That was—" she began but he stopped her.

"No words. Not now. Feel, relax." Or he might bind her to him with the sweetest truth of all, the truth he could never tell her.

Sinking against him, he curved his arms around her and gave way to the sleep that tickled the edges of their minds. The best sleep is the one after making love.

Chapter Six

Toward dawn, when light crept into the apartment from the uncurtained windows, Megan opened her eyes.

She wasn't alone, in mind or in body, but he slept, his mind still locked in hers. Although they'd only made love once last night, the experience had shattered her, broken her defenses and unnerved her. This wasn't the passionate affair she'd expected when she first realized Sandro wanted her. The incredibly hot Italian had given way to a sensitive, caring man who wanted more than sex.

But did she? He overwhelmed her, his power unconsciously displayed so often she wasn't sure she had anything to offer in return. Sex was good but she was mortal, and deep down she knew he wouldn't want to watch another woman he loved age and die. He couldn't want that.

She snuggled back, feeling his arms tighten around her. Still asleep but when she moved to check the time on the digital clock on the nightstand, she felt the first stirrings of a man waking up. Both mentally and lower down, where the beginnings of his morning glory pressed against her bottom. She moved away but he pulled her back with a low growl.

She chuckled. "Good morning."

He moved, swinging up on one arm and pressing her onto her back. "Good morning, beautiful."

She glanced to one side. "Who are you talking to? I thought we were alone."

He turned her head to face him again. "You know we are."

Bending, he kissed her, so gently that he was gone before she could respond. A shadow passed across his eyes but it was gone almost as soon as it appeared, replaced by warmth he couldn't have faked. "Since we're awake so early—" He moved his body suggestively against hers. "Do you think we should keep ourselves busy?"

Her laughter was cut off by his kiss, more invasive this time, opening her mouth with a touch of his tongue against her lips. He explored her at length but he didn't open his mind to her, although she opened to him. He finished the kiss and drew away so he could speak to her. "I think it's time you learned some mental self-defense. I've seen you in street action—you're good, not spectacular but good enough to fend off attack until we can get to you. Now I want to get you to that level mentally."

She felt slightly offended. "Is that all you think I'm capable of?"

He pressed down, resisting her attempt to throw him off. "No, I think it's all we have time for right now. I see no reason why you shouldn't become adept at mental communication eventually. Telepathy can be learned, it's not a natural gift. You need someone to open you to the possibility, breach the mental barrier every baby sets up in the first week of life. But for now, we need to protect you. I'll show you some first aid for the mind."

"Will you stay and teach me after all this is over?" She held still, her heart in her mouth. This was the first time she'd mentioned continuing their affair afterward, when they had Ricardo safe—anything else she refused to consider—and she didn't know how he'd take it.

That shadow crossed his features again, and just as quickly, it cleared and he smiled down at her. "I'd love to. But I'm on active duty. If Ann sends me somewhere, I can't refuse. But Ricardo can look after you while I'm away."

She bit back her instant response—she didn't want Ricardo, not like that, she wanted his brother. "I can wait for you. I like the way you teach things." She wriggled against him, loving the way his body conformed to hers, sheltering and warming her.

He sighed. "Practice, and show me how good you are when I come back."

She stroked his jaw, now prickly with morning stubble. "Do you think they'll send you away?"

His mouth hardened. "Yeah. There's something brewing in Europe and I speak Italian like a native." His grin flashed and he moved his head to one side to kiss her palm. "Ann will keep me on this case until it's over but I know she wants me on the European job as soon as possible." He paused, gazing at her, a hungry look entering his eyes as she watched. "I don't know if I can," he murmured but before she could ask what he meant, he kissed her again, softly. Lovingly, she thought. Or was it hoped?

"Now we have time. What time do you start work today? I've forgotten."

She'd saved this tidbit for him. "Not until one p.m. I'm on a half day."

"Oh baby!" Another kiss, luscious and lavish. "And my only responsibility is you. So let the lessons begin."

He raised up a little and she let her hands slip from his shoulders to smooth over his chest and tangle in the hair there. He glanced down, watching her movements. "You're going to tell me what you want me to do." He looked up. "Mentally. No talking. You can moan, cry out, even scream my name if the fancy takes you. But I won't take instructions any way but telepathically."

Fascinated, she stilled her hands and stared at him. His dark eyes told her nothing, except that he liked what he saw. But when she entered his mind, drawn by his unspoken invitation, she found him waiting. And eager.

"Tell me what you want, *cara*. And don't forget the mirror. It's still there." His low, purring voice incited her beyond reason. Oh yeah, she knew what she wanted.

She watched his mouth curve in a wicked grin before he slid down her body, pausing to briefly nuzzle her breasts, and hovered above her crotch.

Kiss me there, Sandro.

How?

She built the picture in her mind and felt her crotch dampen as she thought of it. His head, lowering to her, taking a deep breath of her feminine perfume, then taking a lick, then another. And a deep draw. She opened her legs.

He bent, and licked, then sucked. Hard but she was ready for him, because she knew what she wanted him to do. When he drew away, tonguing her clit, she nearly lost it. But no teasing this morning. This morning she'd get just what she wanted from him. And give it back.

The next maneuver was hard to picture but she managed it. She wanted to *show* him, not tell him. His groan told her she'd done it right. But he'd promised, and so he pivoted, slowly turning around to bring his cock up to her mouth. Without taking his lips away from her clit.

The swiveling suction nearly drove her insane. Not enough to make her come, more than enough to push her further toward it. Without thinking, she groaned, "Do it, Sandro. Please!"

Immediately he stopped and lifted his head, keeping himself a tantalizing few inches out of reach. He wagged a finger at her. "Humans have no patience."

She reached out to grab him but he moved away, curving his body so she couldn't reach him. "Sandro!" Her voice came out as a high-pitched wail. She wanted him back. Now. Frantically she took a breath, and concentrated.

The picture she sent was detailed and explicit. His chuckle ended on a groan. "You can send spectacularly well, *cara*. I don't think I have anything to teach you there. Okay, now try *not* to think of what you want next. If you do, lock it away, hide it from me. Or you won't get it."

"I'm not sure I can."

"Enjoy. Play the game."

At last, he moved close enough for her to get to him. After she locked her arm around his thighs, making sure he couldn't pull away without an effort, she dragged him close. Close enough to taste.

As he tasted her, she tasted him, running her tongue around the sensitive head and the rim. He opened to her, showing her the sensations she was delivering to him, and she felt his wholehearted enjoyment of her response to him.

He gasped and stiffened his spine, jerking back when she tongued the opening at the head of his cock. "Dear God, you're good!"

Greedily, she lapped the drop of moisture that flowed from the tip, wanting more of him, all of him. But she wasn't to have it, not this morning at any rate. He spun around, his speed telling her he'd partially shifted to take advantage of the creature that lived within him. She knew him so well now. It seemed impossible after such a short time together but he'd let her in so fully she felt she knew all his secrets.

Well, nearly all. She was dimly aware of the darkness at the back of his mind that her presence skittered past whenever she encountered it, like a forbidden door, something that lurked and avoided notice. He was entitled to his secrets but like Bluebeard's wife, every time she neared it, she crept a little closer.

He came back to her, sliding over her opened legs, and she lifted her knees up to open wider for him. His very size demanded it. She adored it. When his eyes met hers, she fell into his spell. "Tell me," he whispered. "Tell me what you want me to do."

"Make love to me, Sandro. Fuck—" His finger across her lips stopped her asking him in terms she thought he'd prefer.

He put his hands on either side of her head and waited. She did as he wanted and sent him the image, his cock sliding inside her, pushing against her body's natural resistance until his balls nestled against her ass. Her vision blurred when he moved closer and her mental picture became reality. He slipped inside her, pushing firmly but with an inevitability neither could stop, even if they'd wanted to.

"I won't fuck you today," he murmured, just before grazing his lips against hers. She moaned from the sensitivity, increased so much from his skin against hers, the sensations her mind sent to her body.

He moved out and in, the rhythm speeding up as both neared completion. Neither forced the pace, which came as natural as breathing. Her backbone stiffened and she pressed her body up to his just as he pushed up to his arms' length, reaching deeply inside her. Their eyes locked, their minds as one, they came, completely in unison.

Poised above her like some fantastic bird, she saw both his forms, the dragon shadowing the man, before the fire in his eyes told her he was definitely changing.

Fear shadowed her but curiosity won. She watched him, this amazing man, and he stared into her mind, her heart. She held nothing back.

He must know she'd fallen in love with him by now. But it seemed not. Either it held no interest for him or he wasn't as aware of her as she was of him. His eyes lightened, then darkened, turning from brown to navy blue, and his skin gleamed as scales appeared.

Then from behind him curled something no man should have. A tail. Long, flexible and scaly with a barbed tip that put real fear into her heart. But she couldn't have moved now. He held her fully within his control.

The tail curled toward her and she knew the barbed tail held death at its tip. Still, she trusted him to keep her safe, even as he wielded the weapon that could be her end.

The barb curved away from her but the tail came down, stroking her skin until she shivered with the pleasure it brought her. The warm, dry scales evoked the time she'd flown on his back and she remembered the tactile sensation of the dragon. She loved it. Everything about him, dragon and man, she loved.

He took a deep breath and the tail whipped back, as if drawn like an electrical cable on a coil, back into his body. The shadowy scales disappeared and his eyes returned to warm brown.

He sighed and sank down onto her body, gathering her close. "I'm sorry. About the last part, I mean."

"No," she murmured, still dazed from the experience. "Don't be. It was incredible."

"You were never in any danger. You never will be with me. But sometimes the animal side wants a share." He tucked her into the warmth of his all-too-human body and she realized they were still joined, although he had softened inside her.

"It's exciting."

He stroked her back soothingly. "Whatever form I take, dragon or man, I'm a sentient being. You can always talk to me, reason with me, and I'll understand. Never forget that, Megan. As the years pass, you'll meet more of my kind and it's better if you know how to manage them."

She opened her mouth then closed it again. He talked as if he wouldn't be there when she met these other beings. How could he be so sure? She certainly wasn't. Commitment shy, or determined not to get too involved with another mortal? She suspected the latter, and so, out of respect for him, she held her tongue.

She curled her leg up over his, ready to doze in his arms, but snatched it back as something as hot as a brand burned her inner thigh. "What the—"

As she sat up, she felt him go still. He stayed completely immobile, except for his chest moving in quiet breaths, as she examined him. "What's this?"

The tattoo was etched on the outside of his upper thigh, the most beautiful she'd ever seen. A small dragon, his tail curled under his body, stared straight ahead, every scale, every fold of skin lovingly depicted on Sandro's tanned skin. The ink must be special, because it glowed, almost as if the creature had been drawn in fire.

She touched it, drawing back immediately when she felt the heat.

"Keep watching."

She did so and saw the image fade until only her memory held the image. She turned her head to look at his face. "What was it?"

"It appears sometimes when I make love," he said. "All shifters have them."

"So if you were a merman—"

"There would be a little merman there. But I'm a dragon, so I have my friend here instead." He reached for her hand. "It means I can convert you to a dragon. If you wish it."

Everything seemed to stop, even her heart. It was real. "I can be like you?"

He lifted her hand to his lips. "If you want to be. But if I do it, you could be weak for several days afterward and you won't come into your full strength for a while. And there's a slight risk of madness, although the way you accepted me just now tells me you shouldn't be susceptible to that particular curse. I don't want to consider it, not while you're in danger, because of the weakness that comes after the conversion. It would make you too vulnerable." He toyed with her fingers, watching their conjoined hands rather than her face.

"Does it mean I had a dragon in my ancestry?"

He didn't look up. "Maybe. We think so, or there is some mutation in your genetic makeup that makes it possible."

"So why—why does the IRDC take people like Ricardo and operate on them?" She repressed a shudder. She needed to know the answer, not show him how much the mention of the labs repelled her. "If you can convert people, surely that's the answer?"

He lifted his eyes to her face, grave and full of sorrow. "It's not enough for them. They want more and they want it under their control, not ours. We want to make the knowledge public when the world is ready, not when this stupid hysteria infects half the population. They'd regard this gift as a weapon, one we could use against you."

"Why don't you?"

He shook his head slightly. "We don't think in that way. Humans have made themselves the most fearsome race on the planet by their insatiable curiosity and their desire to progress. And their ability to procreate, more prolific than all the Talents combined. Though to what and from what they rarely stop to ask themselves. Since they are aggressive by nature, they assume every other race is too. But we're not. Truly we're not. We can kill but we prefer to love. We can destroy but we'd much rather create."

"Most humans are like that."

"Some." He stroked up each finger before tugging her down to lie in his arms. "You."

When they kissed, it felt like coming home but with both of them temporarily spent, it was a kiss of affection. Even of the L word Megan was beginning to banish as soon as it appeared in her mind, because Sandro didn't seem to want it. "So you're offering to convert me?" she said a little breathlessly a minute later.

"When the time is right. If you want me to."

She took in the implications of it. He could convert her. She'd be a dragon and she'd live for hundreds of years. But could she adapt? Did she want to? "Can my family be converted?"

"Probably not. It doesn't seem to run in families equally. Some members have it, some don't. When we think we're nearing the solution, it slides out of reach, at least that's how a scientist tried to explain it to me once."

"Was Jane compatible?" Talking about his late wife seemed natural, she realized with a shock. Jane had belonged to a different Sandro, at a different time. But if she couldn't be converted, that would explain a great deal.

"Yes, she was," he said calmly, completely astounding her.

She gaped. She couldn't help it. Who would refuse to join the one they loved? Well Jane did, obviously. "Did you ask her?"

This time he didn't hide his dark shadow. "Yes I did. She didn't want it. I only shape-shifted in front of her once and she asked me not to do it again. She wanted the man, not the dragon."

"But you're both of them."

He kissed her again, a gentle salute. "Thank you for that. Yes I am. She couldn't understand it. So after a while I accepted her decision and I lived with her as a man."

That must have hurt him. Megan gloried in the dragon side of her lover, not just the man, and she understood, even more now after his recent lovemaking, how the two were really one. "I'm sorry."

He brushed his lips over her once more. "You're addictive, you know that? Don't ever be sorry for something you didn't do."

"I'm sorry you had to go through that experience." She gave up trying to explain when he smoothed his hands down her body, from armpit to hip. "I would never do it to you, ask you to hide what you are."

"I know."

The intensity of his concentration on her almost scared her. She wasn't sure what she was getting into here. Something made her draw back, avoid the connection her body wanted her to make with him. Not just her body. That was the trouble. An affair with somebody as hot as Sandro was every woman's dream but the troubled mind behind the glorious body made her pause from making the ultimate commitment. She needed time. Time to think, to work out what to do, and what he meant with her.

He smiled. "Now for your next lesson. How to lock something away. I can do it for you although it would be much better if you could do it for yourself."

"So the enemy can't read my mind?"

He stroked the tip of her nose, then kissed it. "So other Talents can't. We're not all the good guys, some work for the enemy, and in any case, with Talents coming out into the open, it's going to be a basic skill most people will want to learn. It adds a new dimension to the way the world works. We could always read people but we had a few rules. Never Tell, Never Compel. Now the first part is obsolete."

"And the Never Compel?"

"Some Talents can compel by using the power of their minds, make people do things they don't want to do. That's always been outlawed. The penalty is death, no appeal."

She gasped. "That's a bit hard."

"So it is." He kissed her again. "But it worked. For a long time. Now the politicians want to incorporate it into the law. That means all the attorneys will get involved and all the other leeches." He laughed mirthlessly. "I don't think that will work somehow. I have a feeling some things will stay in the Talented community, at least for now."

"You'd break the law?"

He studied her, watching her closely, and she felt his mind come to attention. "Yes, I would. Talents can withstand Compulsion. Mortals need to be taught how to do it."

"So teach me."

"In time." He kissed her again, a soft, warm touch of his lips to hers. "It takes practice. Now I want to teach you to lock all your secrets away, so nobody can read your name, address and number."

"And PIN number," she murmured. Right now she couldn't care less about her PIN number.

"Two" — kiss — "Seven" — kiss — "Three" — kiss — when he mumbled another number against her lips she didn't have to hear it to know he was right.

Never had a lesson been sweeter! He showed her how to hide her essential details by making her not think of an elephant, then to lock the image of an elephant away in her mind. Their laughter rang around the large room.

Then the lesson turned more intimate. While she was still laughing over the elephant, he turned her over and massaged her body, long, sweeping caresses driving her to fever pitch before he told her not to think of things she couldn't then stop thinking about.

His body touched hers, from shoulders to toes, then to her bottom. When he raised her up to kneel with her back to the mirror, her head resting on a bank of pillows, he sent her an image. His body entering hers. The warm glow of sunrise, streaming in through the windows, bathed her in warmth.

This time he loved her long and slow, sending her the images of his cock sliding nearly all the way out, then in again, deep and hard before driving her to dementia and further. Only then did he allow himself his release, his mind firmly embedded in hers, his hands gripping, stroking, his mouth kissing and finally biting her shoulders and neck.

As he lay next to her in the aftermath, he murmured wickedly, "I'm going to send you images of this in the forefront of your mind, not through our private, deeper channel, every time there's another Talent present. If you don't want to have our love life there for everyone to see, you'll take it and lock it down."

"You beast!" She struck out, only half in jest, but as he caught her fists in his big hands, laughing, the phone rang.

He paused, and she felt him wonder if he should leave it for the answering machine, then change his mind. An image of Ricardo as they'd last seen him appeared, and sighing, he turned to pick up the bedside phone.

"Yes?" When he turned back to her, his jaw was set in a hard line. He handed her the receiver. "It's for you."

Without another word, he got out of bed and headed for the shower.

Chapter Seven

"Yes?"

"Don't snap, darling," Jack's unmistakable tones came back at her. "Did I interrupt something important?"

She felt the blood surge hotly to her face. "No." She tried to keep her voice normal but she obviously failed.

"Okay, don't let the big man faze you. I take it he's great in bed?"

She grinned. Nothing could keep her down for long. If she'd been a cat, she'd be purring. "That would be telling."

"I see. Well you know I want the gory details." A pause. "Well not quite all of them."

"Why are you calling? Is anything wrong?"

"Not exactly. You left your purse in my car that's all. When we went to lunch. I didn't want you to worry, so I called you as soon as I noticed."

She hadn't even noticed. Sandro had picked her up from work, and they'd come straight to bed and been there ever since. He'd even brought food to them in bed. "Oh. Will you bring it in to work today?"

"Sure, no problem."

"Will do." She was about to hang up when she sensed something, a barely suppressed excitement in him. "Hey, Jack? Am I imagining things or did you get lucky with Carilla last night?"

"Very lucky," he purred. "And the night before too."

Happiness filled her. She'd known something simmered between Jack and the sexy cat-woman. Obviously they were working on it as fast as she and Sandro. "Good for you."

"Good for *us*. Megan, I think this is it. I've never felt like this. She says shape-shifters often link fast. I wouldn't have believed it before. We'll never be the same again, you and me."

"Always friends though, Jack."

"Yeah, babe. Always. See you soon."

"Take care, Jack."

Taking the phone away from her ear, she combed her hair back from her face with her fingers and leaned over to put the receiver back. Only then did she see Sandro, back from what must be the fastest shower ever, hair wet and combed straight back, a pair of jeans slung low on his hips.

But it was his expression that made her pause and pull the sheet up over her breasts. Grim, arms folded across his damp chest, he stared at her. "You gave someone this number?"

"Only Jack." Jack didn't count. "You don't mind that, surely?"

"It compromises you. Hell, it compromises this place. Get packed, you can't stay here."

"Sandro—" She paused. "Jack's part of the operation so I didn't think there'd be a problem."

"Kind of."

That made her mind race. He was hiding something. "What do you mean, kind of? Carilla's living in my apartment and Jack's there with her. He knows what's going on. So what's wrong?"

His mouth tightened even more in a grimace she found disturbing but she felt the stirrings of anger inside her. What the hell? "Carilla's there principally to draw the fire meant for you, to take some of your captors, if she can. But she's also keeping an eye on Jack."

"More than an eye," she said before something else occurred to her. Something almost unthinkable. "You mean seduction is part of the job?"

"Sometimes."

She pulled the sheet higher. "Me too?"

He turned away. "No." He took a few paces and then turned back. "That wasn't planned. You're leaving here. Pack and come down to eat. I need to make a few calls. On my cell." He said the last with grim purpose and didn't look at her or smile when he turned away to go downstairs.

He suspected Jack? If he did that, he couldn't understand her completely, especially now she'd told him just what Jack meant to her. The thought that Carilla might have seduced Jack to keep an eye on him made her feel sick. The thought that Sandro did the same to her made her feel worse. Stupid, naïve. No wonder he didn't want to talk about love. It didn't stop her being in love with him although it stopped her being a complete idiot and confessing it.

Numbly, she packed the clothes she'd brought with her except for today's outfit.

She showered and chose an outfit that covered most of her body, feeling suddenly vulnerable and lost. A high-necked sweater and long, soft skirt in black with a silver-buckled belt. When she went downstairs, she was fully armored, ready to do battle.

He had scrambled eggs and grilled bacon for her. His hair was drying, curling in wisps around his head, making him look like some grim-faced, dark angel. He dumped the plate in front of her. "Eat."

The last thing she wanted was food but she wouldn't show him any vulnerability. She longed for a cup of tea, not the mug of coffee he put at the other side of her plate. She'd never been so homesick for England. She'd loved being here in the States, loved the newness of everything, the differences and the liveliness of the city but now she wanted the comfort of home, the old cottage her parents lived in, her bedroom with its small windows and rough plastered walls.

Megan picked up her fork. Sandro sat at the other side of the glass-topped table and picked up his own fork. He ate the American way, fork in his right hand. She still ate the English way, knife in the right, fork in the left, and cut the food as she ate. Even that was different. Sandro was a different species, something out of her experience. Who was she kidding when she thought they had something permanent? Only herself.

Sandro had cut himself off from her completely. Nobody in her head but herself and she felt lonely there. Quite a shock. Sandro had only taken up residence last night, before that he'd entered and left, and fuck, she wanted him back. How pathetic was that?

He put down his fork with a clink of metal against glass that sounded louder than it should have. "Megan, nobody has this apartment's number. Nobody."

She met his eyes. "I'm sorry. But you should have told me. I didn't realize."

He sighed. "Yes, I should have told you. My bad. And I'm sorry I was so angry too. I took that shower cold. It didn't help any. This place is compromised now, and until I can secure it again, I want you away from here."

Relief and tension at the same time. What a strange feeling! "Where?"

"I'll take you to Chase. He can train you better than I can, and the hotel is secured."

"And—Sandro, what about us?" God help her, she had to ask. There couldn't be any errors here, and his last words sounded more as if he cared for her safety still, not just as part of the job. She cursed herself for her own weakness but she couldn't help it.

He got up, taking his half-full plate with him. "There is no 'us'. There never was, not more than the sex. It's not possible, Megan."

"So last night?"

"We enjoyed each other and had fun. I turned what could have been a boring lesson into something else. Just leave it at that, will you?"

The rigid lines of his shoulders and back told her more. Last night, he'd been more than a lover of her body, he'd loved all of her. She knew it.

"That doesn't work for me, Sandro."

"Look." He straightened up from stacking his empty plate in the dishwasher. "You were always Ricardo's. He claimed you first. When I met you, I felt it. What I did was protect you and take advantage of a situation. For which I'm sorry. But when you meet Ricardo—and you *will* meet Ricardo—you'll understand."

She got to her feet, abandoning the attempt to eat. "No, Sandro, *you* look. I'm nobody's. Nobody claims me, nobody has any rights to me that I haven't given them. Understand?"

"Sure." He moved to the door. "But this affects me, not you. He has first claim."

"Like somebody at a dance hall who claims a woman first? Don't you think that's a bit childish?" She'd been wrong. Sandro *was* a Neanderthal.

"It's our way. Besides, you said you felt something with Ricardo, a connection, you said. That's a sign you belong together." He left.

But I was wrong. It's only because Ricardo is your brother I felt anything for him. It's you I want.

Cross my heart and hope to die.

* * * * *

An hour later she was in the Spyder speeding toward town. It was still only nine o'clock. She had plenty of time before she had to be at work. Sandro seemed eager to get rid of her.

Had she misread him? Was sex all he'd wanted from her? That, and Ricardo's location? She'd been wrong before but this time she'd been so damn sure. And his excuse about Ricardo didn't wash. He'd claimed her last night and made her his. She felt sure he'd have fought even his brother for her. She could understand that giving Jack his phone number might have compromised his apartment as a safe house and he was concerned for her safety, she could even understand his wanting to get her to a place of safety but not this total rejection of her.

Shit.

She sat listlessly staring out the window at the stream of traffic, the buildings passing her window but this journey was short and completed in silence.

When she'd thought about the hotel Chase Maynord managed, she'd imagined something small and discreet. Classy, certainly, Chase gave out that aura of quiet confidence that came with wealth but not this.

Chase's hotel wasn't called Maynord's, it was called the Timothy, part of a chain of luxury hotels stretching across the US. There was also one in London, one in Paris and another in Singapore, that she knew of.

She walked through the huge marble lobby, with its centerpiece crystal chandelier, a modern design featuring large tear-shaped drops smoothly flowing to the floor, her mouth slightly open before she remembered to close it.

Sandro had called ahead and Chase waited for them in the lobby, a gold-colored luggage trolley by his side.

His sharp gaze went from Megan to Sandro and back again but he said nothing. He didn't contact her. They greeted each other warmly, not too warmly, and stacked her cases onto the trolley. People watched them cross the palatial lobby toward the elevators. Chase waited for an empty one and they walked inside in silence.

The doors slid closed and Chase spoke to her. "Watch, Megan." Instead of hitting a floor number, he hit a combination of numbers. "Four, three, eight, twenty. Can you remember that without writing it down?"

"Sure." She repeated them silently to herself. Then she felt him in her mind, gently touching her to let her know he was there. Chase's presence felt subtly different, brighter than Sandro's dark, sensual presence. Less personal.

Kinder.

"Can you lock that away on your own?"

She tried. She succeeded. When she turned a smile of triumph onto the men, only Chase gave her an answering grin. "Well done. That number will take you to the secure floor. I change the combination regularly but I'll let you know when it is. If you can't remember, pick up an internal line, they're on every floor, say your name is Jillian Miller and ask if room one-three-nine B is available. They know to put that call straight through to me on a secure line. I'll come get you."

He glanced at Sandro. "Not talking today?"

"Not much to say."

"How about why she's here?"

Sandro glanced at her, his gaze darkly accusatory, then turned his attention to Chase. "My place has been compromised. I need to re-secure it."

"So Megan will be going back to you when you have?"

"Probably not."

"Ah." That single note made it sound as if Chase understood more than Megan did. She hoped so. Then he could tell her what had turned everything sour so fast. She could accept Sandro wanting to move her for her own safety but not breaking off the affair between them.

The elevator doors slid open and she made to get out. Chase pressed the "open" button and grabbed her arm. "Wait. Do you see that picture there?"

She peered out at the watercolor set opposite the elevator doors. "Yes."

"It's a Turner. Very distinctive."

With its bright gold sun gleaming over an impressionistic gleam of red buildings, it was instantly recognizable as the work of the master of color. "There are copies of it opposite all the elevators on this floor. Only on this floor. If you don't see them, don't get out."

Wow. If she hadn't believed a top-class New York hotel was a good place to be secure, she did now. She nodded and only then did Chase release the "open" button and lead them out. Sandro followed last, pulling the luggage trolley behind him.

Chase took her to a suite that looked more like a private apartment than a hotel suite but unlike anything she'd have been able to afford on a librarian's salary. Large windows opened onto a breathtaking vista of Central Park, the green oasis, so important to everyone living and working in Manhattan. It was a beautiful day, the sky blue with fluffy white clouds scudding across it. The only darkness lay in her heart.

"It's a lovely suite, Chase. Do you use this for prisoners?" With this level of security, she guessed STORM used it for more than voluntary guests.

Chase's low chuckle told her she'd guessed right. "Nope. The holding cells don't have windows and they're on a different floor. Settle in and I'll come back in an hour."

"I need to be at work by one."

"I'll arrange for a car." Chase glanced at Sandro who stood gloomily in the center of the room. "I'll go with you. I'll give you a few moments alone now."

He left, not giving them a chance to protest.

The thought that had begun to nag her through the car journey returned in force. "What is it about Jack you don't trust, Sandro?"

He made a sound of exasperation. "Jack came to get you when Paul Johnstone died. Jack made sure you were with him in that apartment. The PHR is always alert for Talents and sensitives they can recruit, and this is a typical way of doing it. He came to you when you were at your most vulnerable and took over your life. Don't you find any of that suspicious?"

She strode toward him. "I don't believe you! Jack is my friend, Sandro. Hear that? My friend!" Because she was standing before him, the only way he could avoid her accusatory glare was to turn his back and walk away.

He stayed where he was and watched her, a new wariness in his eyes. "You have to be more on your guard, Megan. More careful."

"Well if this is your brave new world, a place where nobody can trust their friends, I don't want any of it."

Chase returned, and then, seeing them so close, turned to leave again. They must have looked very intimate like that but she didn't touch Sandro. Only allowed him to see and feel her fury. "Don't go, Chase. I have to get in to work."

Sandro looked at her, once, and she tried to enter his mind. He blocked her. "I'll see you soon, Megan." He left without looking at her again, as if they were just friends, fuck-buddies.

But they were so much more than that. Had been. Blindly Megan turned away, toward the first suitcase but Chase stopped her. "Leave those. I can get someone to do them for you."

"I thought this hallway was secure? Doesn't that mean no help?" She lifted the case off the cart. She needed something to do, to stop her thinking about this mess.

"That's why only two maids work it. Both shape-shifters, sisters actually. I think we have more to talk about than the help."

With a sigh, she turned around to face him. "Okay. Shoot."

He studied her without speaking for a short time before walking to the sofa and taking a seat. "Come and sit down."

She obeyed. The sofa was a long one, plenty of room for five on it.

He reached for a remote and flicked on the wide-screen TV. It flashed onto a daytime drama so he picked up another remote from the table in front of the sofa and switched on the DVD player. The title, *Dragons Exist*, flashed on the screen. "There's a lot you need to know, Megan. About Talents, about dragons in particular. So we'll use this for a prompt. At any time, ask and I'll tell you what you need to know."

They watched in silence, Megan happy for the respite. If Chase wanted to watch it again, that was all right by her. But he hit "pause" part way through the opening shot of the dragon soaring over Central Park.

"There he is," he said. "Sandro Gianetti, in all his arrogance."

"He's not arrogant!" Self-confident, maybe but he'd never struck her as arrogant, and being British, she'd met her share of arrogant in her time.

A sweet smile curved Chase's mouth and ready laughter lines creased the corners of his eyes. "So you're not indifferent to him, despite your breakup. People who know Sandro well know arrogance isn't in his nature. He's reserved, standoffish even. I wanted to know."

"Wanted to know what?"

"How well you know him." Chase lifted his hand. "No, not that. I know you've been sleeping together. Your body language when you're together tells me that. But you can sleep with someone without real closeness. So why are you here and not with him?"

"I don't know."

"He said his apartment was compromised. How?"

"I gave Jack the phone number there." She paused. "And the address."

Chase sucked in a breath through his teeth. "Ah. But he can get it changed. That won't take long, with his contacts. And I could wipe that memory from Jack's mind but he hasn't asked me." He nodded toward the luggage cart, mute witness to her recent peripatetic existence. "This is for a bit more than a day's stay."

"I thought—" She stopped abruptly. "I was wrong."

"Don't you understand how much he feels for you?"

She shrugged. "He cares enough to sleep with me. You already know that. But Jack's my friend, and he has been for nearly ten years now. Sandro could have asked me about him."

"No he couldn't. That would have put you in an impossible position. Sandro wouldn't have allowed you to tell Jack, in case his suspicions were real and then you'd have to keep the secret. Can't you see that?" She couldn't mistake the steel behind his gentle tones.

And now that someone not involved reasoned with her, yes, she could see it. It still hurt that Sandro didn't trust her closest friend, and she suspected jealousy as well but if he wanted to keep her safe, he needed to investigate. And it would be typical of Sandro to take the responsibility himself instead of making someone else shoulder it. She sighed. "Yes. Maybe I can."

"Good. We're not playing games here, Megan. And you should know that I've been looking at Jack as well. So far we haven't found anything."

"I don't think it's just because of Jack. He seemed glad of the chance to get me out but before then—" She felt heat rising, and knew she'd blushed. She'd never blushed so much before but images of their lovemaking the night before appeared unbidden in her mind. She felt sure Chase must have seen something of it before she managed to dismiss them again.

If he did, he pretended not to. "He probably has commitment problems. You know about Jane?" She nodded.

"Jane hurt Sandro more than he cares to admit to anyone. She only accepted part of him. Not the dragon part. Since then, his relationships have been casual and friendly, nothing more. Until you."

Hope rose unbidden in her heart. "What do you mean?"

"He's nuts about you. In my considered opinion." Chase gave a crack of laughter when he saw her face, and spread his arms in an expansive gesture. "Look, don't quote me, okay? Sandro's too old a hand to put his emotions on display and if I pry where I'm not wanted, I'm liable to get hurt. But I've never seen him like this before. He's fighting the attraction." He flicked the documentary back on. "I can't tell you any more."

"Will you tell me if you do find anything else?"

He slid a sideways look at her. "If I'm not breaking any confidences. I won't come running if Sandro doesn't want me to, only if I think you have a right to know."

That seemed fair but she wanted more. She needed to know so badly. Had she done something wrong? "He said Ricardo had a prior claim on me, like I was a prize in a competition."

"Did he now?" The image of the dragon on the screen had disappeared, replaced by a talking head, a man in a suit discussing the spate of headlines that led to the outing of Talents. Suspicion had been growing for some time, only to culminate in the final acceptance that not all humans were alike.

Well, duh. They never had been.

"Yes, he said I would have a link with Ricardo that made the one with Sandro look feeble. Or words to that effect."

Chase snorted. "Nonsense. He was trying to fool you. All that 'one mate' stuff is for novels. It doesn't happen."

"One mate?"

"Don't you read romance novels?" He stretched an arm along the back of the chair.

"I like the historical ones."

"Ah. Well there's a common storyline in the paranormals that there's one woman for every man. They're fated, meant to be, and they won't be complete until they've joined together."

She raised a brow. "So you read them?"

Unabashed, he grinned. "Some of them are great reads. I'll lend you a few. But don't kid yourself that happens in real life. It doesn't. You can meet someone, fall in love and split a few years later. It happens in the Talented community, same as everywhere else. Love is love, whether it happens to shapeshifters, vampires or Sorcerers like me. In the old days, we were executed for witchcraft, or if we were clever, we managed to find ourselves positions of power." Chase shrugged. "It was just an absence of the natural barrier most humans develop in the first week of birth. A deformity, nothing more. And the subsequent increase in our psi gifts. So the title is kind of ironic. Sensitives exist in every degree, we just have the gifts in spades."

"I see. And Sorcerers don't have soul mates either?"

He watched her, for once the smile absent from his face. "No, we don't, at least not pre-ordained ones. We can love and lose. I sometimes think it might be nice to live for five hundred years, like shifters and vampires, but then I think of all that time alone, or watching the loved one age and die. Then I know we have the best of it."

She frowned, glancing at the TV. "So why—"

"If he isn't in love with you, he's well on the way."

Sandro left the hotel, knowing he was walking away from the woman he wanted, the one he'd found too late. The best he could do was keep her from harm and get his brother back. Ricardo would have time to love her, and if they decided to bond, they would have many years together. Unlike him.

But he wouldn't feel sorry for himself. How sick, to end a long productive life in a frenzy of self-pity! Instead, he'd do what he could and then retire to the place he loved more than any other, his villa in Tuscany, to end his days watching the sunsets and drinking wine from his vineyard. He'd try to persuade Ann to return to New York before the end. He'd feel more comfortable hiring a nurse, someone unconnected to him in any way to attend him as he knew he'd need.

The thought made him feel a little better. Maybe he'd finally give that TV interview. Ever since his appearance in the skies, the media had been on the hunt. Advertisements in the press, appeals on TV and other inducements all had given way to simple appeals, "for the good of mankind". Sandro ignored them all until now. Perhaps his last hurrah would be to try to explain shape-shifter existence for those who wanted to listen.

Yes, he liked that idea. But only after this case concluded. It would keep him busy. Keep his mind off Megan. For a while at least but he knew he'd continue to think about her at the vulnerable times. Just before he fell asleep, on waking and when he was relaxing or trying to relax. Then the memories would come and he'd either have to fight them or face them.

He found a lot of paperwork waiting for him in his office. Ann thrived on paper, he swore sometimes that she ate it instead of regular food and he was only half joking. He drew the first sheet toward him and got to work but his mind kept drifting away.

Last night, she'd been on the brink of telling him she loved him. If that happened, he wouldn't be able to stop himself telling her how he really felt, and that wouldn't be fair. He'd still convert her as a proxy for Ricardo, who'd used up his one chance at converting, and he'd do it in Ricardo's presence.

When and if they got Ricardo back. He turned his attention to the graphs quartering New York, detailed scans of every inch of the city. Every Talent would be investigated, every presence until they narrowed down the search. Then they'd raid the addresses they targeted, a clean, simultaneous swoop, giving none of the locations any notice. With any luck, they'd flush out more than one nest of the bastards who only wanted to make money from Talents.

But damn, the scans were boring and he had to work hard to concentrate on them. His mind ticked down the time until he could leave for his shift watching Megan. His last. He'd rearrange the shifts so he'd never be alone with her again.

He was saved by the bell when his P.A. rang through. "Chase Maynord to see you, Sandro."

Not saved enough but Chase wouldn't go away without seeing him. "Okay, let him in."

Chase walked in, his hands thrust into the pockets of the trousers of his navy suit. Even then, it was obvious the suit was quality. His working wardrobe.

"You're smitten, big guy."

If anyone noticed how far gone he was, it would be Chase. "Maybe. But she can't stay with me."

"Why not?"

He wondered if he should tell Chase but before he made his decision, Chase's sharp intake of breath told him he'd noticed. "Oh fuck." Eyes wide open, Chase stared at him and Sandro felt his mind invaded. He allowed it.

"Don't tell anybody. You hear me?"

"Sure. If that's the way you want to play it. Does Ann know?"

He nodded. "Okay then, I guess I won't tell anybody. Yet. You could have a couple of years, you know."

"Not enough and too much. I won't do that to her. I'll let her think it's a casual affair, two people brought together by circumstance."

"I'm sorry, Sandro."

He jerked his head in a tight nod. He'd manage. He always did.

"You're not doing her justice, you know. Don't you think that two years together is better than none at all? I'm betting that she does. Give her a chance, Sandro, tell her the truth."

He shook his head. "I've already told her Ann is sending me to Europe on a case after this one. I'll go and then let her know I've been killed. You haven't seen a shape-shifter at the end, Chase. It's not gentle and it's not pretty."

"Let her in. That's my advice."

"I can't, Chase. I can't do that to her."

"Or you can't do it to yourself."

* * * * *

At work, Jack watched Megan with a gravity that told her he knew something was troubling her. Eventually, she promised to meet him out in the yard at break time, at around seven. Just at the change of shift, when her minders switched.

What made matters worse was Sheryl's breathy questioning. She was behaving like a ditz. Were there any more like Sandro at home? Was he really rich? All said with much flicking back of her dyed blonde hair, which Sheryl generally wore tied back or pinned up for work.

Megan nearly snapped a couple of times. The last time she strode off without speaking, making her way to the small yard where she'd arranged to meet Jack for a private chat. It was a quarter to seven p.m. and she was due to finish at eight.

She leaned against the wall, closing her eyes, the better to enjoy the weak sunshine struggling through the clouds and past the two tall buildings on the university campus. The library was situated in one of the older sites but that only meant it dated back to the 1930s. Yesterday by British standards. The house her parents lived in was two hundred years older than that. Maybe more.

What had the country been like when Sandro arrived, less than a hundred years into independence? All the hopes, mistakes and successes still ahead. Slaves still worked the fields and houses. She'd have done anything to visit—just visit. Today's comforts suited her much better for a permanent existence. Did they suit Sandro?

That morning Chase had patiently answered all her questions about Talents, inspired by the documentary she realized she hadn't watched properly before. Questions she wanted to ask her lover—ex-lover now. Her admiration for him and understanding of what he'd been through increased but it was too late now. She wouldn't know how to tell him without sounding like a complete idiot.

Depression spread its black wings over her and drew her in. Although never welcome, she half expected it this time. The black despair that had descended on her after Paul's death had exacerbated the way she felt to utter listlessness, too apathetic to consider killing herself. After saving for years to afford the post-graduate course, finding it all she expected and more, then losing Paul on the very day of her last exam, her dream had collapsed around her like a pack of cards and blackness took its place.

The door to the small space scraped open and she opened her eyes to see who was interrupting her thoughts. They were welcome, even if it was Sheryl bent on asking yet more questions about Sandro, pushing the dagger further into her heart and giving it a twist.

But the man who'd helped her to break her last spiral of despair stepped out into the light. Jack, her best friend. Always her best friend. His grin lit up his face, sent a shaft of light into the darkness that threatened to plunge her back into apathy.

"Hi. So tell me. What's happening?"

She didn't hesitate to tell him. If Sandro suspected Jack, that was Sandro's problem, not hers. "Sandro said I compromised his apartment by giving you his number and address. I'm staying at the hotel with Chase."

His eyebrows went up. "*With* Chase or just at his hotel?"

"What do you take me for?" she demanded indignantly.

Her attitude abashed him not one bit. "A woman with eyes to see two good-looking men panting for her."

"Chase?"

"He wouldn't say no if he got the chance." He shrugged. "Sorry." Jack shoved his hands into the pockets of his jacket. Black, nondescript, it contrasted with the expensive, tailored suits hanging in Sandro's closet and, she was guessing, the numerous designer suits in Chase's. Megan welcomed the change. Clothes meant little to Jack, he was at his happiest in worn denims and casual slacks. "Chase is probably holding off because he wants to leave you to Sandro. So are you going back when he's had the number changed?"

"You mean you believe that stupid explanation?"

"Yeah, sure. Don't you read? We have a whole legal section and there are some very interesting books there about the secret services. A good safe house is completely secure and that old need-to-know thing comes into play. A phone number is a lever, a way in."

"Oh."

Jack moved closer and tilted her chin up. "You didn't split with him because of that? Tell me you didn't."

"He split with me. Last night was a bit intense — it scared him, I think." She bit her lip, realizing how right Chase was. She couldn't tell Jack Sandro was investigating him because it would compromise the whole operation. But Jack was her friend and keeping something like that from him hurt her.

"How about you?"

"Me too." At least she wasn't too proud to admit it. "I've not known him long enough to get in that deep."

"Yes you do." He took a pace back but didn't take his close regard away from her. "I'm ready to commit to Carilla."

That shocked her out of the last of her depression. Or almost the last of it. A shred remained, a touch of blackness at the back of her mind, in the depths of her heart. "But you've only known her—"

"She opened to me completely. And I did to her. There is nothing between us. Nothing except the secrets of her job. She's only the same age I am, you know, almost exactly. We have a lot in common."

"Except you're different species."

He turned away then and kicked at the paving under their feet. "Maybe not."

"What?"

"I agreed to let her convert me." He lifted his head. "We're soul mates, whatever you want to call it. Normally I'd say wait but I wanted to do this. And you know me, always jumping in first."

His effort at a careless grin didn't fool her for a second. Jack really cared. She'd never seen him so involved with anyone else before.

"Jack, are you sure? Don't you want to wait awhile?"

"No." Grim-faced, Jack seemed older, his laughter lines fading into nothing. "Please don't, Megan. I know you mean well but I've never been more certain of anything in my life. I want her, and I want her for keeps. I'll do anything to achieve that. I know it sounds stupid but I'm in love, for the first time in my life, truly in love."

She had a choice. She could continue to protest, advise caution or she could stop now and preserve their friendship.

If she stopped, she wouldn't be able to live with herself. "Jack, Sandro offered me the same thing. For Ricardo, he said. He advised me to wait. Until I was sure, and because a newly converted shape-shifter is vulnerable."

"I've thought about it."

Megan was still worried Jack was about to plunge into something he might regret bitterly later. She had seen this boyish enthusiasm in Jack before. He tended to dive into new projects with enthusiasm, only to abandon them just as suddenly later. This was like the half-completed model of the *Victory*, the two watercolors that were supposed to be three.

Some things remained as constants in Jack's life but not many. And at this stage in a relationship nobody had a way of telling which was which. Least of all, Jack.

She opened her mouth but the words didn't emerge as the door scraped again and someone else entered the small, enclosed yard.

Not anyone they were expecting. Holding Sheryl in front of him, like a goodwill gesture, was one of the largest men she'd ever seen. The red-haired joker from the hospital.

He wasn't laughing now. She doubted he'd cracked a smile in years from the expression on his weatherworn face. Except on seeing her, something lightened a little in his creepy gray eyes. Relief or pleasure, she couldn't tell which and in any case, it didn't matter.

"Our patient," he rumbled in a voice as low as a Russian bass singer without the accent. "Come along now. Can't have you running around any longer without treatment."

She didn't like the sound of his "treatment". "I'm nobody's patient. I'm not going anywhere with you."

"Sure?" The man advanced on her, totally ignoring Jack, who bared his teeth in a humorless grin.

"You heard the lady."

Jack bent in the stance of a karate master. And he was a black belt, first Dan, so he had a good claim to the title. She widened her legs, difficult in the tight pencil skirt she wore but she managed a useful balance.

Ginger looked at them and a broad grin spread over his face. Not good.

He came at her first, throwing Sheryl aside so he could leap over the distance between them, giving himself the impetus to take her down. Megan kicked high, trying to knock his arm up and get him off-balance. At the same time, Jack struck hard at his neck.

Neither action worked. The bastard spun around, growling, and caught Jack's wrist, spinning him over on to his back. Jack let out a single cry and bounced back on to his feet. That fall must have hurt him.

Before Jack regained his footing, she struck out, striking at Ginger's side, at the fleshy part below his ribs.

Sheryl screamed and froze. Jack called out, drowning her voice. "Sheryl, run! Get my cell and hit speed dial!"

His voice provided the release she needed and Sheryl scrambled for the door. Jack stepped between their attacker and the door, giving her the chance to get away, but that gave the giant the chance to strike out. All he had to do was swing one meaty arm in a backhander that caught Jack completely off balance and sent him down again.

He sprang up again slower this time. Nothing she could do would stop Ginger for long but if she did nothing, he'd kill Jack and overpower her too easily. No Sandro to rescue her this time. So she attacked, kicking out arms and legs in a desperate attempt to overpower him.

She feared anything she did might not be enough. But she had to do something.

At least if he killed her, they wouldn't be able to find out what she knew and what she didn't.

Chapter Eight

༃

"Library! Attack!"

"Hey, who is this?" Sandro pulled his cell phone away from his ear to stop instant deafness and stared at it as if he could see through it.

"Sheryl!"

By then logic had clicked in. Library, Sheryl—Megan. God, Megan!

He didn't need any more. Thank God this office had opening windows. He flung his open, ignoring the flurry of papers stirred by the breeze. A particularly strong gust took most of them off his desk. Even better.

He registered the flutter and flap of escaping paperwork as he ripped open his shirt and tore the clothes off his upper body. He unzipped his fly, changing the upper part of his body as he stripped, and took to the air, kicking off his shoes, pants and underwear. When he heard fabric rip, he didn't bother to check what he'd destroyed this time.

The cell phone lay on his desk, about the only thing left on it, squawking to itself, because Sandro was about a hundred feet away. A hundred feet up.

Instead of the phone, he used his mind. *Library. Anyone who's free get there now!*

I'm on my way. Any details? from Carilla, hiding out in Megan's apartment while she was at work.

Nothing. Just get there.

I'll be there.

Johann responded. *I hear you, man. Any clear pictures?* Vampires needed a clear image of a place to flash to, otherwise the journey could be fatal for them. The sun would set very soon, in the next half-hour, and Johann would come into his powers. Thank God. Regretfully, he couldn't guarantee anyone would be in the places he'd memorized. *Stand by. I'll send as soon as I get there.*

Sure thing. I'm outside Megan's apartment staking it out. No action.

On my way. That, briefly, from Chase, who had to drive. *Carilla, how long?*

Don't wait for me, get going.

Okay.

Other Talents responded, none of them in the vicinity of the library, none of them trained agents.

He fuzzed. Behind the image, he grew to his full size to take advantage of the increased power of his wings and concentrated on making his body as streamlined as possible. Dear Lord, what had happened? Sheryl had sounded scared, really scared. No prank then. Maybe the IRDC had moved in force to surround the library, so he'd better take a circuit around it before he landed.

Trying to think rationally, fighting the panic that threatened to close his throat, Sandro concentrated on flying straight and true, wishing the hours back. Who was supposed to be watching her? He'd put his team on to the job and they were all seasoned professionals, not only Talents but ex-FBI and CIA. Hell, he'd even got an ex MI6 man working for him.

The time, seven, so an hour short of her shift ending. Chase was due to take over guard duty at seven. Hopefully that meant he was on the way already. Five until seven—yes, it was Angie Mulhaven, a wyvern shape-shifter.

Angie!

No response. Dear God, let him be on time! He kept calling out to her, trying to contact her with no response. They hadn't parted on good terms and now he wished his last words to Megan had been "I love you", not "I'll see you". He couldn't contact her, couldn't touch her mind. Perhaps she was dead. No, he couldn't go there. If that happened, he'd take the fucking library apart and then start on the hospital.

Sandro had never flown so strongly, so powerfully here in New York City. He'd never had this kind of motivation before.

Not knowing made the journey worse. When he arrived, nothing seemed out of place, unusual. No suspicious people standing by the library entrance, no cars parked out front, the library car lot full of the usual vehicles, no new ones.

Before he landed he made a slow circuit, low down. He'd shift naked. The people who watched him would have to cope with that. He might be able to grab a coat or something on his way past. It wasn't his main focus right now.

As he soared above the buildings he saw a small, enclosed paved area, completely enclosed by the building, a kind of courtyard. He'd never noticed it before but he did now. Several white splashes dotted with red lay on the gray paved stones. *Jesus.*

He folded his wings against his body and dove, the quickest way of landing, reducing his size as he flew so he could land in the small space without disturbing anything.

By the time he landed, he'd almost completely shifted, only his wings left, before they too morphed back into arms. Only a naked man now, one with red before his eyes, metaphorically and literally.

Three bodies. He leaped over the body of the red-haired man from the hospital to get to Megan. Blood pumped from a wound slashed in her thigh, and if he didn't get to it fast, it was all over. When he pressed on the wound, leaning on it with both hands, he felt the sickening grind of shattered bone. She must have fought back.

"Oh God, why?"

The door burst open and Chase hurtled into the courtyard, a quivering Sheryl hovering at the entrance. He took in the situation at a glance. "Sending Johann the picture," he snapped and went to the nearest body. Jack Hargreaves lay twisted like a marionette with its strings cut, limbs sprawled in a sickening way that said most of them were broken. "It must have been a hell of a fight," Chase muttered. He bent. "He's breathing. I'm calling an ambulance. One of ours."

Johann arrived in a sudden excess of energy at the corner of the yard and a scream from Sheryl, which he ignored. "Christ." His attention went from Chase to Megan and he crossed to Megan, going to her head. "Oh fucking hell. How the fuck did this happen?"

"Chase felt for a pulse on Jack's broken body. Angie Mulhaven's dead in her seat. The bastard must have broken her neck. I can't do anything more for him, just make sure he's breathing."

"Then do that."

Chase indicated the red-haired man with a jerk of his chin. "What about him?"

Johann scanned him briefly. "Dead."

After a brief surge of triumph, that at least they'd achieved that, Sandro murmured, "Fuck. We could have done something with him alive. Now we can't question him. I would have enjoyed that." He lifted his hands slightly and was rewarded by a definite lessening of the blood flow. "Come on, Megan, you can't leave me now!" He didn't care if the others heard the yearning in his voice, open and raw.

"Sandro, get inside her head," Johann said quietly and Sandro looked up.

The vampire met his gaze steadily. "Her skull is broken. If you don't get in there and hold her together, she'll die before the ambulance gets here. It has to be you, Sandro. You know why."

Yes, he knew why. He loved her. He kept his hands on her thigh wound but moved his presence inside her head.

At first he couldn't find anything. No signs of life, nothing, just dead tissue, then he found her. A small spark, right at the back, like a child cowering in fear. He surrounded her, pushed all thoughts but positive ones out of her head. That meant hatred, fear and pain all had to go.

He worked at it but couldn't dispel his anger, his absolute fury that the team he led had let her down. Megan, the most precious thing to come into his life since — since forever.

Then he felt another presence with him. Chase. This was his territory and Sandro's only hope. He surrendered to his friend and let Chase clear his mind for him, leaving a tranquil floating sensation. He suspected Chase had used extreme hypnosis on him, an advanced technique only skilled Sorcerers could achieve, something he'd normally fight against. This time he didn't care. Chase made it possible for him to help the woman he loved. That was all that mattered now.

Retaining the dreamy, floaty feeling, he tried contacting her again. This time the small spark didn't retreat from him, scared of the negative emotions he projected, but came toward him, drawn to the comfort he offered. He enclosed her, the mental equivalent of taking her in his arms and covering her body with his, protection and love the only emotions he allowed to touch her.

He could still see and observe the action going on around him but knowing any violent efforts would dispel the semi-hypnotic state Chase had induced in him, he left the directions to Johann.

The ambulance arrived. He let one of the paramedics take over her thigh wound, heard Chase explain what was happening. The paras, being Talents or used to treating them, took it in stride. One handed Sandro a set of scrubs and he clambered into them without taking his attention from Megan. That spark wavered but he kept it alive, like a man blowing on a flame to make fire, he wouldn't let her go. She belonged here, with him.

One of the medics went to Megan's head and gently probed what he found there. The spark wavered but Sandro held it tight. *You will not leave me, you will not!*

He heard, as if from a distance, "This one's a newly converted jaguar. I'm going to help him to shift, then he'll heal."

What the fuck was with that? The information shot through his consciousness and broke the semi-trance. But now he had Megan's essence within his embrace, he retained it, tucked it carefully in the front of his mind. He'd recovered from his initial blaze of fury. He could control his emotions better now.

"What are you talking about?"

"No mistake," said the medic. "I've probed his mind and it's there. The mark of the cat."

Sandro skimmed Jack's mind and saw it, the seal that identified Jack as a cat. But the medic was right, the mark was fresh, like a new tattoo that still glowed red from the needles. Shit, Carilla! So sure of herself, and her decisions, she hadn't waited. And he knew why. If he'd found out, he'd have pulled her out of that apartment, not giving her the opportunity to convert Jack until after the operation, after they found Ricardo and the institution holding him. A newly converted shapeshifter was more of a liability than an asset.

"Do what you have to."

He turned away, no longer interested for the time being. He filed the information away for later. When Megan came back to him. But the spark he held was no bigger, no stronger. If anything, it was fading. There was nothing he could do to bring it back once it had gone for good.

"Convert her."

"What?" He stared into Johann's dark eyes, gaping at the vampire.

"If you don't convert her, she's going to die. The medics say that head injury will kill her in the next half hour. Nothing can stop it in a human. If you convert her, she has a chance. But only a chance. Nothing is definite, Sandro. She could still die."

Typical of Johann to face reality head-on and be the one to present him with the only solution. He valued Johann as a member of his team because of his ability to think twisted, to work out solutions nobody else would have considered because they were too outlandish or just plain outside the law. And for his straightforward honesty.

Now Johann showed him the answer. The only one possible.

Sandro got to his feet, stripping off the scrubs he'd so recently donned. "Chase, remove your thrall from me. Every scrap of it."

"Sure." He felt a presence strong in his mind, carefully avoiding the core where his essence wrapped Megan's, and then it left him. "All gone."

"Johann, you will be our proxy."

"Most definitely." Megan couldn't take from him, so Johann would have to do it.

He shifted, taking as near his full size as he could in this cramped place, keeping his wings tight against his body, curving his long neck down to compress his body as far as possible.

He locked his mind into Johann's and the vampire stepped forward. "I take this for Megan," he said, running his hand over the scales on Sandro's chest. That should have been a sensual gesture, a gesture of love, but Johann did it to locate Sandro's strongly beating heart. He couldn't afford to make a mistake.

Johann wrenched a scale from the dragon's body, directly over his heart. The pain pierced Sandro. He lost scales sometimes but this was different. Freely given, this was the single part of him that held the power to convert another.

He shifted back and bent down to Megan. The spark faded, nearly gone now. Oblivious to the silent watchers, he opened his hand and took the scale when Johann pressed it into his palm. The warmth radiating from it told him it held his essence. He lifted her hand, trying to ignore the crunch of broken bones. She must have hit the bastard hard and broken bones in her hand doing it. Her arm was broken too, shattered when she fell head first onto the hard paved surface and held her hands out to break her fall. He read it all, like a newly written letter in the forefront of her mind. He felt her pain as if it were his. It was, or would be soon.

As if that would deter him.

When he pressed the scale into her palm, her fingers curled around it and he took it as a good omen. And as consent. If—when—she recovered, if she claimed he did it against her will, he'd be accused of compulsion and executed. It would be worth it if Megan lived. He was going to die soon enough anyway. A clean death might be better.

Her hand felt cold against his when he held it against her upper thigh, bared when her skirt had torn. But warmth radiated from the scale. He put his whole mind and thoughts into the place they joined, both hands pressed against her thigh, hers in acceptance, his in aiding her. The whole process usually occurred in privacy, often just after making love, and that was how it should be. Not like this, with Megan's broken and bleeding body half-dressed and disheveled, her limbs sprawled on the hard, cold ground.

The warmth increased until it burned. He welcomed the pain. That meant the process was working. It became almost unbearable but he bore it, kept his hand pressed over hers, holding the scale firmly in place.

He had no idea how long it took, he concentrated on nurturing her spirit and bringing her back to him. *Please, God, whoever and whatever you are, hear me now. Save her. Take me if that means she lives. I'll take anything you send for me.*

The heat ebbed and faded away to warmth once more, then nothing. Cautiously, he moved his hand, then pulled hers away.

A beautiful sight greeted him. A small, glowing mark on her thigh, like an intricately detailed tattoo. As he watched, it burned, then glowed, then faded to nothing.

But everyone had seen it. The conversion was a success. Megan was now a dragon.

This should have taken place with love and full consent, not here, with broken, bleeding bodies around them but for all that, it was a beautiful act, given and received with love.

One of the paramedics broke the awed silence. "Help her to shape-shift and regulate her form to human-sized. Otherwise we can't get her out of here."

All emotion gone except one, Sandro entered his love and gave her the picture of the dragon she needed to shape-shift. He felt Chase in his head, lending him strength, and he accepted it, giving her the burst of energy that changed her from woman to she-dragon.

So lovely. Even unconscious, eyes closed, her scales gleamed. She was azure blue although when the light from the medic's torches hit them, she gleamed golden. One of the rarest combinations and utterly, ethereally beautiful.

After that, the medics worked fast. They loaded the small cat that was Jack onto a stretcher and while Sandro recalled time and place and scrambled back into his scrubs, they placed the new dragon carefully on another, strapping her in so she couldn't damage herself any further.

Sandro dispassionately admired their professionalism as they methodically set a thrall around the stretchers. Anyone watching would see people, injured but not as badly as they really were, being loaded into the ambulances that waited outside. He climbed into the one holding Jack and Megan.

He wouldn't leave her now until she either recovered or died. If she died, he was going with her, as soon as he'd located Ricardo. There would be nothing left for him to do.

Chapter Nine

ஐ

As a dragon, Megan's survival was fifty-fifty and the next forty-eight hours would be the decider. They kept her in dragon form, the better to accelerate recovery.

At the hospital, the doctors finished their work and the nurses settled her in to the bed, broader than the usual hospital bed to take account of her shape-shifted form. This special wing of the Syon hospital had been here as long as Sandro could remember, disguised as a research unit. He supposed it wouldn't need the disguise anymore.

Dawn spread tentacles over the sky and he sat watching Megan, helping her in any way he could. Dragon or woman, she was beautiful to him and he loved her above all others. He left her secrets and explored the parts of her mind that opened to him, gently trying to smooth away her pain, calming her so she could heal.

Her superficial injuries were well on the way to being healed by daybreak. That, the doctor told him, was a very good sign.

Fatigue hit just as morning light streamed in through the windows. By then he knew he could rest. He kept his mind locked in hers and let his head fall onto the bed in front of him. An uncomfortable position but he'd known worse. He wasn't complaining. She was still alive.

The sound of an opening door awoke him not long after. The sun hadn't crossed over to afternoon, he saw that as soon as he opened his bleary eyes. She still lay, scales gleaming dully in the morning light, still except for the regular rise and fall of her chest.

"How is she?"

He nodded to Chase as he came into view. "Still with us. Improving. I think she'll live."

"Good."

But he didn't see the relief he knew he should be seeing. He sat up, alerted by Chase's expression. "Chase? What's wrong? Is Jack dead?"

"No, Jack's recovering."

"Can you send Carilla to me? I need to pull her out of her position at Megan's apartment."

It was obvious now that the operation, or at least this part of it, was over. Carilla couldn't pose as Megan anymore.

"No, my friend, I can't send Carilla to you."

For the first time he took his attention away from Megan. His head jerked up, and he stared into Chase's stark, wide-open eyes. "What's happened?"

"As Carilla approached the university, they attacked her. She fought them off but they came in numbers at her. It was a possibility we should have foreseen." He shook his head at Sandro's unspoken question. "She's okay but she was badly hurt and she needs to rest. She's in the bed next to Jack's. That suits them both." He flashed a tired grin. "Who would have thought it? That she and Jack…"

"Yeah." Sandro leaned back and pinched the bridge of his nose in a desperate effort to fend off his budding headache. "So what now? Do we go around in pairs?"

"I don't think so." Chase leaned wearily against the wall. He'd had a bad night too, and probably less sleep than Sandro. Chase's usually immaculate appearance had given way to tousled hair and a creased suit. His tie rode at half-mast, though it was typical of Chase not to have discarded it completely. "I think the bastards want to replenish their lab."

Sandro went back over his plans, running them through his mind. "Shit. Oh shit. How could they have taken us so off guard?"

"They must have gone in force to find the Talents and they know how to approach us. They sent one big man to collect or kill Jack and Megan."

"Why so determined?"

Without further words, Chase picked up the remote for the TV that hung from a bracket on the wall and switched it on. A familiar face filled the screen. Dominic Murdoch, senator and merman. "These horrific laboratories must be searched out and destroyed. Whether people calling themselves Talents are human or animal, this treatment is unacceptable. It must stop."

Sandro watched in silence for five minutes until he'd seen all he needed. Pictures of Talents hooked up to machinery, heavily censored because of the time of day and the possibility of children watching. But they showed enough and Sandro felt sick to his stomach. They'd gone public. "Someone has upped the game. Who could that be, I wonder?"

Chase grimaced. "She'd never admit to it but I think—"

"Ann." Sandro swore long and colorfully but it didn't make him feel any better. "She's playing politics. They leaked, so she's leaking too."

"She's always said it would come to that in the end," Chase said. "So they're increasing their attacks instead of backing off. They're increasing their pressure on Congress to pass the law calling all shape-shifters animals so Ann needed some heavy ammunition. She chose the labs."

"And the foot soldiers get to clear up the mess. In case you were wondering, that's us."

"Sure. I guessed." Chase swore colorfully and thumped the wall. The dull thud disturbed the occupant of the bed.

Megan stirred and groaned. Instantly all Sandro's attention turned to her. He stood and smoothed the pillow under her head, where a deep crease had formed in the fabric, and waited until she settled again.

"Why didn't Ann warn us? Surely she must have assessed the possibility of them stepping up the action."

Sandro cleared his mind and thought. "I need to see Ann."

"You're seeing her."

He hadn't even heard her come in. She stood by the door, as if she'd flashed in. Although he tried to contain his shock, he failed, and he knew she'd noticed. One strike to her.

"You were so engrossed you didn't notice, that's all."

"It's not like you to excuse anyone," he noted laconically.

"I've been acting out of character for the last twenty-four hours," she replied, just as dryly. "I've told the other teams. I didn't want you to leave Megan's bedside. Besides, I doubted you would." That was quite an admission from the hard-headed boss of STORM. "So I came to you."

She did look weary. Her immaculate makeup didn't quite hide the shadows under her eyes or the skin around her chin that sagged with fatigue. "So tell me what you did and what you expect from us. Then go get some sleep."

"I leaked some pictures but not all. Senator Murdoch got some others, leaked or stolen. I'm still looking for the mole." Despite her tiredness, Ann could still do a good savage growl. "Remember the San Francisco lab?"

"Sure." One place he'd never forget. The memories still gave him the occasional nightmare. Room after room containing Talents or what was left of them. They'd destroyed it completely, taken the records that mostly led to dead ends although many of the staff had got away. He'd have given them the same treatment they meted out. See how they liked it. But he'd been a good Company man and he'd done his job. And regretted it ever since. He should have killed them all.

"If you remember, we took a few shortcuts with that one." She pinched the bridge of her nose and then lifted her head wearily to look Sandro in the eye. "I suspected trouble but not like this. The pictures Murdoch leaked had most of our agents shaded out but not you. Anyone who knows you would know it was you taking out two doctors on the film. I didn't see it until yesterday. You're feted, Sandro, a hero but it meant the IRDC had a picture, someone to go after. They came after you, and failing that, your team."

"That include Carilla?"

"Yes it does. Though the person they really want is you."

He bared his teeth. "Bring it on."

She bit out a brief sound of exasperation. "Oh no. That's what they want. They want you, Sandro. Not that it'll be important for too much longer."

She glanced at Chase, who spread his hands in a placating gesture. "If you're talking about his gray hairs, yes, I noticed. Not many but for a shifter, that's all it takes."

"I'll be out of here after this operation." Sandro carefully avoided looking at them. "And that goes for Megan too. I'm hoping that when we find Ricardo, she'll stay with him but it's her life. Especially now. Subject closed, okay?"

"Sure."

Sandro didn't trust Chase's easy assurances. He'd have to watch his back, make sure nothing got back to Megan. If he told her, it would be on his own terms, not forced into it by anyone else. "But this does put an extra twist on this operation, doesn't it? And a lever. Me."

* * * * *

"Hey, *cara*."

Megan opened her eyes on to the ones she yearned for most. She blinked, clearing her sight.

Sandro held her hand, and smiled down at her. He sat next to the bed but it wasn't her bed, nor was it his. The hotel? She struggled to remember and felt his mind in hers, holding her warmly.

"Don't try. Let me tell you what happened." His voice came soft and low, and when a shaft of pain lanced through her head, he smoothed it away for her. "Just relax. Do you remember the fight?"

Fight. Fight, yes. That red-haired bastard taking on everything she and Jack could hit him with and coming back for more. "Did we kill him?"

"Yes. But he nearly killed you. You're in hospital, Megan. He broke your arm, your hand, some ribs, gashed your thigh down to the artery and put a dent in your head."

She tried to smile, make a joke but that hurt too. "So you brought me here?"

"Straight away. You're going to get better, Megan, though it was touch and go for a while."

She blinked again and concentrated on her body, moving her limbs very slightly. One arm, two. Strange, she could feel the slight roughness of the sheets against her sensitized flesh on both arms, all the way down. Shouldn't one of them be plastered if she'd broken it?

Her legs were bare beneath the sheets and very sensitive to the fabric covering them. She lifted her hand, the one not clutching Sandro's, and touched her forehead. It was hot but she couldn't feel any bruises. "Which arm did he break?"

Sandro touched her hand gently, the one covering her forehead. "This one. Two places. Clean breaks."

There was only one way to heal broken limbs. Set them and wait. "How long have I been asleep?"

"You were hurt on Monday. This is Wednesday."

"But a different month, right?"

"Wrong. You've been under for a couple of days."

She lowered her arm and stared at him. He'd locked his mind down but when she touched it with hers, he opened to her.

Only concern and warmth there. Everything else tucked away, the way he'd taught her. She was too tired to ask for more, and anyway, Sandro knew all her secrets. "What—how is that possible? Have the doctors harnessed Talents' healing powers?" She licked her dry lips.

He pressed a button on the side of the bed and it lifted at the head before he grabbed pillows and stacked them around and behind her.

Speculation filled her mind, as she recalled more about the fight and the events before it, like a story unfolding backward. He filled a glass with water and held it to her lips. "Drink, *cara.*" Gratefully she sipped, then gulped. He refilled the glass for her and she drank that too, before he put the glass down on the bedside table.

Was it her imagination or was he avoiding her eyes? No, he looked everywhere but at her. "What is it, Sandro?" Fear coursed through her veins. "Jack? Is it Jack?"

He lifted his gaze then and she saw remorse there. Oh God. "No, he's recovered well. Did he tell you?"

"What?" She tried to remember, then it came to her. "Oh the shape-shifter thing?"

"Yes." He seemed almost relieved. "He told you Carilla had converted him?"

"What?" Her heart beat a little faster. "He *did* it?" She couldn't believe it. "He let her convert him? He told me he was thinking about it, that's all."

Sandro's mouth settled in a grim line. "It's done now. It can't be changed. In any case, if Jack wasn't a shape-shifter, he would have died. That operative the IRDC sent after you was a killer. No mistake, Megan, he meant to kill both of you." He glanced at the glass on the table and reached for the water jug.

"So Jack's okay?"

"He is now." He poured water and this time took a sip for himself. "Shape-shifters can heal very quickly in their shifter form. He's out of bed now, ready to go back to work." He took another sip. "Not that we're about to let him."

"He can't go back to work?" She felt stupid, her brain clogged and confused.

Sandro shook his head. "He's a marked man. So he's taking leave from the university and going away."

Jack was leaving her. That was all she could think of, and the remembrance of all they'd been through together came back to her, bringing back the tears. She blinked them away. "Can I see him before he goes?"

"Of course." Sandro put the glass down and reached for her hand. "There's something else you should know, Megan."

By the way his shoulders tensed under his soft t-shirt she knew he was about to tell her something he didn't want to. "Just tell me, Sandro. Please."

His hands tightened over hers, then he released them and withdrew. She felt bereft but said nothing, watching him carefully. She got the feeling that after his next words her life would change forever.

"Megan, remember what I said. The assassin meant to kill you. And if you and Jack had been mortals, he would have done just that. By the time we got to you, you'd bled out, your lung was punctured and your skull was crushed." He swallowed. "I had a choice. I could let you die or—"

"Convert me," she finished, her voice hardly disturbing the air around them, but he heard her.

"Yes."

She still felt the same, still felt like Megan Armstrong. "Are you kidding me?"

"I wish I were. It was the only way to save you. That head injury would have killed you." He swallowed. "And I couldn't have borne that."

"Why?" Still confused about his motives, she'd never have a better time to find out.

Slowly, he shook his head. "I care for you, Megan." He lifted his head and met her eyes.

They stared at each other for a full minute. She didn't try to read him, she didn't know if she could, and he didn't intrude on her thoughts. So they stared.

Could she confess she loved him? For her, there was no other man.

Accepting the fact brought a kind of peace.

He squeezed her hand. "Right now, it's all about you. We need to get you better. We'll talk later, I promise."

She lifted her hand and touched her head, grimacing when she realized what a state her hair was in. At the top, just toward the back, she felt it. A hard ridge that hadn't been there before, like a scar left by a horrific injury. But the wound, although tender, was closed and healed.

It was true, it was all true. As if she needed that tactile confirmation, the reality of what Sandro had done crashed in on her. Her mind opened, panicking, and she reached out.

At once he took her hands, entered her mind. "Listen," he said, his voice low but penetrating, his whole attention fixed on her in a way that gave her delicious shivers, even now when she felt weak and knew she looked like shit. "Listen to me, Megan. You don't have to change a thing. If you want to live as a mortal, you can. You only have to shift form three times a month, at the full moon and the days either side of it. That's all, and those shape-shifts can be as brief as you please. Five minutes if you want."

"But how will I cope? You're stronger, you live longer."

"*We're* stronger, *we* live longer. Accept it and that will help too. It's not that bad, really."

She leaned forward, intending a hug but she was still weak and she ended up falling into his arms. They closed around her, holding her safe. Safer than she'd been for a long time. Sandro offered her a respite from the stress her life had become, a moment to rest. She took it until he stood and eased her back against the pillows.

Megan had to force herself to let go, to free him so he could return to his chair but she kept hold of his hands. His touch brought comfort to her, a soothing presence in this world that had somehow turned itself on its head.

His smile was bittersweet. He looked away, staring at nothing before he turned his attention back to her. "When you leave here, you need to come home with me. Not to resume what—what we had before but so I can train you. I'm the only dragon available." He ruffled his hair again. "It's probably best if we try to keep this professional." He glanced up but she saw the disconnection in his eyes. Sandro couldn't look at her, not directly.

So that was how it was going to be. "Saving me for Ricardo, Sandro?" she said, a bitter twist to her mouth. "Don't I get to make my own mind up? I'm a big girl, even bigger now."

"No, Megan, it's not that." His expression softened. "I was losing control of the operation, losing sight of the objective. I do enjoy being with you, maybe too much, so I have to step back for a while. When I got word you were injured, in danger, I shape-shifted without thinking and headed out. I didn't pause as I should have done to set something up, to protect my team and they all came under attack." He traced the lifeline on her hand, and she found herself wondering how much it had lengthened, or if it had gone decimal. Stupid thing to think at a time like this. It took her that long to catch up with what he was saying.

"They were attacked?"

He nodded, still not meeting her eyes. "They got away but the IRDC planned better than I did. They attacked you and Jack, putting two of us with connections to you in danger—Carilla and me. We were heading for you, without thinking of anything else. That was wrong. I'm a team leader. I should always *think* first, always, and I didn't. Because of that, I could have lost the team."

She felt the tension in him and wondered that she could do this so easily. "Sandro. What else happened?"

He looked up then, and the bleakness in his eyes made her gasp. "Angelica, the shape-shifter looking after you, was killed. Garroted."

She inhaled sharply but used the moment to retain control of her emotions. "That can't be your fault."

He grimaced. "Not entirely. She should have scanned the area constantly but her killer must have taken her by surprise."

"And you can't let that happen again, can you?"

"No." His abject misery struck right at her heart. "So I have to think of that first, Megan. *Have* to. I can't let you—no, that's not fair—I can't let myself be distracted again."

Despite the sick fear that seized her every time she thought of Ricardo and now Carilla and Angelica, Sandro's last words filled her with another feeling—dismay. "Is that all I am to you? A distraction?"

"No." He gripped her hand again and she loved the connection. "Much more than that, Megan. But although I'll take you home with me again, this time we keep to our own bedrooms at night."

"But you sleep on the platform."

"I'll use the other bedroom," he bit out. "Megan, I mean it."

"Yes." The exhilaration, the sheer pleasure of waking up with Sandro next to her, the feel of his bare skin against hers, all that was gone. "But when all this is over, I'll come back. I won't go away."

He blinked. "I know." Why did she get the feeling he was about to say something else?

He touched his open hand to her forehead, blessedly cool against her feverish heat. "I can tell you're tired. Sleep again, Megan. The more you rest, the faster you'll heal."

She slept.

* * * * *

Megan couldn't believe how quickly she healed. The following day found her dressed, sitting on the bed waiting for Sandro to come get her.

She hadn't realized Jack was there until she looked up and saw him, his arm around a pale but whole Carilla. When she'd first met the jaguar shape-shifter, Megan had thought her dangerous. Now she looked vulnerable and sweet, her sharp features softened with love.

She held her hand out in welcome and Jack stepped into the room.

"You don't mind, do you?"

She gave a short laugh. "What does it have to do with me? Jack, I'm happy for you, really I am." She let her gaze encompass Carilla. "And if you're making Jack happy, I'm happy for you too." Seeing them together, looking as if it was somehow meant, made her heart ache. "And you'll want the apartment to yourselves, won't you?"

Jack shrugged. "We might move out to Carilla's." He looked wary but his eyes told her something else.

Trying her newly developed powers, she felt for his mind. She knew by his smile that she'd succeeded. Jack opened to her. The first time she'd tried this with anyone but Sandro.

Love and happiness filled him. She couldn't take that from him, couldn't begin to question what was happening to Jack, taking him away from her. As was right. "We'll always be friends, won't we, Jack?"

"The best. Always." Jack released Carilla to bend down and slide his arms around Megan's waist for a gentle hug. It felt good to feel his arms around her, simple friendship instead of complex love and all the tempestuous emotions that brought. She hugged him back, a bit less gently. "It's okay, Jack."

He stepped back, still smiling and reached for Carilla's hand, threading his fingers between hers. As if they couldn't bear not to touch. "We will. It's better now. You're with Sandro—"

She felt rather than saw Carilla's flinch. So the cat-woman knew her affair with Sandro was going nowhere. "We're taking a step back, so he can concentrate on rescuing Ricardo and finding the lab."

For the first time a shadow crossed Jack's features and it was for her. "It's okay, Jack, it's temporary. I hope. He's a complex man, and he needs some space." Even as she said it, she doubted her own words. They still didn't sit right with her. There was something else, she felt it every time Sandro shielded his expression or kept himself apart from her. But she had to give him the space he wanted or if they lost Ricardo, if they didn't find the lab in time, they'd have no future at all.

She smiled for Jack and Carilla, wished them well but wanted them out of it, away from the trouble she knew was coming. Otherwise, why would Sandro be so preoccupied, so worried?

Two days later, Sandro took Megan back to his apartment. It was almost like coming home. Even the smell of the apartment, a mixture of leather, aftershave and Sandro, felt familiar. And good. Her body seemed to open to welcome it in as if it was part of her already. She would never smell this particular combination again without wanting to weep if Sandro put an end to their affair.

Unfair to let her love him, then pull back. Even more unfair to pull back for a reason she couldn't quarrel with. If he felt their affair was preventing him doing his job properly and his brother was involved, then his priorities were clear. She only wished she featured a little higher on his list. Just a little.

Abruptly she turned and he nearly collided with her, preventing it only by throwing out his hands to retain his balance. He raised a brow. "Something wrong?"

"I want to call my parents."

He sighed heavily. "Our UK unit is talking to them, explaining everything. They'll put them in witness protection or provide bodyguards for them until the danger is over. They're incommunicado."

"So I don't even get to tell them about my conversion."

He watched her warily and she knew he thought she'd cry. So she swallowed back her tears. When she would have pushed past him, he caught her waist in his hands. He didn't pull her close, his chest to her back, and link his arms around her. How she wished he would, even now. "When all this is over, you can tell your family everything."

"Too damn right I will." Angrily she dashed the tears from her eyes before turning to face him. She didn't want him to see her so vulnerable. But it seemed she'd missed one, because he lifted his hand and traced it under one eye, catching the moisture there.

"I'm sorry, Megan. It's for the best."

"So why not send me into a safe place too?"

He paused and caught his lower lip between his teeth in a sensuous gesture she yearned to follow up with a kiss. Even now, when he made it clear he didn't want her, she wanted him. "Because the fact remains—you are the only person who can contact Ricardo. We still need you, Megan." He stepped away and walked around her but he stopped at the door. "I've had the phone number changed for this place. It's as safe as it ever was. I can look after you here and I'm your mentor, at least for now. I'm the only dragon shape-shifter available."

He said that as if he didn't care, as if she were a nuisance. Perhaps she was, but remembering their passionate encounters, a seed of doubt entered her mind. Perhaps he just wished she was.

She watched him, then listened to his steps on the wooden floor of the mezzanine outside. They were steady, determined.

Walking away from her.

Chapter Ten

"Hold that image in your mind."

Already she was improving, getting better at holding the image of the dragon. He'd seen that dragon although Megan hadn't, not yet. She'd see it today.

Sandro feared she wouldn't like the beast. The way Jane had looked at him when he'd shape-shifted for her that one time had seared itself into his memory, with him until the day he died. He'd seen contempt, fear and disgust. To Jane, he'd been an animal.

Megan might feel the same. Not about him, about herself. All very well to accept the difference in others but he was terribly afraid she wouldn't accept it in herself. So he'd delayed the final move, spending the day helping her to train her telepathic powers.

She felt the dragon. She was almost ready. Normally they'd wait until the full moon, until the transformation happened naturally to show a newly converted or newly matured shape-shifter her other form. But it was weeks away and this time they couldn't wait.

He got to his feet and strolled to the kitchen to fetch them coffee, his mind resting in hers, although she thought he'd gone. He never went, not now, because like it or not, she needed him to ensure her safety. Soon she wouldn't need him anymore. When they'd found the laboratory holding Ricardo, when she'd developed her skills. She'd leave him then, hopefully with Ricardo.

No, he would have left her. The gray hair at his temples was thickening every day and he'd taken to covering it with a temporary dye so no one else would notice. Yasmin, Carilla,

Johann, Chase and Ann knew—that was three more people than he'd intended. He felt a weakness in his limbs, a more insidious precursor of what was to come. It would only increase—there was no cure for old age.

Time rushed with an urgency he'd never felt before. He had to find his brother before his weakness became apparent to everyone. And more particularly, Megan.

He took his time pouring the coffee, giving Megan a chance to hold the dragon in her mind on her own. It was the first step toward the shape-shift, and she did it well. Sandro wanted to see the dragon again, wanted to fly with her. Perhaps he'd find contentment doing that since he would no longer make love with her.

She took the coffee mug with a slight smile and sipped at the steaming liquid. "I tried so hard last night," she said. "I really thought I could contact him."

He already knew. He never left her mind but last night neither of them could contact Ricardo. "It doesn't matter. He might have been unconscious or asleep."

"Or dead."

"No."

She turned fierce eyes on to him. "Sandro, you must accept Ricardo might be dead. Those people did terrible things to him. He couldn't withstand it forever."

She took her hand away from her cup and put it gently on his forearm, just above his shirt cuff. He wanted to put his own hand over it.

"He's not dead, Megan. If he dies, I will know it. That isn't some kind of mystic belief, it's the truth. We're of the same flesh and our family bond can't be broken this side of death."

"Do all shape-shifters feel like that?"

He shrugged. "I have no idea. But children are very precious to us and siblings often have a close bond. We don't have so many children we can afford to take them for granted." He stopped, realizing what he'd just told her. "I'm sorry, Megan. For a moment I forgot. You're a shape-shifter now. I've reduced your fertility."

She forced a smile, he could see her lips quiver with the effort before it firmed again. "I only ever wanted two. Or none at all. I thought I'd wait and see how I felt. After I lost Paul I decided I didn't want children. A little while afterward I realized maybe I did. My biological clock started ticking but I always had other things to do."

"You're not that old, even by human standards. You had years ahead of you to make up your mind. Now it's made up for you."

"I have five hundred years to decide if I want children?"

He grimaced. "They kind of expect it."

"Who do? The community? It's compulsory?"

"No." He sipped his coffee, more for something to do than because he really wanted it. "Some do, some don't. Vampires are very protective about family although their fertility rates are even lower than ours. But you're a new shape-shifter and word will get around. You do have time but you'll be popular." He took another sip. He didn't like the thought of other shape-shifters courting Megan. The thought didn't sit well in his mind. All the more reason to bring her together with Ricardo, a mature dragon, ready to protect her and give her the freedom she needed to explore her new world.

"So as a new shape-shifter, can I convert someone?"

Reluctantly, he shook his head. "Only shifters born can do that."

She looked as if she were going to say something else but shut her mouth with a snap. She was getting better at hiding her thoughts. He should be glad.

Abruptly, he got to his feet. "It's time, Megan. Get to your feet and take your clothes off."

She shot him a startled glance and he felt his lips quirk briefly. "Unless you want to destroy what you're wearing. Nudity is natural to shape-shifters, they will strip anywhere if they need to shift form." He studied her closely to see how she'd take it.

To his surprise, she smiled. "I remember the first time I met you. You were nude within the first ten minutes and when you shape-shifted on the STORM roof, you behaved as if it was the most natural thing in the world."

"I know, I saw you blush." The remembrance brought a rush of desire to his whole body. Her skin, flushed with passion, under his hands, in his bed.

No. He had to stop thinking that way. Because she'd want him naked too, and he'd need to be if he was going to help her. Instead, he remembered when he shape-shifted and her astonishment, followed by her ready acceptance of him.

He couldn't appear before her half-hard this time. He had to preserve the distance between them. So he projected his thoughts on to her, imagined she was just another shape-shifter.

That didn't work. Her strip wasn't exactly sensual, she took off her clothes with brisk efficiency but somehow it seemed more erotic than any other strip he'd ever seen. Except this time she obviously didn't want to turn him on.

He turned away and stripped, trying to keep his mind on anything but her, anything but what happened not long ago in that bed on the mezzanine. Nothing worked. Nothing.

"You're sure Ricardo isn't dead?"

A vision of his brother, strapped to a bed, his arms flayed and cut open, flashed into his mind.

Yes, that worked. He turned around and faced her, his dick flaccid once more.

The sight of her nearly did it again but he drew a deep breath, closed his eyes and conjured Ricardo's image. It hurt so much to see it but it reminded him this was for him. If he got his brother out and safe he'd count this operation a success. It was all that mattered to him now.

He kept his attention on her face. "You still have the image?"

She cleared her throat. "Yes."

For an instant he let his gaze stray and caught a glimpse of the dew on her pubic hair before he gasped and brought the image back to his mind. She wanted him. The sight was enough to remind him, that and her scent coming faintly to him across the room—

He groaned low in his throat before he wet his lips to continue. "Okay. Hold the image. Close your eyes and examine it closely. Look at every scale, every gleaming inch of it. Stroke it, feel it. Now *be* it."

He watched and waited. Felt her trying so hard, and realized what was wrong. "No, *cara*, feel it and relax into it. If you try, it won't happen."

When he entered her mind he touched her softly, soothing her. He'd promised himself he wouldn't help but this time, this first time, she might need it.

Keeping his eyes open, he saw a shimmer, a sheen over her body, starting at her navel and spreading out. Bluish-gold at first, darkening as she sank into the beast that was now her other half.

He'd seen her and helped her transform to heal but he hadn't seen her do it for herself and he found it fascinating. Watching a shape-shifter change form for the very first time was a privilege few witnessed. He'd had that honor twice, with Ricardo and now with Megan. Both people he loved more than any other in the world.

He was glad he'd lived to see it.

Now Megan was almost all dragon but he saw the essential grace she carried around unconsciously and he loved her. He wanted the dragon to belong to him, he wanted to fly with her, caress her body with his wings, adore her.

That didn't hurt. She sounded surprised.

He shape-shifted, aware she watched him because she turned her gleaming head to one side to get a better view. *Are you coping with the vision? You've lost stereoscopic vision unless you look straight ahead, which you'll find more difficult, and you can see different things out of each eye.*

I'll keep looking forward then.

Yeah. It was getting harder to remain laconic and detached. He'd already locked his more profound thoughts deep in his mind although his physical body reacted to her, in dragon form or mortal.

He'd never had dragon sex. Human was his basic form, as it was for all shape-shifters. He'd just never wanted to before. Now he wondered what it would be like.

He cut himself off. Dragon or man, he still had a penis and it could still become erect. But she was so beautiful, so stunning to him.

Her dragon form was like his, which was only to be expected since he'd made her, but it didn't always turn out that way. So she had blue scales that shimmered gold in the light instead of his blue and green combination, heavily clawed feet and she was a Western dragon. Dragons had their species too, and Western dragons were heavier, less sleek than their Eastern counterparts.

But both flew, and both breathed fire. Maybe he'd save the fire part for another day. But today she'd fly.

* * * * *

Megan's mouth went dry. As a man he was desirable but as a dragon he was arrogant, invincible—and irresistible. Of course, she thought wryly, as a female dragon she would think that. Did dragons have alphas, leaders of the pack?

No. On the whole, we're solitary beings. Except when we mate.

He turned his great head. *I'm regulating your size for you, because that's harder to learn and in your full size you'd probably damage the furniture. Remember what I told you once — we change size by expanding or contracting our body mass, so the possibilities aren't infinite.*

She heard the smile in his voice and relaxed imperceptibly. *I thought I was to do this on my own?*

You are. All I'm doing is regulating your size to save my furniture. You shape-shifted yourself.

I felt a bit dizzy.

That's normal. You'll learn to control that.

She should be panicking, surely. Changing her form, changing from one being into another? A year ago she would have scoffed.

You hid, all those years?

Can you blame us? He sent her a picture, then retracted it. She didn't get more than a flash of bloodstained scales. *Dragons were worshipped, then slaughtered.*

He paused and she felt him in her mind, just being there. It felt right.

Megan, you're delaying. You know I'll answer all your questions about Talents but not now. Don't be scared, babe, you're doing really well. Do you want to change back or do you want to try a flight?

I want to fly. The thought filled her with exhilaration. From dreams of flying to lying back on the grass of the village green at home watching the planes soar overhead, she'd always wanted to fly, as long as she could remember.

We use air currents to help us but we don't have any in this apartment. So I want you to take off the old-fashioned way.

How's that?

Take a run at it.

Nothing ventured. She sighted down the long center area of the room and realized why it was relatively bare. A runway.

Okay, she could do that. Taking a deep breath, she began to run.

Five minutes and twice as many turns later she paused to draw breath and heard his chuckle.

Are you laughing at me?

A pause. *Yes. Do you mind?*

She thought and got an instant mental vision of herself, head and neck forward, brow-ridges heavily frowning, determination on every feature, running up and down the long living area. *How can I, when I look like that?*

You look adorable.

He cut himself off and drew out of her mind with a suddenness that made her gasp. Only then did she realize he'd been there all the time, because there was now a void in her mind where he'd been. A Sandro-shaped void.

He returned just as quickly. *I'm sorry. Shall we continue?*

So he was finding it as hard as she was not to touch and caress.

Let's try the motions.

Flap my wings?

Precisely.

She stood in the middle of the floor, feeling more than stupid, and flapped her arms—wings. The air stirred pleasantly around her but nothing else happened.

Make it rhythmic. Get into a pattern, your own pattern, the way you feel most comfortable.

Nothing ventured, nothing gained, her Cockney grandmother used to tell her. She felt the spirit of that indomitable woman spark deep inside her. The determination that had gone through five years of war and faced the Blitz, when her home and everything she owned had been smashed to pieces, the courage to get up and start again when the war was over, now filled Megan with energy and resolution. She'd make her forebears proud of her if they were watching. Both grandmothers, so different but both so tough. Her Welsh grandmother had lost her husband and a son in a mining disaster and then sent her younger sons down the mines too. All to earn a living. Until one had broken away and gone to London to seek his fortune. Which he'd found.

Now she was delaying. She closed her eyes and felt a flicker when she opened them again. Startled, she jumped back a foot.

He chuckled again, warmly filling her mind with it. *That's your inner eyelid. We have two in this form.*

She remembered a natural world film about a chameleon, and the way it had flicked a cover over its eye to protect it from the dry, sandy atmosphere. *Cool. Does that mean I won't need sunglasses?*

Not in this form.

Wow. So much to learn.

He soothed her and it felt like soft hands stroking her inner being. So sensuous she could give herself over to it completely. *After this crisis is done, you can explore what you are.*

Yes.

She had to concentrate. Remembering what he'd told her, she flapped her wings, experiencing the muscles flexing and relaxing, learning her new form. She closed her eyes to concentrate on the sensation and leaned into the action.

But when she lifted her feet, she flumped onto her belly. Opening her eyes once more, she glared at Sandro. *So what good did that do?*

It showed you the action of flying. A bit like dry swimming. Now follow me.

The fastest way to move without flying was to heave her weight from side to side and push her feet forward. Her claws grated against the wooden floor.

Sandro's exasperation flickered and made her laugh. She stopped when a weird howling sound emerged from between her jaws. *What the hell was that?*

You. Your voice box has changed. You can howl and roar but you can't speak. Why else would we have telepathy?

Staggering along in his wake, she considered the question. They'd need something if they couldn't talk. *So do other creatures have it?*

Only shape-shifters have the full telepathic gift, because we're fully sentient but yes, birds and other creatures have a primitive form.

Does that mean we can talk to them? The image of Dr. Doolittle crooning a song to a seal took hold of her imagination.

Not like that but we can communicate at their level. You'd be surprised how stupid some cats can be. They always seem so clever and enigmatic if you can't communicate with them.

Her parents had a cat, imaginatively called Tibbles. Tibbles ate the best morsels, slept in front of the fire and spent most of the day being cosseted and petted. Not a bad life, however stupid you happen to be.

I always wanted to be a cat.

You should have stuck with Carilla then.

And she remembered Jack was a cat now.

Dragon, cat—sometimes the shock of the whole thing stunned her.

But not now. Now she had to concentrate on being the strongest shape-shifter she could be, so Sandro could find his brother, so she wouldn't have to lean on him for protection anymore. Maybe she could move back to the hotel, and share Chase's undemanding company instead. Rest from the constant agony being close to Sandro brought her now, the need to touch him and the knowledge that she couldn't.

Going upstairs was awkward. She had to concentrate on folding her wings close to her body, and she soon found it was easier to jump from step to step than to try to walk upstairs. *These stairs weren't made for dragons.*

This time his laugh was external as well as internal, a weird wheezing sound. *No they weren't. In this form I don't usually use them.*

He flew. Of course.

Why are we going upstairs?

You're going to jump off the balcony.

What?

They'd reached the mezzanine but before she could back up and hurry down again, she felt the dizziness of a transformation. She closed her eyes and steadied herself. When she opened them again, the floor was a lot closer.

Something lifted her and she squawked in panic but then she realized it was Sandro, lifting her on the tip of one great wing. And she'd shrunk to the size of an eagle. *Won't I kill myself at this size?*

No.

He perched her on the top of the balcony, and waited until she swayed backward to balance herself. To her surprise, it came naturally to use her tail to achieve that. *Wow.*

Yeah.

With a sweep of wings and a rush of air Sandro flew. Just like that. One minute he was standing next to her on the mezzanine next to his bed, the next he was in the air, hovering above her. He swooped down in a graceful glide to just below the level where she perched. *Now fly. Use your wings just as you did on the ground and drop. I'll catch you, if you need me to.*

Twice she needed him. The first time she jumped, then plummeted like a stone, to land on his warm, safe back. He gently restored her to her perch. The second time she managed a foot before the thought struck her. *Jesus, I'm flying!* Before she lost it and plunged once more.

Third time was the charm. This time, although Sandro stayed a couple of feet under her all the time, she managed a circuit of the room. With him below, she couldn't feel the whole flying thing properly but she got the idea.

Oh Sandro, thank you for this!

* * * * *

Sandro heard her thanks with mixed feelings. This mentoring only increased his tenderness toward her, made him want to fold her in his wings and take care nobody came within a foot of her but he wouldn't be doing her any service if he did that. She needed to learn how to take care of herself and how to defend herself. Grimly he put the thought in the forefront of his mind, like a knot in a handkerchief, something he couldn't afford to forget.

He made her work. When her wings ached from flying he made her land and work at blocking attacks. Her karate training helped, improving her balance even in this new form and helping her to sense danger when it surrounded her. That would be the most useful skill of all.

Only toward the end of the afternoon, when sunlight slanted into the windows did he let her change back to human form. Only to make her transform again until he was sure she could do it on her own. Eventually the shape-shift would become almost instinctive, like driving a car or walking or writing a note. She wouldn't have to engage her brain to force her body into the shape. Picture the dragon—be the dragon. Just like that.

Back in human form, Megan ran upstairs and twenty minutes later emerged dressed in sweatpants and t-shirt, her dark hair damp and spiky from the shower. He'd showered too and dressed in slacks and shirt. He didn't want to show off any of his body, give her any temptation, so the shirt was a large, baggy one, left over from a summer holiday in Florida. Bright blue, with suns and palm trees scattered over it in a dazzling display of Floridian taste. Or rather, what tourists usually assumed was Floridian taste.

She stopped short and stared, eyes wide with what looked like shock.

"What's wrong?"

"I thought you were a man of refinement."

He smiled and went to the coffee machine to pour one for her. "This took my fancy."

"Not all your taste is good then."

He turned around and handed her a cup of steaming java. "I like this shirt. So be careful what you say."

"Sure. But I still think it would look better in a bonfire."

"That would ruin the elegant design." It would look better on her, preferably with all the buttons undone. He'd enjoy exploring that particular island paradise.

Taking a deep draught of steaming hot coffee took his mind off the vision that came too vividly to his mind. He almost choked on the scalding heat but it did the job.

He forced his mind to the purpose of this afternoon's exercises. "If you're attacked, the first thing you do is to shape-shift. We don't have to worry about keeping our form secret anymore so the first priority is your safety. In the dragon form you're almost invincible. You have one vulnerable spot, just under your throat. Over the years even that will harden up."

"What about all those legends about knights killing dragons?"

"They lied."

She choked on her coffee. "What, all of them?"

"Not all. If you're hurt, you shape-shift. The healing process will begin immediately and you won't die."

"Lord! So shape-shifters mainly die of old age?"

He winced. "Mainly. But they can be taken by surprise, as Angelica was in the library, and killed in human form." He didn't allow himself to dwell on the dead operative. It happened rarely but all too often for his liking. That alone made it imperative they close this laboratory and find all the perpetrators.

"What about the guys we captured after we went out to dinner?"

He grimaced. "Nothing. They were hired muscle and knew very little about the people who wanted us taken captive, just that they paid well." That had been a severe disappointment but the Sorcerers had questioned them well before wiping their most recent memories and putting them back on the street.

He sipped his coffee, now at a comfortable temperature, enjoying the sensation of the hot liquid finding its way to his stomach. When time suddenly became short, every experience became a revelation.

"We're going to practice your shape-shifting, so you can do it under pressure, in any circumstances. In an emergency, you don't need to worry about regulating your form but we'll make a start on that skill, just in case. Second, you open your telepathic channels and *scream*. Call for help."

"Does it have to be in a particular form, you know, SOS or something?"

He bared his teeth in a feral grin. "No. Just open up. The Talents nearby will read you loud and clear. Third, fly out of there. While you have the connection with Ricardo, you're valuable to STORM." He carefully avoided letting her know how valuable she was to him.

She put her empty cup down on the pristine white work surface and stared at it as if it held the answers to all her questions. "What if I don't?"

"Pardon me?"

She lifted her head, and the bleak expression in her eyes almost floored him. "What if I can't contact Ricardo anymore? What if my transformation stopped it? I couldn't get near him last night."

Christ, he never thought of that. He'd just put her inability to connect down to her inexperience, or maybe Ricardo had been asleep. But he would still have done it. "You were dying, Megan. The choice was to convert you or let you die. I didn't want to do that."

"Why not?"

"You know why." He stared at her, keeping his mind carefully separate but allowing her to see the warmth in his eyes. He might not be able to make good on his desires and needs but he knew she was feeling alone and maybe, deep down, a little scared. She needed his friendship, at least for the time being.

That was all he could give her. Soon he wouldn't be there anymore, for her or for anyone else.

Enough.

"You mean too much to me, Megan. I won't watch you die."

He watched her reaction, the way her blue eyes dilated just a little as she absorbed what he said. She didn't look away. "Why can't you promise me anything?"

He took her hand and stroked the palm, following the strong lifeline making its way right around the thumb-pad. Her touch soothed him. He wanted her so much it hurt his chest when he breathed. Her touch eased the ache a little. "I have—commitments, arrangements."

"You mean there's hope for us?"

Again he chickened out of telling her. Because that was what it had come to—he didn't want to see her expression when he told her exactly how hopeless their love was. He could disappear so she'd never find him but that, he now knew, was the coward's way out. He'd tell her before he left. Just not today.

"Megan, I want you to meet Ricardo before we go any further. I want him in your life. You dreamed of him first and the connection between you might be stronger than the one between us. Our relationship could be the pale shadow. I would never forgive myself if I closed that off for you. Believe it, love, because it's true."

Shit, he'd just let the endearment slip. He could only hope she'd take it in the British sense, where they called each other "love" as a fondness, not as the stark truth.

She blinked and he caught the tail end of joy as she put it away behind her newly erected barriers. Barriers he'd helped her erect. "I see. So if, once I've met Ricardo, it isn't him but you, will you let me speak then?"

"Sure." It wouldn't happen. He'd have told her the truth by then.

Chapter Eleven

Watching Sandro strip and transform into the dragon became unbearably erotic to Megan. Deprived of his touch, surrounded by him here in his apartment, she thought she'd go mad.

After another flying session, she stood before the window, watching the sun slide down below the level of the buildings opposite. "What must it be like to be a vampire?" How strange, to wonder about people that she had no idea existed such a short time before. But she did. She'd met one, she'd seen one. Maybe more but she'd not been aware of it before.

He came up behind her. She felt his heat through her toweling robe, his presence electrically charging the air around her. "I haven't the least idea. I never had much to do with them until I joined STORM. Vampires used to keep to their own communities until relatively recently."

"Relatively?" She turned her head to look at him, bracing herself for the sight as she always did. Every time she looked at him she wanted him, every time she longed to reach out and touch, her fingertips tingling with the need. As usual, she resisted the almost overwhelming temptation, clenching her fingers tightly to stop herself reaching for him.

"They're big on family," he said with a grimace. "Most vampires have very passionate natures, impulsive and fiery. Others, like Johann, rein all that in deliberately. Turn into a kind of vampire Spock."

The allusion made her laugh. "I always thought Spock was hot."

He raised a brow. "As hot as me?"

He turned away abruptly. She replied anyway. "Nobody's as hot as you, Sandro. Nobody."

Would he pretend to ignore her or listen? Taking her bottom lip between her teeth, she bit hard, stemming the tears that threatened to overflow, scolding herself for her stupidity.

He stopped walking but kept his back to her. His shoulders straightened, the muscles under his thin robe clearly visible, taut with tension. She heard his deep breath, clearly audible in the nervous silence.

"I never meant to make you unhappy," he said, his voice low and measured so she knew he was making an effort to control it. "I wanted you but I wanted you to think it was a passing thing, friendship and comfort. Nothing more. Please, Megan, let it go."

"I can't." She stared at his back but didn't enter his mind, afraid of what she might find there. "Sandro, you can walk away, that's your choice. I can't stop you. I'm sorry you don't feel for me what I feel for you and I daresay I'll learn to live with it. At the moment it's a struggle."

He accompanied his choked laugh with a brief shake of his head. "Megan, this is driving me crazy. I don't know what to do." He turned around, slowly pivoting on one heel.

His face showed only bleakness and despair and her heart sank. This was it then. She'd have to put up with his lack of feelings for her, at least feelings not as strong as hers were for him. Megan blinked hard and swallowed. "I'm sorry, Sandro. I'll do my best not to intrude."

"Intrude?" He gave a short, humorless laugh. "Megan, you intrude on my thoughts day and night, whether you're here or not, whether I'm with you or not. I thought if I put some distance between us, if I could make you believe—" He tipped his head up, stared at the ceiling so far above them. "What's the use?" he asked the unseeing space. "It makes no difference." He lowered his chin.

The intensity in his dark eyes consumed her. All his careful distance had gone, replaced by yearning and want, so much she didn't know how either of them could stand it. "How could I expect that the woman who catapulted into my life that day would take me over so completely? And why now, of all times?"

As if driven by an outside, unseen force, he took the three strides separating them and reached for her. She went, opening her own arms to stretch them around him, encompassing his back. His heat seared her skin and she welcomed it.

"Megan, how could I resist this? I'm sorry, so sorry but this changes nothing. I still can't promise you anything."

"Did I ask for anything?" She looked up at him and he seemed unable to resist. Staring at her for a brief, hungry moment, he took her mouth as if compelled to do it.

It felt like coming home. Megan leaned her head against his supporting arm and opened her mouth to him. Sandro didn't hesitate to take her invitation and plundered deeply. He tasted every part of her, devouring her as if this was his last chance at a long-desired treat.

Megan reveled in his taking. She felt cherished and wanted, although there was nothing gentle about his kiss. His low groan of surrender gave her all she wanted to know about desire and needing. Eventually, he slowly drew away, just far enough to speak. "Can we have tonight? If I promise to tell you tomorrow, will you let me love you tonight with no more questions?"

His eyes burned her with passion but she saw a hint of anxiety too. If she refused to do this, he might pull away again. She couldn't bear that. "Yes. Tonight."

He closed his arms around her tightly and kissed her again, this time gentler, with more tenderness. When he drew back, he smiled at her. "Thank you. You won't know what it means until tomorrow. I'll tell you, I promise."

When he released her, he took her hand and led her upstairs. They walked past the bed on the platform. "Maybe we should christen the other bedroom tonight," he murmured as they passed.

"You haven't...?"

"No." He turned to smile at her. "I've slept there occasionally but not shared it. This is the night."

When he opened the door to the bedroom she'd never been in, she gasped in surprise.

The room was larger than she'd thought and it needed to be. The rest of the apartment was spacious and sparely furnished in natural woods and neutral colors. This was the opposite. A four-poster bed dominated the space, the dark wood enhanced by gilt. A serpent wound its way up each of the bottom posts, the head forming part of the elaborate canopy. Crimson draperies enhanced the crimson and gold coverlet and cushions, brocade on brocade, velvet on satin.

The rest of the furniture enhanced and reflected the bed and a huge gilt mirror hung over the marble fireplace. No other fireplaces existed in the apartment, so that in itself was a surprise.

Megan walked into the room, staring around her. By the bed, on the side nearest the windows, she saw a painting of a young man. Gorgeously arrayed in elaborate court garments in the style of the eighteenth century, the man stared down his arrogant nose at her, as if daring her to comment on the cerulean blue coat and gold-laced waistcoat. For all the lace and satin, the subject of the painting looked dangerous. And he carried a sword that didn't look as if it was just for show.

When he came up behind her, she felt his presence, heat radiating through her. "Is that you?"

"Uh-huh." He nuzzled her hair, more interested in her than the portrait, though through her enhanced senses she felt a thread of tension in him.

"Before you met your wife?"

"Yes." He lifted away and slid his arms around her waist. "I was living in Venice when that portrait was done."

"What did you call yourself then?" She loved Italian names, a liquid language. More the language of love than French, she'd always thought.

"Giacomo."

"Giacomo, were you good in bed then as well?"

He sighed and lifted his head, leaving a breath of hot air behind. "I was fun, I never asked for more than I got and I was adventurous. What do you think?"

"I think you're a different person now. I would have loved to have known you then."

He chuckled. "No you wouldn't. I did some really stupid things, and I lived far too recklessly for you."

She turned in his arms and pushed her palms against his chest but he held her too tightly for her to get away. "You think I'm staid, is that it?"

"Far from it." His expression melted her, love and care where before he'd only allowed friendship. "I think you have too much sense, is all. I did some bad things, Megan, but I don't do them now. I'm ready for you, ready to love you as you deserve."

She considered his answer. Okay, he'd sweet-talked his way out of that one. For now. And she hadn't realized who he'd been. One day she'd make him tell her all the things he'd seen, all the places he'd been. Perhaps she could visit them with him. Whatever he was about to tell her in the morning couldn't stop her loving him, fighting to be with him.

"Is that where you were really born, Venice?" She had a vision of him among the canals and old palazzos. He fitted.

"No, I'm from Tuscany originally. I was born near Florence."

"Don't you miss it?"

"Italy? No. These days I can go there regularly. I still own some property." He stopped abruptly.

"What is it? Do you own a palace?"

He chuckled and drew her closer. "Nothing so grand. This room is the reminder of my previous existence. Before anyone knew Talents existed, it was wiser to let material things go, to go from one life to the next with the minimum of baggage. I bought that painting back at auction a few years ago. It was labeled 'unknown male'. I hadn't thought to see it again."

"It's beautiful." She turned in his arms to face him. "You're beautiful."

"No, you are." He kissed her, gently touching his lips to the tip of her nose and her forehead.

"This room is so different."

"Fulfill a fantasy of mine. Take off that robe and go lie on the bed. I want to see you there." He kissed her one more time before he released her.

She blinked then her hands went to the tie of her robe. Why was it so difficult to undress now, when she'd spent most of the day naked in front of him?

Because there was naked and there was nude. This was nude.

He watched her, dark eyes burning with intent and she felt almost shy under his gaze. But she did as he asked. Her hands trembling only slightly, she managed to pull the tie undone and let the robe open of its own accord. She only had to lower her shoulders a little to make the soft fabric slip. Feeling it slide down her arms, she sensed every thread of the weave. Maybe her new state had enhanced her sense of touch but she thought it was more likely to be Sandro, standing absolutely still, watching her with an expression that made her shiver.

She left the robe where it fell on the Persian carpet and walked around to the side of the bed. It was higher than she was used to and she wondered if she'd have to make an undignified hop to get some purchase on it then she saw an upholstered footstool, obviously placed there to help the would-be sleeper up. Except she wouldn't be sleeping for a while. If at all.

So her ascent to the bed was more elegant than she'd thought it would be, although she had to scramble a little at the end to get her feet up. On all fours, she paused to glance at him, still standing between the two base posts, watching her silently.

A smile flickered across his lips but he said nothing. She didn't return the smile but pushed a couple of cushions to support her back when she turned and sat on the soft, velvet brocade cover. She kept her legs together and stretched them out, aping a demure pose, her hands quietly clasped in her lap.

He watched.

She pushed her heels together hard, so when she relaxed, her knees naturally fell apart. She kept up the impetus, bending her knees as her legs separated more, lifting them slowly up allowing her hands to slide between her thighs, covering her sex and at the same time tightening her arms either side of her breasts, bringing them into focus and pushing them together to deepen her cleavage. Only then did she smile.

"Something like this?"

"Exactly like that." His voice, low and purring, held the throb of passion promised but not delivered. "Now on your stomach. Lie over some of the cushions."

She slid a couple under her and he growled. "Cloth of gold. Appropriate. Did you know at one point in history only kings were allowed to wear cloth of gold?"

"Were you ever a king?"

He gave a crack of laughter. "Not hardly. But you make me feel like one now."

Actually the pillow under her stomach, the gleaming cloth of gold one, felt slightly scratchy. She'd have thought kings would prefer silk or velvet. Maybe appearance was more important to them than comfort.

She pushed another pillow under her breasts and let her legs fall open. She heard his indrawn breath. "Now that is any man's wet dream. More, darling. Another pose. Your choice."

She was beginning to enjoy this. Never particularly proud of her body, Sandro's admiration made her feel wanted and sexy, more than any lover before.

The Venus pose. One of her favorite paintings was the "Venus of Urbino", so she took that pose now. Ostensibly modest, all it did was emphasize her sexuality. One of the sexiest poses ever, especially with the small touches she planned to add.

So she shoved the pillows to one side and lay on the bed, her upper body propped up by the stack of pillows at the head of the bed. She crooked one elbow, lifting her arm next to her, and rested her other hand over her intimate curls.

Then she gazed down at Sandro, watching him closely as she bent one knee and tucked her right foot under her left thigh. He stood at the foot of the bed and he could see her slowly reveal herself to him, confronting him with a challenging stare.

He shook his head slightly. "Woman, you are irresistible like that. So simple a pose!" His hands went to the belt of his robe. "Wait." A slow smile crept over his face. "Titian, right?"

She nodded, slowly.

"Like I said before. Any man's wet dream." He slid the robe off his shoulders, heedless of where it fell, and climbed up to her level. Once his knees were on the bed, he kneeled up and looked down at her. "Open your legs for me, *carissima*. Wide." He growled the last word, a command, not a request. Megan obeyed, uncurling her legs and lifting her knees to give him what he wanted.

He took a deep breath through his nose, as if savoring her scent. Between his legs, his cock twitched, as though it too got her scent and wanted more. Slowly, he crawled up the bed over her, a predatory animal claiming its natural mate. He didn't touch her until the head of his straining phallus touched her stomach, before he took it in one hand and moved it down to nestle between her thighs. His responsive shudder quivered against her hot flesh. "God, you are so wet!"

"You did that. I've never liked a man to look at me before but you—you make me melt, Sandro."

"Literally," he purred and lowered his cock into her hot crease, keeping his weight off her by propping his upper body on his elbows. All this time he never took his gaze off her face, his eyes glowing with want and need. "Open to me, love. All of you, all of me."

He paused and she felt him at the forefront of her mind, poised as he was at the opening to her body. "I love you, Megan."

She reached up to cradle his cheek in her palm, his beard stubble lightly abrading it, providing a contrast to his silky cock head, wet with her arousal and with his own. "I love you too, Sandro. So—"

He cut her question off with a kiss and at the same time, slid into her.

Her back arched and he held her down, exploring her mouth, his body in hers. Then he merged their minds, entered her mind, invited her into his. She touched his tongue with her own in greeting and slid past to caress it, and enter his mouth.

Together as she hadn't been with anyone else in her life before. Love and tenderness filled her, completed her. Every cell of her body merged with his, except, as they neared totality, he withdrew and drove hard into her pussy.

She jerked, arching up to him, and he lifted off her so he could push harder. Because she was so deeply merged with him she felt a flash of lightning across his mind, as if anger had prevented their complete joining or maybe fear. Anger and fear were close allies, difficult to separate. But his deep, hard strokes made it difficult for her to keep anything in her mind except what Sandro was doing to her.

He found her sweet spot and drew her along the paths of ecstasy, paths that weren't strewn with roses but edged with fire and led up into the sky.

"You want roses?" he murmured after he lifted his mouth away from hers. He gave her a soft kiss. "You shall have roses, my love. Anything you want, it's yours."

The room filled with the scent of roses, and she saw, in her mind, lush armfuls of the blossoms, in shades of crimson and pink, spilling over. She even felt the velvety touch of petals on her body.

"How do you do that?"

He grinned. "Practice."

The touch disappeared and the flames returned when she arched back up and clenched her body to clasp him intimately deep inside. He gasped, laughing in delight and thrust.

The roses faded away and Megan saw stars.

* * * * *

"Open."

She smiled and opened her mouth like a fledgling chick.

Sandro popped a morsel of shrimp into it. The prawn salad lay decimated on the delicate ormolu table by the bed, together with a container of strawberries and raspberries and a cup of double cream. The champagne sat upended in the ice bucket, the last of its fizz sipped from a shared glass five minutes before.

He followed the shrimp with a kiss, sharing the taste, lingering to enjoy her flavor. Everything about her delighted him. With his mind firmly barred against the coming dawn, he would have this night against the coming struggle. Every minute of it.

"Need any more?"

She shook her head, her cheeks flushed slightly from their recent bout of loving. "Only you."

That low, sultry voice drove him crazy. Every time he heard her, felt her, smelled her, his body went into overdrive. They'd made love three times, each better than the last, each accompanied by her throaty moans and sighs. He wanted more and yet more.

"That works for me." He kissed her again. The flavor of their recent impromptu meal dissipated, all but the slight sparkle of the champagne. Or that might have been the bright sparks of their loving returning to intoxicate him yet again. He didn't know and cared less.

Her body rose to meet his, pressing invitingly against the erection that hadn't worked so hard for many years. Here and now was all that mattered, all that existed.

He curved his hands either side of Megan's waist, stroking up the sinuous curves to the slopes of her breasts. Cupping them in each hand, he balanced on his elbows and lifted his body over hers. They'd made love in several positions tonight but he adored the feel of her under him, her skin pressed close to his. The old-fashioned conservative in him reveled in the way she surrendered to him when he loved her. She was a dragon now, as strong as he was, did she but know it, and that curvaceous body covered a form that could turn to steel in an instant. She'd learn in time. Perhaps he'd live long enough to see it, or at least hear about it.

Now here she was, under his hands. He stroked up to her nipples, plucking the tips between his forefingers and thumbs, smiling when she moaned deep in her throat. "Like that?" His kisses barely touched her cheeks, her lips, her throat, then he slid lower to take a nipple in his mouth and suck hard before delivering an unexpected nip.

"Ah!" The choked-off cry drove him to suck harder and caress the oversensitive tip with his tongue, stroking and curling around her to stimulate every part of it. It hardened and he let it slip from his mouth with some reluctance. He wanted to taste other parts of her even more. It glistened from his mouth, dark and hard.

He lingered at the secret spot just inside her hipbone until she twisted in his arms, trying to get away, then he released her from the exquisite torture with a gentle kiss before moving toward the place that invited and enticed him.

She was wet, as she'd been all night, slick with her juices and his, their combined scents driving him mad with wanting her, just to sink into her and forget everything else in the glory of this woman.

He touched his tongue to the tip of her clit in greeting, feeling the firm flesh under the soft, slick skin. One long lick from opening to clit and just beyond made her squirm then he lowered his hands to her hips, anchoring her in place while he took his pleasure of her.

Glorious wet woman. Every tiny fraction of a centimeter, all hers, all his. Leaving his mind lingering at the edge of hers so he could enjoy the sensations coursing through it, he set himself to drive her up, up, up—then no further. The first time he sucked her, holding her clit in place with his teeth, careful not to hurt her, lapping at the crest until she screamed her pleasure but just before her climax, he stopped, eased off and moved farther down. He wanted more.

Sandro, what are you doing?

Making you mine. But he didn't articulate his thought. It wouldn't be fair. He concentrated on lapping at her, savoring her luscious taste before he slipped his tongue inside her—and partially shifted.

He could control any part of his body and make that part the dragon's without transforming anything else, a skill it took some time to learn. This time he lengthened his tongue, made it the dragon's, that flickering, *long* tongue with the forked ends. This tongue was athletic, the muscles strong and he could reach deep inside her.

Megan's moans, increasing in volume, told him she enjoyed what he was doing. He tortured her with loving licks, swirling caresses, and then tickled the spot just inside her, the one that drove her mad, with both parts of his tongue-tip. She writhed, trying to get away, but he wouldn't let her. He deepened the mind contact and felt her whole being pulse with her rising climax until it exploded in fluttering, showering sparks of light.

She'd told him she'd seen stars the first time tonight. He'd thought it an amusing conceit but now he saw it was only the truth. Stars indeed. Shooting stars, even.

With a roar worthy of any dragon she shoved at him, finding his shoulders. She pushed him off and away. He fell on his back and before he could sit upright, she was on him, pushing the place his tongue had so recently caressed onto his straining cock.

Now it was his turn to moan, until she stopped. He opened his eyes to see her staring at him. He flicked his tongue into his mouth and changed it back. "Whoops."

"Is that what—how—"

He nodded, watching her reaction carefully. Her mind had stilled. Pleasure still moved in her but no more peaks.

A grin transformed her features, turning shock into delight. "Wow, there are more advantages to being a dragon than I thought."

She resumed rocking on him and while relief coursed through his anxious mind, he became increasingly aware of her actions. She lifted and plunged, sensitizing his cock even more, hurling him into new sensations.

He'd never enjoyed a woman taking control but he loved it now. Leaning back against the pillows, he let her do whatever she wanted, knowing he could never invent anything better. "*Carissima*, you are the—most—sexiest—

passionate—" He lost his thread and ended on a deep moan of fulfillment. He could do no more than take what she gave him. And he loved every thrilling moment.

"Turnabout is fair play, my Cockney grandmother used to say," she purred. Her movements became rhythmic and he raised his knees slightly, pushing his heels against the bed to meet her plunges.

When he held up his hands, she took them, using them to work him harder, deeper inside her. He felt the extra length grow inside her. Never before had that happened on its own, he'd always controlled it but that part of his body rose eagerly to meet his love, as the rest of him did.

"I think I love your Cockney grandmother," he managed. "But I love you more."

"I love you most." Her smile held only joy. He gave himself up to the *now*, to the ecstatic moment of eternity that existed when they came together, exploding in unison. The wonderful pulses of light thrummed between them, neither his nor hers but theirs.

She fell on to him and he welcomed her, holding her tightly as if he'd never let her go.

That was when his phone rang. This time his groan held nothing of pleasure, everything of regret.

He rolled over, depositing her on the sheets with a tender kiss before rolling the other way, off the bed toward his discarded robe.

"Yes?" He didn't care how brusque he sounded. Too soon, tomorrow was here.

Chapter Twelve

Chase's clipped tones came down the line, succinct and chilling. "Someone took Carilla and Jack."

"Christ!" He sat up and dragged his robe over his shoulders. "How? When?"

"Last night, just before Johann went on duty at the apartment."

"Fuck, she's an experienced agent! How could she let them?"

"Hey, man, calm down. It happens, you know?"

Sandro took a deep breath. "Okay. Now tell me." He felt hands on his shoulders, gentle, soothing hands. He opened to her, so he wouldn't have to tell her, so she could listen in to the conversation.

"Johann arrived, just checking in, making sure everything was okay. All quiet. It stayed that way through the night and he decided to check again," a pause, "an hour and a quarter ago. He got a hunch, he said, a gut feeling so he rounded up some agents and took them with him. He got in touch with me, since you said your first priority is getting Megan up to speed. I went immediately."

"He's a *vampire*, for Christ's sake! What did he do, invite them in?"

"Cool it, Sandro. No, he fought, of course he did. But the two men with him didn't last long and then they got to him. The place is a mess, Sandro, but Johann didn't let them take Carilla and Jack easily."

"What do you mean, they didn't last long? Didn't Johann have Talents with him?"

"No. We're short-handed. They were regular agents."

Sandro swore, long and loud. "So we know what kind of priority Ann Reynolds gives on keeping our people safe." How could he have forgotten what an operator, what a player Ann was? Sure, her friendship was steadfast but her leadership had all kinds of nuances to it.

"Not fair, Sandro. With this coming out shit, we're more than short-handed. We're hanging on by a thread."

Her touch, gentle on his shoulder, helped him immeasurably. Instead of smashing something, he held on. "Yeah." And Chase had a point. Protecting Talented journos, politicians, even the media, their remit had increased tenfold overnight. And now they were out in the open, their enemies knew where to find them. "So how is Johann?"

"He'll recover but he's out of action for a few days."

"Any leads?"

"Not yet but there has to be something. I have people going over the safe house. And I'm trying to track them." With a Sorcerer of Chase's caliber on the case, that was the best prospect they had.

"Stay on it."

"I'm at STORM, I'll call you if that changes."

"Give us twenty minutes."

Chase hung up. It took a few seconds for Sandro to realize he still held the phone in a death grip. When he released it, the pieces fell to the floor. "Shit."

"We need to shower and change, don't we?" Although her voice was filled with anxiety, it still brought him comfort. She was here.

"Yes. But forgive me, *carissima*, not together."

"No."

He turned and took her hand in his. "I think you should stay here," he said without much hope.

"You're joking, aren't you? In any case, wouldn't I be safer with you?"

He'd considered that. "I'll be busy, love. You're always first with me but I need to be sharp."

"I won't get in your way. You've taught me enough to take care of myself and I still have the self-defense classes." She smiled hopefully and he recognized it as an attempt to cheer him. And she was right, she was probably safer wherever he was.

Her bravery struck him to the heart. He got to his feet and drew her close for a gentle kiss. "I love you, Megan."

"I know."

* * * * *

Half an hour later, in the Spyder on the way to STORM, his cell rang. He had more than one, which was just as well. If he had to leave them behind when he shape-shifted, he smashed them to destroy ID.

He put it on speakers. "Hi."

"Come to the airport," Chase said, his voice stripped of emotion.

"What's up?"

"Just come. LaGuardia. I'll have someone meet you at the gate. He'll ask you if your name is Anemone."

Basic security. Glad Chase had remembered that much, Sandro spun in a squeal of tires to a chorus of car horns and u-turned into the traffic heading for Queens.

He kicked the car up as fast as he dared. Any cops he picked up were welcome to come with him. Right now he didn't care. The first jam they hit, he'd shape-shift and finish the journey by air.

There proved to be no need and he got to LaGuardia in twenty minutes flat. Rather disappointingly, no cops followed. A siren parade might have made his journey faster. Yeah, he was in a Spyder but however battered cop cars might look, the engines were often tuned to within an inch of their lives.

An ordinary-looking African-American stood by the main entrance, looking bored, holding a sign that actually said "Amenome". Chase's joke, or maybe a genuine mistake. He didn't care.

"Sandro Gianetti and Megan Armstrong." Why use a geeky password when his name meant more? The bored look disappeared, replaced by keen interest.

"You were on the TV, weren't you? You're a—"

"We like to call ourselves Talents. Yeah. Lead on. Care to tell me what this is about?"

"I have orders not to," the man said, albeit reluctantly. "Mr. Maynord wants to update you himself."

They passed through the airport, past the queues of passengers by the check-in desks, and through a side door. Bare, shabby hallways led to a door labeled "Freight" in old-fashioned lettering. Past that, a yard holding row after row of containers, some sealed, a few gaping open to the suddenly chilly spring day.

So far Sandro had kept his mind off what waited for him. Now he realized only one thing would stop Chase briefing him over the phone. And he didn't want it to be that. Anything but that.

Chase met them at the end of a row, his tie slightly askew, his jacket obviously not meant to be one to match jeans. His state of relative dishevelment alerted Sandro to Chase's agitated state just before he touched Chase's mind in greeting. His startled gaze went from Sandro to Megan and back. "I didn't think you'd bring Megan."

"She's safer here."

Chase shook his head. "Not necessarily."

"So tell me."

Chase swallowed. "We found Carilla."

All hope left him then. They followed Chase in silence. He reached for Megan's hand, not caring how it looked. He'd need this. He partially shape-shifted to enhance his sense of smell. His hearing was better in his human form, so he left it as it was. That was how he smelled the blood.

He halted. "Stay here, Megan."

"No."

"Please, love. For me." He couldn't bear her distress as well as his own.

She regarded him silently for a second or two and then nodded. "But come back to me, tell me. Promise."

"I swear."

When he reached the container and stepped around the doors that shielded the view, he was glad he'd asked her to stay behind.

Slumped at the entrance, blood covering her half-naked body, lay the lacerated form of Carilla. Half jaguar, her claws extended, her lower legs still in jaguar form, no doubt to take advantage of the powerful muscles. She wouldn't give him backchat any more.

Or breathe.

They'd torn her apart. One arm was almost severed and deep cuts and bruises covered her body. What had killed her was the bullet to her brain.

"She must have been in the process of shape-shifting when the gunman hit," Chase said from behind him. "There's only one way she'd fight to the death."

There was only one way he'd fight with quite that intensity, blindly, without calling for help. For the person he loved. "Jack."

"He's gone too but he's not here."

"They took him." He had to tear his attention away from Carilla. Staring wouldn't bring her back. "Any idea who?"

"The M.O. is the same way they took Ricardo, efficient and fast."

"We're losing this one, Chase. Our techs haven't found anything, our sensitives have come up blank and the lab is still there. Suggestions? Frankly I'll take anything at this point."

Chase grimaced. "I'd say find the bastards and torch them but it's finding them that's the problem. The first thing I did was scan the place. But the regular cops got here first."

"And they saw her?" Of course they did.

"Freaked them out." Chase shrugged. "They better get used to it. I spoiled all the pictures they insisted on taking. We don't need all that, chances are they'd end up on the nightly news as well."

"Good thinking."

"Still, their presence tainted the air and I couldn't get anything much. Violence, of course. A bunch of men, maybe ten. They were taking no chances. They had syringes, knives, guns. A sense of triumph." He almost spat the word. "Nothing definite, no faces, no ID. Fuck!" He turned away.

Sandro gave him a much-needed minute before he spoke again. "Didn't Carilla take any out?"

"Two. Around here."

Chase led Sandro to the other side of the container. Behind the open door lay two men, neither of whom Sandro recognized. Deep lacerations to their throats showing where Carilla had achieved a clean kill. "Nothing from either of them. By the time we found them all traces of life had gone, nothing we can use."

Staring at them, Sandro began to reconstruct what happened. "They captured Carilla and Jack. Then they brought them here, and Carilla came around, maybe while they were trying to load her into something for transport. She fought, they fought back. Sound reasonable to you?"

"Yeah."

"It's me they want."

Sandro spun around, trying vainly to block the sight of the two dead men from Megan. She shrugged. "Don't bother. Whatever they got, they had it coming."

"*Cara*, I don't want you to—"

She gave him a wry grin. "It seems to go with the territory. At least, with *your* territory. First I find I'm not afraid of heights after all, then that I can fight back, then that the sight of dead bodies doesn't paralyze me. Unless—" She glanced back but the open door blocked her view. When she turned back the expression on her face made Sandro glad she couldn't see. "Unless you know that person. Sandro, is Jack—"

"No, he's not." There was no way he could keep the truth from her, so he told her straight. "They killed Carilla and took Jack."

He reached out for her, and thankfully, she let him steady her, his hand under her elbow. He needed the touch as much as she did. Her next words jolted him right back into shock mode.

"If they want me, they can have me. I'm the only way you're going to get to them fast enough, before they kill Ricardo and Jack. Wave me at them, Sandro."

His first reaction was to haul her close, never let her go but that was reaction. He wanted to keep her safe but he couldn't, not forever. Instead, he had to teach her how to be strong on her own, for when he wasn't there anymore.

Staring at her in sheer horror, he slowly became aware that Chase was speaking. "You could be right, Megan, but let's step back and think. Try to find another way. Our techs are quartering New York, working through it, and we might get lucky."

"Not in time, they won't. Look, I know it's stupid to go for it on my own but I'm desperate enough to try it."

She meant it. How could he bring himself to help her? There was only one way. "If they take you, they take me too.

They might want to kill you, and I can at least stop that. As far as they know, you're a leak and that's all. They must have realized you're with us. You're weak and you're a security risk. If you visit Ricardo again, you might be able to pinpoint where he is, so they'll fight hard for you."

"But they only k-killed Carilla when she fought back."

She was right. They'd taken her with Jack, not killed her first. "Why am I even thinking of this?"

Her face brightened slightly. "You are?" She seized his hands. "Please, Sandro. You've taught me so much. I can hold on until you come. Plant a bug in me, a real, live electronic device."

"They have jamming devices." He tried to stem the hope rising in him. It might work. Tempting them as they had before. Bluffing them that they knew more than they actually did.

"You'll be able to track me until they jam me. Anyway, haven't your techs got more than one bug? One designed to bypass jamming, different frequencies or something like that? *Please*, Sandro. Please. I can't wait and know they're doing to Jack what they did to Ricardo. I can't bear to go through that again."

Both men stared at her, hope dawning on them both. He felt Chase in the deep contact level he reserved for the team. *She could do it.*

Fuck.

The worst thing was, she was right. She was their only chance of finding the lab early enough to save his brother and her best friend. They would eventually find it but not soon enough.

Before today, he'd been so sure they could find Ricardo but seeing Carilla laid out like that, doubt assailed him with tooth and claw. The world was changing so radically he didn't know if he wanted to see any more changes. He'd weathered the coming of mechanized transport, not being alone in the skies with the birds anymore, radical changes in social structure. He wasn't sure he could cope with the populace at general knowing his kind existed.

If it weren't for Megan, he'd be content to die, to leave and discover what came next.

She made the difference. So if this would be his last act, he'd make sure, absolutely-fucking-sure she was cared for and safe. And with these bastards after her, she wouldn't be safe. So yes, a chance to make sure she was fine.

He dropped her hands. "Okay, we go with it." He turned away, sick of it all, eager to have everything done with.

So he could die in peace. Or at least with no regrets.

The rapid way Sandro swung into action made Megan dizzy. Once he'd made his mind up he didn't hesitate, didn't pause in his decisions. Maybe that was what made him a leader. Chase, and later Johann, listened, nodded and agreed with the plan he outlined to them in a boardroom at STORM HQ on East Thirty-fourth Street.

If she hadn't felt so sick, Megan would be enjoying this. After shopping at Tiffany's (where they bought nothing but browsed) and Saks, where they spent far too much, he took her to lunch at a fashionable Italian bistro.

"What did we just buy?"

He gave her a quizzical smile. "You can't remember?"

She shook her head. "Not a thing." She glanced out the window and back at Sandro, who smiled and put his hand over hers.

"Don't look. They aren't there. We gave them plenty of time to find us, now all we have to do is wait. Don't forget to go down fast. I'll fight a little but the faster we go down, the less we're hurt." His smile turned grim. "They better pray they don't hurt you."

"Hey." She squeezed his hand. "I'm not made of glass."

"But you're scared."

She couldn't hide that from him with his mind locked in hers. She'd pushed her fear away a couple of times. Not before he'd noticed. "So why aren't you scared?"

"Because I'm angry. Angry they've taken your friend and my brother, angry they think they have the right to do what they're doing to any human being, whether he's a shapeshifter, vampire, Sorcerer or mortal. Who made them God?"

A wry smile twitched one corner of her mouth but she suppressed it. She loved him so, his sense of honor and justice made her proud, as well as angry with him. Suddenly she'd become a member of a minority, one that many members of society wanted to eliminate or use as if they were less than human. She didn't feel less human after her conversion. Everything that made her Megan was still there, still strongly in place. "Nobody. And we're about to stop them."

"We are."

She rubbed her arm where one of the subcutaneous implants rested. They'd put another in the top of her leg and yet another just under the skin on her skull. Tiny appliances, with others in one of her earrings and another in her watch for their enemies to take away from her. Just where they would expect to find them. Sandro was similarly festooned but these were backup. And in case they were discovered, they weren't deep under the skin. All except the one in Sandro's stomach.

He leaned forward, took her hand and raised it to his lips in an old-fashioned courtly gesture. "I wish you'd go with Chase instead of staying here."

"No, Sandro. They want me. They won't come after you, they'll come for me. Though I still don't know why."

"You have—had—an extra special ability to get through the sonic jamming equipment that kept Talents from locating others after they were taken prisoner. Nobody else could reach Ricardo. You could. They'll want to know how. They won't just want to plug the leak, they want to find out in case it's useful to them." He kissed her hand once more before releasing it. "I could still keep you out of it."

In the split second before he put the thought firmly away, she saw he meant to do his best to let them take him alone. Any way he could.

That wasn't going to happen. If she had to wait for Sandro, Ricardo and Jack, unable to do anything at all, she'd go insane. Chase waited outside in an unmarked vehicle and other agents were stationed in places around the bistro, all with orders not to interfere but to follow. Chase locked into both their minds and now all they could do was wait.

The IRDC had attacked them before as they left a restaurant but they might decide to take a different approach this time.

Sandro leaned back to allow the waiter to put their food in front of them. The waiter arrived with the Chianti Sandro had ordered and he moved the white wineglasses away.

Sandro took a sip of wine and paused before glancing up at the waiter, giving him permission to pour. At the same time he sent her a message, deep down in the part of her only they shared. *Eat before you drink,* cara. *They've drugged the wine.*

Do you know what it is?

No. He paused. *It isn't poison. I could detect poison, so I guess it's something to make us drowsy or sick. Something to get us out of here.*

Her appetite for the delectable pasta dish steaming in front of her shrank to nothing. She might as well get it over with. She picked up her glass.

Eat something. You hardly touched your starter.

That was true. She'd taken one look at the mussels, shells cracked open, wafting their fragrance up to her nostrils, and pushed the plate aside after nibbling at some of the watercress and tomato salad it came with.

For him, she picked up her fork and managed two mouthfuls of the meal. The impoverished student who still lingered in the recesses of her mind, the budget-conscious librarian who still lived there, protested at such a waste of good food but she couldn't. Soon this nightmare would be over and then she'd eat as much as Sandro wanted her to. So she drank and let Sandro refill her glass, his mouth set in a hard line.

That should be enough. The minute you feel anything, stop.

It's a shame. This wine is good.

Sandro was making a good meal. He'd probably been in similar situations before. "Sandro, will you carry on doing this when—"

He took a deep breath. "No."

"What will you do?"

She could read nothing in his mind and that made her pause. He must be hiding something. Had he plans? Or maybe he still wanted her to go on with Ricardo?

Do you feel anything yet?

No. She took another sip. *Yes.*

Dizziness, a slight wooziness but nothing she might not expect if she drank on an empty stomach. Except this was subtly different. No doubt their would-be kidnappers wanted them to drink the whole bottle so they'd be firmly under.

Don't drink any more.

"Duh," she muttered and heard his chuckle.

Half an hour later they left the restaurant, Sandro's arm slung loosely across her shoulders, their gait laxer than when they'd entered. Sandro hailed a passing taxicab. "Here we go, darling."

So she was ready when he got into the cab first, leaving her to follow. That would have alerted her. Sandro had the remnants of his upbringing and an old-fashioned regard for good manners, so he would normally have let her in first. When she tried to follow, he held the door against her and sent her a mental message of apology. She was ready for that too.

Then she released the door handle but as the cab began to move again, wrenched it open and got in, catching Sandro unawares.

His eyes flared with anger. She shook her head. "There is no way you're doing this on your own."

He closed his eyes and lifted his hand to his forehead. "I have to."

"No. I'm not waiting at home for you. I'm not some Victorian lady, delicate and shy. I'm trained and I'm ready." Already the drug had taken hold. She felt dreamy, strangely detached from reality. But she held on. Until she heard the click that meant the doors had locked and she couldn't get away now if she wanted to.

* * * * *

"Darling, are you awake?"

The low voice woke her. She blinked a couple of times. Her mascara had glued her eyelashes together but once she realized that was all it was, she could force them open.

She felt surprisingly unaffected but that was until she moved. Then the strange, dimly lit world she found herself in seemed to jolt an inch sideways and she reeled.

Only to find herself hauled into Sandro's arms. She nestled in, glad to find herself with him, at least. "What's that noise?"

"An engine. We're in a crate, loaded onto the back of a pickup."

"On our way then." She remembered everything, the restaurant, the taxicab and his anger when he realized he wasn't getting rid of her that easily.

"I didn't want you here."

"I know." She snuggled closer. "It's a two-person gig, Sandro. Always was."

He bent and whispered directly in her ear. "Megan, speak to me, mind to mind."

"Why?" They were close enough to murmur quietly. She trusted Sandro well enough to know he would have scanned for bugs in whatever container they were in and it was a small one.

"Just do it."

Like this?

Yes, just like that. Now stay in my mind. Can you do that?

Sure, just like you taught me. What's wrong, Sandro?

Cephalox.

"Huh?"

They've injected me with the stuff. I'm just a man, sweetheart, I can't tap into the other part of me. You'll have to keep the contact with me, not the other way about because my telepathy is passive now. The fact that you can keep the contact means they haven't injected you with it.

Her fogged mind fought to make sense of what he was telling her. "They used it on you? Why didn't they—" He cut her off with a hand across her mouth before she could finish— *use it on me?*

Using her link, he replied. *Because they don't know you're a shape-shifter. As far as they're aware, you're my lover, a librarian with an ability they want to tap. That means you're psychic although without the power of a shape-shifter or a trained agent. We faked some scan and test results and let them steal them earlier today. They said you had nothing special, except a strange reaction to high-pitched sounds.*

She nodded to show she understood.

He pressed a soft kiss to her forehead. *How wrong they were! Even before your conversion, you were special.*

They sat together, huddled in the packing case, and she'd never been so happy. "I love you, Sandro."

"You're my life, Megan. My heart." Their kiss was almost spiritual but its intensity was no less than any of the others they'd shared.

"Sandro?"

"Yes, *mia adorata*?"

"How long?"

He sighed. *Not long.*

"Why haven't they tied us up, secured us in some way?"

"They did." He lifted his hand and showed her some plastic ties, hanging loosely between his fingers. *I have other skills, not just the ones from my Talent.*

"I thought it was impossible to get out of these things?"

When you have a razor blade in your coat lining, it's not.

She chuckled. "And when we get out the other end?"

"I brought more ties in the same place as the razor blade. They won't be as tight. Black, white and transparent ones."

"What if they'd been red?"

He chuckled again, and smoothed her hair. "Then we would have had to think of something else."

She shouldn't have felt this content but this respite, a chance to hold him and rest before the ordeal ahead, gave her the peace she hadn't felt in the bistro. They had at last started on their way to finding Ricardo, and Jack too, with any luck. And they deserved luck now. It had eluded them so far — it was time they had it on their side.

"God, I wish you hadn't come!"

The anguish he felt was all in his voice but when she lifted her chin she saw the pain in his eyes, even in this gloom. "Sandro, why?"

He gazed at her, watching her silently for at least five minutes, time she didn't try to break. Decision firmed his expression and flattened his mouth. "Because I'm a swelled-headed fool. I wanted you to remember me as a hero. Gone to rescue the people you care for, a knight on a charger." He huffed a short, mirthless laugh. "I've always been a romantic. But darling, it's tomorrow. I promised to tell you why we can't make future plans."

"I hadn't forgotten." She lifted her hand and cradled his chin, her palm prickling with the stubble beginning to grow through after his morning shave. "So tell me what this secret is, why you won't commit, what you're not telling me."

He moved so she palmed his cheek, rubbing himself against her caress, more a cat than a dragon. "I left a letter for you. When you get back, you'll find it."

"What about you?"

"I'm not going back. This is my last mission. I'm dying, Megan."

Content, happiness, all went in the flick of an eyelid, in the voicing of one word. "No, no! You're lying!"

"No, sweet, I'm not." He lowered his voice even more. "I should tell you the other way but I can't. I want you to hear the words, *really* hear them. And believe me. Please, love, believe me. When I knew I was coming here, doing this, I knew I could finally tell you how I feel about you, because it wouldn't matter. I wanted to go out in a blaze of glory." He laughed again, this time a self-deprecating huff of hot air. "What an idiot. Just like a dragon."

She tightened her hold on him, as if she could hold him back from his fate but she didn't take her gaze off his, didn't take her mind from his. "Tell me. What is it?"

"I'm dying, my love. Simple old age."

She began to shake her head but he caught her chin and made her look at him. "Do you remember, I told you how old I am?"

"Four hundred and fifty two."

His smile was tender. "You did remember. When I first met you, I thought we might find some happiness together. A human lifetime. Fifty years. It would be enough to have that.

Then I realized what was happening to me. I'm dyeing my hair, love, underneath the gray has started to come through. It's not vanity, I didn't want people to notice."

"How about Ann Reynolds?"

"She noticed."

She grimaced. "She would."

"Yeah." He gave a short laugh. "She knows this is my last mission."

"Do you think I'll hate you because you get older?"

"Shape-shifters age rapidly and only at the end. I have between six months and two years left and I'm hoping for the shorter timespan. The last months aren't good ones."

She moved closer still, felt the hard wall of his chest under her hands. His arms tightened around her. "I originally planned to go away, just disappear but this might be better." He put his hands on either side of her head and pulled her away so she was looking up at his face. Intensity and sincerity burned into her soul. "Megan, I'm going to take risks out there. If it means you and Ricardo and the others get away clean, I'll put myself in the line of fire. Please, please let me."

The way he held her meant she couldn't hide her tears from him, so she let them fall unchecked. "Don't ask me to do that."

"I'm asking. Let me do this, let my death mean something. I can't shape-shift, so I'm just a man but you can. We're going to get them out, get the coordinates, and I will see my brother free. I don't ask any more. I've entered an irreversible process, Megan. Nothing will save me now. Do you understand?"

Numbly, she nodded.

"Old age, darling. It gets us all in the end. There is no cure, no remedy. And I'd far rather go out in a blaze of glory than slowly rotting my time away."

They stared at each other, he dry-eyed, she weeping openly. "Sandro, I love you so much."

He kissed her tears away but she produced more. "I love you too, Megan. More than anyone else. I'll never regret meeting you, just that I met you too late for us. Remember me as someone you loved, remember that you have my blessing if you find someone else who can make you happy. Remember what we had with thanks, not regret. Can you do that?"

"Maybe, in time." She could only croak the words, her throat clogged with emotion, her heart full. He'd given her life, only to lose it himself. "I can't bear it."

"Yes you can. I wouldn't have told you if I didn't think you were brave enough to bear it. I didn't want you to see me throwing myself into danger and think I was always like that. Most of all I don't want you to try to save me."

The air lay heavy between them as she slowly made sense of recent happenings. He couldn't commit. Not wouldn't but couldn't. "When did you first realize you loved me?"

His intimate smile showed her his thoughts went in the same direction as hers. "The day after our first night together. I'd followed you for weeks, investigated you and allowed myself a few mild fantasies but the reality was so completely mind-blowing I knew I was in deep."

She wet her lips. "Yes."

His gaze followed her motion and he bent forward, touching his lips to hers, sharing her taste. Then he drew back. His hands slid down, caressing her cheeks with soft touches before he curved them around her shoulders, enclosing her in vital male warmth. How would she ever live without him, without this?

Five hundred years of life suddenly seemed five hundred years too long.

She kneeled up and kissed him, softly, sweetly, trying to show him all she felt but without passion. Their love went far deeper than what they did in bed, although that was an important part of what they had. "I love you, Sandro. Always. And though it breaks my heart, I'll do what you want. I won't get in the way, I promise. If you promise me one thing."

"What's that, *carissima?*"

The word caressed her as softly as his arms. "That you won't take unnecessary risks. You'll only do it if you have no other choice, if it means my life or Ricardo's."

He regarded her gravely for a few minutes before jerking his head once in a brief nod. "Yes. I promise."

"Thank you."

He kissed her again and this time the edge of passion returned. They felt the heat course between them and she slid her hands around his t-shirt and underneath to touch his skin. He growled low in his throat but he didn't stop her. Neither did he initiate his own caress on bare skin but let her touch him, curving his body to allow her more access.

"And you say you've been losing muscle tone?" She lifted the shirt so she could touch her lips to his bare skin.

"Hey." He lifted her away. "We can't do anything here."

"I want to touch you. To remember everything about you." Time, which she'd thought stretched in front of them for a long time to come, telescoped right down into the next hour, the next five minutes, depending on when they landed. Their guards were still in the other compartment, she found when she extended her senses. Three of them seemed relaxed, maybe sleeping. How could they be so blasé? They had a dragon in a crate. Two, did they but know it.

"Darling, we said our goodbyes that way last night."

"There are things we've never done."

One corner of his mouth crooked. "We hardly had time and I was always too keen to get inside you. We've loved. That's what's important."

She saw sense. Although she still wanted him, this wasn't the time or the place, even though it might be their last. She had to accept that love was all they had left now. Touching, holding and words of love.

"We're slowing down."

"Time to tie your hands together again." He made her turn around so he could fasten one of the ties around her wrists. It held her but not too tightly. She could get out by shape-shifting. He managed to maneuver himself around and together they did his hands too. They turned back to each other and gazed into each other's eyes, their communication too deep for anyone except themselves to read.

Tension seized her, freezing her stomach before sending it lurching into uncomfortable stress. This was the beginning of the end. He might never hold her again as he was holding her now, never touch her with the gentle care he used, or the rough touch of passion.

The game was on.

Chapter Thirteen

A strange excitement mingled with Megan's fear. After all, she was a powerful ancient beast, or part of her was. It existed with her at all times, was part of her nature now, in a way she found difficult to explain. Sometimes, when she had an instinctive reaction, she found her dragon there as well, ready to respond in a way she, the human Megan, would not.

Now the dragon reared its head, growling, aware they were close and its presence might be required.

The vehicle carrying them took a sharp turn to the left and then another to the right.

She recognized that turn, awkward and tricky. She should recognize it, she took it every day. Sandro had cursed when the Spyder nearly missed it.

She'd been almost sure they'd take her to the hospital, the one the sleep clinic had sent her to that very first day. Instead, she was right back where all this had started. Back at her place of work.

Instead of driving into the small car lot behind the library, the pickup truck carried on to the heart of the campus and into a different spot.

She felt the whining she'd only ever heard in her visions of Ricardo. An inhibitor, meant to destroy telepathy but perhaps her telepathy operated differently because she still felt Sandro resting in her mind. The sound grated against her senses, intensely irritating but not incapacitating.

Where are we?

His voice rumbling into her mind gave her a visceral shiver. Sandro would always be able to do that with her, waken her arousal just by talking to her. She let him see it, feel it. *We're at the university. The sleep clinic.*

Silence while he absorbed the information, then a single word. *Shit.* A pause, and she felt him register the information and scan his memories. *We concentrated our research on the hospital, not the clinic. We scanned the clinic and investigated the staff. Obviously not thoroughly enough.*

It could be another red herring.

We'll soon find out. Baby, I know you're the muscle but please let me take the lead. I'm the experienced one, I've been here before, taken a lab down.

Sure. But remember your promise.

This was his, all his. He'd found her, saved her from death twice, taught her lovingly and tenderly how to accept her new nature, embrace it, even. He'd probably prevented other Talents from suffering the same fate as his brother. She couldn't imagine how he could have functioned, much less provided strong leadership, but he had. Pride for him, for the man she loved filled her to the exclusion of all else. Except love, which was with her always and always would remain. She pushed back the desperation she felt when she recalled his confession, her sheer panic when she thought he would leave her.

The crate jolted again and his body nudged hers, hard and resistant. She melted against him, even in this situation. Ridiculous but all at once his mind, seated within hers, surrounded her with love, a mental embrace.

She would miss that. She'd miss everything about him.

Megan cautiously stretched out her senses.

Be careful. We don't think they have sensors although they do have sensitives working for them. Some Talents too.

Bastards.

Copy that.

His dry tone almost roused an instinctive laugh but she choked it back.

If you feel any conscious presences meeting yours, don't trust them and withdraw.

Okay.

She felt none, and then a gentle intrusion made her realize what Sandro meant. The newcomer, a touch she'd never felt before, had a faint Talent compared to her own. *Hello. Who are you?*

While faint, the touch felt healthy, so it was unlikely to be any of the prisoners in this hellhole. She remained blank, tried to make her mind akin to a rabbit caught in the headlights, and in the background, checked her mental shields were holding firm. Sandro was there, behind the first set of shields, and the others were strong. Anyone trying to read her mind would only see what she wanted them to see. A scared librarian, someone with no Talent who happened to be the lover of a powerful dragon, currently incapacitated by a shot of Cephalox.

They were lifted, dropped and then the movement became smooth, so they must be on a trolley of some kind. After a sharp turn, the crate was lifted and dumped on a hard floor, the reverberations jarring her bones. Then a muffled order and a door closed.

After that, she heard the rattle of buckles as straps were removed, and the unmistakable click of two padlocks. Then someone opened the lid and light flooded in on them.

Still half lying over Sandro, she stared up into two pairs of curious eyes.

Dr. Jones, the man she'd last seen at the hospital. And Dr. Bennett, the man who ran the sleep lab.

"What are we doing here?" she managed, blinking against the strong light.

"The time for innocence is over," Dr. Bennett said flatly. "I knew you were sensitive and when I saw Gianetti, I knew he knew too. Get out."

She stood up, using the side of the crate to brace her hands, still lashed behind her back, against the wincing pain in her cramped legs, letting her captors see her grimace. They ought to know they'd caused her some discomfort.

Dr. Bennett produced a scalpel and she kept her eyes blank, knowing he'd note any sign of fear in her. But he walked around the crate, taking his time, and sliced through the binding at her wrists.

Dr. Jones watched. Although she didn't meet his gaze, she felt his eyes on her, avidly waiting for a response. Working in a place like this must involve a degree of sadism and both doctors demonstrated this in abundance. Bastards.

Sandro got to his feet and stood silently beside her. When Bennett sliced through his bonds, he winced and she knew Bennett had cut him. She wanted to tear him apart. Perhaps that was the idea, to unsettle her enough to reveal any Talent she might have. She had some passive telepathy as far as they knew but it could be developed. Would they kill her if she were of no immediate use to them?

Undoubtedly. So she allowed a small amount of mental fear to leak through and saw the slight change in Jones' expression. He was a sensitive then, able to pick up mental images.

But not the ones between her and Sandro, carefully locked down in the private area they shared in each other's minds.

We improvise and wait for Chase's word.

How will we know?

The sensors. Or he'll try to break a mental path through, though I suspect that's not possible. They've sealed this facility or we'd have found it months ago.

How can they do that?

He managed a mental shrug, an image of his shoulders and it came so naturally into her mind she nearly laughed. *Various methods. Silver can be an inhibitor and many Talents are* allergic to it, so they sometimes use a paint with silver suspended in it.

She'd like to see silver paint. *Why haven't they scanned us for electronic bugs?*

They have. They took our watches and your earrings, where the obvious ones were. The rest are subtler, state-of-the-art, less easy to detect. Arrogance probably had a part in it.

"Has this place always had this facility?" she asked. She genuinely wanted to know. The sleep clinic here had an international reputation for detecting and curing sleep disorders. Had that led to this abomination?

Dr. Jones smirked. "There's a synergy between sleep and telepathy and one led to another when a few patients who showed no telepathic abilities awake did when they slept. Our new sponsor—" He stopped and his gaze shifted away from her. He'd said too much.

"Mr. Cornwell?" The mysterious benefactor who endowed several medical facilities across the country. Sandro's inner roar of triumph reached her. This was important. A link, a someone, a lead to maybe a network of laboratories and research facilities.

Jones turned away. "You showed very little telepathic capacity when we tested you but enough to make us interested. Then you told us the name of the man you dreamed about. That made all the difference. That was when we discovered your particular gift, to operate telepathically at the extremes of the scale."

"So you watched me?" Why should she suspect, when all that had been wrong with her was vivid nightmares? Still, she cursed herself when she recalled all the sessions she'd had, telling Dr. Bennett all her dreams, and the sleep sessions she'd taken part in.

Bennett walked around the crate. "Come out of there. You should have regained your footing by now."

"My ankles are tied together."

After a sound of exasperation, Bennett came around to her side and grasped her waist. He ignored Sandro's low growl of warning.

Megan swung her legs up so Bennett could slice through the plastic binding her ankles. Then he dragged her out of the crate, none too gently, and took a step back, one arm lashed around her waist, the other one, holding the scalpel, held against her neck. Now Megan had bruises forming on her thighs and several wood splinters embedded in her legs but at least she was out of that wooden box.

Megan felt the edge of the blade against her throat. "I'm keeping her like this, Gianetti. One bad move from you and this goes straight into her jugular."

"Bastard." But Sandro lifted his legs and allowed Jones to slice his bonds with another blade, not kicking up as he might have done if Bennett weren't holding a knife to her throat. "What do you want?"

"You." Bennett's voice sounded uncomfortably close, his breath heating Megan's ear. "We have the report your organization carried out on her. You missed something." His voice turned slimy, triumphant. "You have a spy in your office. Not that you'll live long enough to tell anyone." So that had worked. Good. "We want you because this gives us the chance to study brothers, siblings. We haven't had any of those before. Siblings are rare in your world, aren't they?"

"Depends." Sandro rubbed his wrists, his body relaxed. From her karate training, Megan knew this meant he was readying himself to attack if he saw an opening. If she could slip away. Shape-shifting took more effort on her part, and without Sandro's help, she wasn't sure she could do it slickly, and with the knife to her throat it had to be slick or not at all.

"What's with the talk?" Bennett said. "Time we tidied this up."

Pressure against her neck. She thought the cut would hurt but she only felt the pulse in her head increase, throb and then—nothing.

* * * * *

"Megan!"

A voice she thought she wouldn't hear again, after their grisly discovery at the airport that morning. "Jack!" She lifted her hand to her forehead and groaned. "God, my head!"

More carefully, she turned her head to one side and saw him.

Despite the bruises covering the side of his face, he managed to grin, although he winced and made a small sound of pain. But he was alive. "I can't say I'm glad to see you, Megan. Did they lure you here to rescue me?"

She opened her mouth to speak but closed it again. How could she tell him about Carilla? Not here, not now. They had to get out of this place. So instead, she said, "Do you know where we are?"

"In their lair."

They must have brought him in here unconscious. "In the sleep lab."

"At the university?" Jack gave a harsh laugh. "God, that's rich! We were on top of it all this time?"

"What happened, Jack?"

"A sneak attack. They got Carilla first and then me. They think I'm—"

She cut him off. *This place could be bugged. They have sensitives on staff. Be careful, Jack.*

He got the danger at once. *You're good at this telepathy stuff, aren't you?*

I had a good teacher.

Did they capture you with him?

She remembered Sandro's warning. They might have sensitives listening in. *Yeah.*

She closed her eyes and visualized, just as Sandro had taught her, and managed to burrow deep. She almost chuckled when Jack yelped.

Jesus, how did you do that?

I told you, I had a good teacher. This level should be safe. I'm bugged, they found the obvious ones but I have them injected under the skin too. So has Sandro. We let them take us. Listen, Jack, do they know you're jaguar?

I don't think so. Carilla and I agreed we'd keep it quiet until this was over. I'm beginning to understand why. Another pause. *Have you seen her in this place? They drugged us and I haven't been able to contact her.*

She so didn't want to tell him. The shock might render him incapable, she told herself, or he might go nuts. But the real reason was she didn't want to be the person who told him. So she was a coward. No, she wasn't. "Jack, we found Carilla at the airport."

"So where is she? Is she okay?"

"No." She swallowed. "She's dead, Jack. They killed her."

He turned away from her violently and his cry came loud and long. "Nooooo!"

Megan had no difficulty imagining how he felt. To lose Sandro would hurt her so much she still wasn't sure she could bear it. "Jack, I can't tell you how sorry I am and how I didn't want to tell you. But if I didn't tell you that might be even more unkind."

He lifted his arm and gave her the finger. "How do you know how I feel?"

She reverted to telepathy. *This they didn't know. They mustn't. Because Sandro's dying, Jack. He has two years, max, and they won't be good years. That's how I know.*

God. His inner voice came hollow and empty and he rolled on his back, turning his head to meet her anguished gaze, his own filled with tears for his lost love. "So what do we do now, Megan? How do we manage?"

"The way we always have. Friends, supporting each other. We've been here before, Jack."

"Yes." They both thought of Paul for a moment and Megan knew she'd always remember him with fondness. But she'd moved on. "Sandro—I love him so much, Jack!"

"Yes."

"We need to get out of this first." *Are you badly hurt?*

I was but I shape-shifted. I had a broken bone in my arm. That's mended now. Not completely healed but it'll do.

Can you fight?

Oh yeah. To the death.

No, Jack. Not you as well. I can't bear it. Too much for her. Love meant so much. So did friendship.

Hey. His inner voice sounded softer now, as though he were hugging here. *Friends, Megan. Always.*

Yes, Jack. We always end up holding each other's hands, don't we?

We do. His response was warm but held a dryness she valued in Jack. So he'd decided to fight. He'd better.

We're getting out of here. The primary objective is to rescue the prisoners. Then we want to try to stop them destroying the hardware. That could take us to other labs, other prisoners.

Us? Jack's amused tone kept her grounded. Kept her sane.

Us. I'm with them. Are you?

I don't know. Right now I'm so confused I daren't go deep.

She knew exactly what he meant. Right now she didn't want to think further than the next few hours.

Jack rolled so they nestled close and they took warmth from each other. Pressing a quick kiss to his forehead, she took strength from their closeness, their warmth. They were close enough to murmur now, and although telepathy was the safest option, it was still too new to her for her to feel comfortable using it all the time. "Thanks, Jack."

"You're welcome." The edge of distraction in his voice told her he was thinking about Carilla.

"Don't, Jack. Not yet. Later we'll grab a drink and talk about it. Lots of drinks."

"Promise?"

"You bet." She tried to smile but found the corners of her mouth wavering.

"Don't. You don't want to see a grown man cry." Despite the bantering tone, she heard the sob at the back of it all and had no doubt she and Jack would cry together. That wouldn't be for the first time either.

But not here, not now.

So what now?

We improvise. Sandro leads from in here, Chase from outside.

Okay.

The minutes ticked by and slowly her tension climbed to screaming point. When the door opened she nearly leaped out of her skin but Jones' low chuckle brought her right back down to earth.

"So, Megan Armstrong, we'd like to know just how you could contact Ricardo Gianetti when this building is state-of-the-art secure."

Slowly, taking her time, she rolled over to face the loathsome man. "I don't know." She gave him a sweet smile for good measure.

He raised a shaggy brow. "You're going to be reasonable?"

She shrugged. "Why shouldn't I tell you? It's a complete mystery to me. I honestly don't know."

Jones frowned down at her. "We saw the notes STORM made about you, the results of the tests you took. They show nothing except an ability to receive telepathic messages, which is probably the most common there is. But you can receive at ultra-high frequencies. We're only beginning to understand the way telepathy works and you could be a key. Megan, you're one of us, not one of them. Help us."

He didn't sound very conciliatory, more dictatorial, even though his words were soft. As if she had no choice. She kept her voice low and added a tremble. "Do you think they mean us harm?"

"Oh yes. Talents will take control if we're not careful. Humans are weak, so we need all the weapons we can find. So you, a human, have a gift we haven't come across before. If you can help us, that will give us an advantage."

"So what if I agree to help? What do you want to do?"

He pursed his mouth in thought and checked his clipboard, more for something to do than for real information. She knew he was going to lie to her.

"You will take part in some controlled experiments with Gianetti. Maybe with both of them, now we have the set."

"The set?" It took her a moment to get his meaning.

"Siblings." Jones glanced at her and the excitement in his eyes was unmistakable. "They're rare, you know, or they hide themselves very well. But they're our first. We can extract DNA, find out if they have the same patterns as normal people and maybe find out what makes them different. That would give us the advantage. To have their extra strength, their extra lifespan."

"But wouldn't that make *us* into *them?*"

Jones tsked. "No. It would make us more than human but still human."

"I see." Megan frowned. "I need to think about this."

"I thought you might say that. I'll prepare the siblings. One way or another we need to get started."

She swallowed. "If I agree to this, will you put off the—worst experiments?"

He sneered at her. "Soft-hearted, are we?"

"I saw what you did. I don't want to see that again." Try as she might, she couldn't take the edge of repulsion out of her voice.

Pursing his thin lips, he stared at her in an expressionless, chilling way before giving a brief nod. He believed her. After checking his clipboard again, he made a note. "We could leave the other procedures until after the telepathy experiments."

"Take me to them. Let me see."

She didn't stretch out her mind to his. She didn't need to, she merely put herself into his shoes. Jones still didn't trust her but why should he? She'd become Sandro's lover, despite knowing he was a shape-shifter. He still couldn't be sure what side she was on or if she could be persuaded.

An assistant stepped cautiously forward and sliced through the bonds holding their ankles together. After handing the knife to the doctor, he went to her head and gripped her under the armpits, hauling her to her feet. He managed to cop a feel as well, cupping a breast and squeezing hard before releasing her suddenly.

Megan was determined not to stagger, despite the pins and needles in her legs threatening to drop her where she stood. She bore the pain, wishing she could shape-shift. She wasn't at all sure that, when the time came, she could do it. Sandro couldn't shape-shift but could he help her?

Only one way to find out.

The man didn't linger over Jack as he had over her but dragged him to his feet and let go as if he were poison. Jack staggered before taking a wide-legged stance to keep his balance. His face remained stoic but she saw a twitch as he set his jaw against the inevitable cramp after lying so long on a hard stone floor. She sent a message, right to a spot deep inside him, and watched their captors. The message didn't matter—what did was their reactions.

Nothing.

She managed to suppress her sigh of relief.

"Let's go."

Jones led and his goon followed them. Despite his white jacket, the man was a goon, no more a doctor than she was. Megan would put money on him not knowing what to do with a stethoscope but she wouldn't bet against his dexterity with a knife, sterile or not.

The hallway outside was gray, long and featureless, with several doors leading off it, some with small glass panels set in them, some with spy holes. Megan didn't look to the right or the left, although she supposed a good agent would but she was too afraid she'd see something else that would haunt her nightmares.

At the end of the hallway was another, equally featureless, but halfway down, Dr. Jones produced a key and unlocked a door before standing aside to let them in. She didn't hear him lock the door behind them.

Sandro lay in a bed, naked under a thin sheet. She could see the outline of his cock, lying soft against his thigh, and his bare feet poked out the end. Ricardo lay where he always had, in his bed nearer to the door. Her throat tightened when she saw the room exactly as in her dream. She was standing more or less where she always stood, by the door, staring at Ricardo.

"Hi," he said, and he smiled, breaking her heart.

"I'm glad they let you heal."

He nodded. "They were saving me for when they caught Sandro." *Can you hear me?*

Yes. She felt a small mental caress, as if he'd hugged her. *Welcome to the family.*

Faint pink lines criss-crossed his arms, reminders of the terrible injuries he'd suffered. Similar, deeper red ones adorned his chest

Fire boiled in her gut, threatening to burst forth in sheer, unthinking rage. She had to hold everything she was carefully inside her. And it wasn't the dragon, it was the woman, forced to watch and do nothing. Well today that would change. Dragon and woman, both would make these sadists pay.

She clenched her fists, digging her nails into her palms to give herself a bite of pain. Rage wasn't her friend, not now. Not yet.

But it would be.

Chapter Fourteen

Ricardo gave her the heartbreaking smile of reassurance she'd seen so often in her dreams. "Hey, kid, nothing's ever that bad."

His voice, not quite as low as Sandro's, clearer, with a lilting quality all his own.

"Hey." She didn't know what else to say because sometimes it *was* that bad. She could only pray the electronic bugs still worked because she couldn't break through to the outside world to contact Chase. From here on in, they'd have to work blind, not knowing if anyone else knew where they were or if they'd get here on time.

She recited the objectives of the operation, centered herself on it. Talents first, and if there were enough, if they were in any state to fight back, they wouldn't need Chase and the rest of the cavalry. Then save the computer hardware. Third, capture the staff.

Capture, hell. These bastards weren't going anywhere.

She avoided looking at Jack. She didn't need to look at him to understand him and their captors hadn't detected their telepathic communication. *I think we take the doctors and the assistants now. Sandro and Ricardo can help once we free them.*

Sure. Can you do it without them calling for help?

We wait until we can. Until they're close.

"What now?" Jack asked, his voice flat.

Dr. Jones smiled.

Then Sandro turned his head and locked gazes with her. From his expression she knew the Sandro she loved had gone, perhaps forever. Now the professional agent was the only one that remained, his mind a calculating machine of risks and probabilities.

Deep inside, she began to mourn.

Jack's sharp tones broke into Dr. Jones' leering. "What are you planning to do?"

Jones' tones smoothed in response. "I have a whole schedule of tests planned." This man was overconfident. That was good for them.

"This isn't war," Jack continued.

"Yes it is." At last the doctor moved, walking across the room to stand at the foot of Sandro's bed. "And these — things — are animals. Less than animals. But they have so much wealth locked up inside them." He shoved Sandro's bare foot. Sandro let it flop to one side and stared at the doctor expressionlessly.

"Have you seen them change?" Megan stood completely still. She braced her feet, bending her knees slightly to allow for flexibility and balance.

"A couple of times. Disgusting. But bearable, if one gets the other benefits." The doctor consulted his clipboard and she felt a definite disturbance in the atmosphere. Strange to describe but his aura, his space, seemed to ripple. He was afraid of them in their other form or of watching them shape-shift. Good.

She tried a gentle probe. Nothing too much, because he would probably detect it, then she changed her mind, drew back and instead tried to touch the goon's mind. They could take the doctor easily, even with both hands tied behind their backs. Which was the truth.

Jack?

Yeah?

I'll take the goon in the white coat, you go for the beds and get the guys free.

Sounds like a plan.

The idiot was wide open. Was he so arrogant he didn't think he needed mental shields or didn't the staff here care enough about their muscle to look after them properly? Either way, that was their best break. They'd be criminal not to take advantage of it.

She wasn't a criminal. Concentrating hard, she developed an image of a fine, steel blade, sharp enough to slice a hair floated over its surface.

Yes, she thought as she saw the dark hair split into two when it drifted over the blade. Perfect. It glinted as she turned it, pointed it. And pushed it straight into the mind of the man standing behind her.

She sprang up to kick him under the jaw, prepared for a counterstrike that wasn't long in coming.

The man screamed in pain and his hands went up as if he didn't have to think about it, reaching for her foot. She deflected, trying for anything she could reach, and struck.

He grabbed her, twisting her foot painfully, wrenching to break her ankle. So Megan did the only thing she could. She shape-shifted.

True, her full dragon size was larger than this room but maybe she wouldn't do too much damage. She concentrated on halving herself, shrinking. It only partly worked. Over twenty feet from head to tail full-sized, she managed to get herself small enough not to crush the room's occupants. Except for the bodyguard who didn't have time to scream before she crushed him against the wall next to the door.

Moving aside, she went for his neck with her claws and felt the soft flesh give. Savage triumph filled her veins.

Just as well blood didn't faze her because there was a lot of it now, spurting from the artery in the man's neck. She turned away and shape-shifted, faintly surprised at how easy the process had become. Maybe fury or tension or sheer adrenaline helped the change just as it sharpened perception.

Only then did she realize the men were free and the doctor on the floor, his head lying at an unusual angle. Jack looked different with claws, sharp, curved ones that retracted as she stared, fascinated at them. He was staring at her. "You know you're naked," he said, his voice warming a little. But not enough. His eyes were still haunted. She longed for that look to leave him but it wouldn't. Not for a long time.

Any humor she might have felt drained out of her and she turned to catch Jones' white coat that Ricardo threw at her. Jack must have had time to slash the leather straps holding the Gianetti brothers down because they were both on their feet now. The guy she'd just killed had clothes but they were a bit too messy to consider stealing. Her own clothes lay shredded on the floor. "I'm beginning to feel like the bloody Hulk," she said.

"A lot more good-looking," Ricardo said warmly. She caught the glance he shot Sandro but the older dragon had no response for him. The humanity of the man was locked up deep inside where even she couldn't pierce. The open, loving person of the night before last was as distant as if it had happened last year or ten years ago. In his place was the cool, powerful commander, the man with astute, dark eyes quickly assessing the situation and coming to a conclusion.

"I haven't had word from Chase, so I have no idea if we have backup or not. But we can fight and with two functioning shape-shifters on our side we can get through. Remember the objectives. We stay together unless I order the split, and listen to me—we do as I say at all times. No maverick actions, no heroic gestures. Understand?" His impartial gaze swept them all.

They nodded.

"Jack and Megan, you're in control of your abilities. Keep in touch with us mentally and try to contact the others, though I think this place is locked off. It has to be sonic. Somewhere there's a machine, probably with a backup and once we take that out we can contact other Talents outside." He glanced at

Megan. "They'll have put a silver mesh or paint around the crate. Some Talents are allergic to silver and unfortunately I'm one of them. And since I gave you my Talent, that will work for you too."

His dark, impersonal gaze flicked past her to the door. "We have a little time. I want to move out of this room in the next five minutes, so here's what we do. Try to take them alive. Try not to kill but if you have to, don't hesitate. It's them or us. Understand? Anyone have any idea of the way out?"

They shook their heads. Even unable to shape-shift form, Sandro Gianetti was a powerful man. Her gaze drifted to his bare buttocks and her memory gave her a mental image. Her hands digging in as he made love to her with all the intensity in his heart. She couldn't give that up. Not yet. She'd do everything she could to ensure he got out with her.

His face was set in grim lines. "We're going out of here fighting. When you drop somebody, make sure they're not going to get up again but keep going."

"This unit can't be very large," Jack frowned in thought. "The sleep clinic is only one block. They could have some of the building next to it but that's not large either. And we're close to the ground."

"Good, because only one of us can fly," Sandro replied. He glanced at her. "Which, if you get in trouble, is what you do. Shape-shift and fly. Take Ricardo out with you if you can. Jack can shape-shift and run."

"What about you?" Jack asked.

Nobody answered. She exchanged a quick look with Ricardo. He returned her regard with a grave nod. He knew.

"Jack first, I'll go next, then Ricardo, then Megan. When we're out of here, we go right. Then keep going. Liberate all the Talents we can and head for the entrance or the exit. Clear?"

"Good plan," Jack muttered but went to the door. They took their places before Jack opened the door and went out. They followed close behind, careful not to lose sight of each other.

It was anticlimactic at first. Nobody approached them for the length of maybe ten seconds but when they got to the next glass-paneled door in the hallway, all hell broke loose.

Jack opened the door and somebody screamed. Although he leaped in and stifled the sound, someone else must have been inside too, because almost immediately came the high-pitched wail of an alarm.

The deafening electronic scream, meant to temporarily paralyze the intruder, had the effect of paralyzing everyone, freezing them in their places.

Sandro recovered first and the sound of soft thuds inside the room heralded more white-coated technicians hitting the floor.

A soft groan told them of another occupant. Sandro and Jack came out of the room. Jack's face was pale and Sandro's mouth was set in a hard, grim line. "That Talent can't help us now but maybe if we can get help, we can save him. Maybe."

Megan avoided looking into the room as they went past.

The hallway opened at both ends onto crossways passages and around the corners poured security staff, their dark blue uniforms sickeningly familiar to Megan and Jack. Three nude people, one of them female, made a couple temporarily pause but that lasted all of half a second. Long enough to spread out and take on their attackers.

Megan found the fight almost too easy. Three hard strikes with a satisfactory sensation of hard bone against soft flesh and both guards coming at her lay on the ground, unconscious. By her side, Ricardo proved equally efficient. Then they had weapons because the guards carried firearms.

The alarms cut off with a vicious abruptness, leaving her ears ringing.

"Why didn't they shoot us?" she wondered, only after remembering to lower her voice. She must have deafened Ricardo.

He didn't complain. "Probably under orders to do as little harm as possible. Look." He shoved a guard's hand aside with his foot, revealing a primed syringe. "They expected us to be weak. A woman and three men, two of them pumped full of various drugs, and they wanted to capture us. Not that easy though, was it?" His mouth slid into a slight, wicked grin. "I'm a better actor than I thought." She noticed blood staining the fresh white bandage covering one of his arms but that hadn't slowed him down any.

Ricardo lifted the gun and fired. A guard hurtling around the corner fell hard. In the aftermath, she heard Sandro's disgusted snort. "I said alive."

"Can't preserve them all," Ricardo said. "Besides, that one deserved to die."

After that the guards came thick and fast and they downed them all, working their way up the hallway. It seemed to go in slow motion, each man going down like a stylized puppet in a video.

But at the end of the hallway things went a little crazy. If it hadn't been for Sandro flinging out his arms and stopping their forward impetus they might have walked straight into the ambush waiting for them.

The first they knew was a bullet zinging past them to bury itself into the wall just above Megan's head as she moved to the other side of the hallway.

"Jesus!" from Sandro. "Down!"

Since they all had firearms and there were more on the six security staff lying slumbering or dead behind them, the firefight could have gone on until one of them was killed. So Megan judged it time for her to go into action, and besides, she was getting tired of men gawping at her naked body.

She shape-shifted. It wasn't as easy this time. Her system had settled into a pumping, adrenaline-filled rhythm and she had to concentrate, as Sandro had taught her. The thought of how he'd taught her broke her attention and she had to start again.

Then she had it. She felt the scales forming and that strange feeling of *growing*. This time she managed to keep herself to about half her size, and before she remembered his detachment from her, she turned to show Sandro. He pursed his lips and nodded. "Good idea. Stay that way."

Because she wouldn't be hurt. Not because she could hurt others that much better.

A chill that had nothing to do with her new form crept through her bones. He really meant to do this. How would she manage without him? Who would wake her in the mornings, laugh at her attempts at cooking, then kiss her and make her sit while he showed her how to flip an omelet?

Nobody, that was who.

Shoving the thought aside, she walked into the corridor. Nice sharp intakes of breath and a few gasps rewarded her before a sting in her side alerted her to the presence of one of those white-coated nuisances. She roared, the first time she'd tried that, and almost stunned herself with its force. With a casual swipe of one clawed arm, she swept the man and his syringe aside. "Stop it, you idiots!" she heard an irascible male voice snarl. "You want it to stay like that? Go for the kill, gentlemen. We have two dragons, we can afford to waste one!"

So they didn't know that much. She forged forward, pausing to hit out at anyone who tried to shoot her or stop her. One idiot even walked forward and threw his hand up, as if he was a cowboy facing a Red Indian in an old-time movie. Well unlike the actors playing the natives, she was for real, not a heavily made-up fake.

In the course of the next five minutes, she proved it. They passed through two more hallways, and with Jack in his jaguar form, between them they could pause to go into the rooms and deal with any of the technicians lurking in there with syringes and scalpels.

At the end of the second hallway lay a smaller one and at the end of that, another door. No rooms led off it. It could be a trap.

Sandro glanced up both parts of the hallway. His eyes narrowed and Megan entered his mind to read his thoughts. *Why aren't there any people coming at us from there?*

A moment and he'd made his decision. "That way!"

He led and she backed up but the hallway narrowed and she found she couldn't reduce her size any more. So she shape-shifted back to human. Now that she had the knack of it, she could shape-shift back once through the door if she needed to.

The door exploded open. She wasn't looking but she guessed someone had kicked it. Her money would be on Sandro. She backed up, glancing over her shoulder to make sure she wasn't going into something worse. With guards on their tails, they spilled out into the new environment.

"Shit, we're out!"

Sensations flooded into her brain and for a moment she found it difficult to control her reaction. Voices spoke in her head and then one became clearer. Chase. *I've got you! On our way.* A brief pause. *ETA ten minutes.*

She stepped forward and stared around. A dozen pairs of eyes stared back at them, belonging to a group of people seated on plastic chairs and one woman sitting behind a receptionist's desk under a sign suspended from the ceiling reading "Enquiries".

"We're out," she breathed. "I've been here many times. We're in the main sleep clinic."

"Bet you've never been here naked before," Ricardo said laconically.

She couldn't help it. Her laughter rose up unbounded, fueled at least partially by relief. "Only in my dreams!"

Jack, now back in human form and also completely naked, gave a howl of unrestrained laughter. They were out, they'd found the clinic and help was on the way.

Until the guards burst through the door and showed no signs of slowing down.

"Everybody out!" somebody yelled. "These people are dangerous!"

Their audience needed no more warning. They surged to their feet with a clatter of chairs and accompanying screams. Megan, caught in the real-life situation of a well-known nightmare, feared her mind might fragment any minute. She could feel everyone in her head, her wide-open mind vulnerable to any nuance, and standing naked in a place she knew well, had visited twice a week since her nightmares began, wondered if anything was real.

A hand clasped her lower arm and she didn't have to look down to know who it was. "It's real, Megan. It's all real." His voice, meant for her alone, purred through her and she felt her nerves steady. His hand, warm and so desired, stopped her skittering senses and brought her back down to this place, this time and the danger they were still in.

"We need to get out of here."

"We need to get through them to get out of here."

Half a dozen guards now stood between them and the open air. The doors could have been locked but as she recalled, the university security was hardly state-of-the-art. Besides, Chase had locked into her. She felt him, a presence in her mind, firm and reassuring.

"Here we go again," Jack muttered but it wasn't quite the same this time. Every guard held a gun, and they were all pointed at them. Jack shape-shifted, fluidly rippling into the large cat and Megan followed suit, planning to stand between Sandro and the guns, but as she shape-shifted she saw more guards. "How many of those bastards do we have to kill?" she wanted to say but her vocal chords had already gone beyond speech and what came out was a muted roar.

Interesting. The guards on her side stood back. She roared again and watched them move. This time forward, some lifting their guns to aim at her throat. Just where St. George was supposed to have skewered his dragon, she remembered wryly.

Jack, now a jaguar-god, larger than the animal but just as intimidating, golden fur shading into creamy white on his underbelly and dark brown rosettes traced around the whole, stood on the other side of Ricardo and Sandro. As a jaguar shape-shifter, he was just as invulnerable as the dragon, so his protective shield was just as effective as hers.

The guards fired so she crouched to cover Ricardo and Sandro from the front and the bullets bounced off her hide.

How wonderful! Exhilaration filled her, despite their situation. They were going to get out of this alive. The guards fired again, this time from the other side and Jack roared, the sound higher than her full-throated deep cry but just as intimidating.

But they had accustomed themselves, it seemed, because the next volley came faster. She felt Sandro giving orders but after hearing *Megan, stay put,* listened only peripherally to the others, giving their attackers more attention. They were spreading out. No doubt they hoped to come at her front and back. Well, she was wise to that and, sure she could still get them with a lunge and one sweep of her tail, she'd let them play.

She watched. Someone took a photo. She didn't bother to look in the direction of the flash, as it could well be a diversionary tactic.

Sandro gave the word, yelled into their minds. *Now!*

And they moved. Megan took two guards out with a massive sweep of her tail while yells and shots mingled with

The demand, louder than a shout, echoed in her head and in unthinking obedience, she shape-shifted back to Megan.

She slipped and fell into a pool of blood. "Shit, I didn't think..." Faintness assaulted her, a black dizziness that warned her she wouldn't last much longer. But when she put her hand to her throat, she found a small cut, fairly deep but easy to staunch in her human form. She put her hand over the wound and pressed. Almost immediately the seepage lessened.

"Go." Sandro touched her arm and stroked his finger along her pulse in an unmistakable lover's caress. She stared at him and for one fraught moment she met his dark gaze. Love joined them, total, unfathomable and complete. There was no need for words.

Two shots rang out and two more came from behind her head, the succession so fast she didn't hear them as separate shots. She felt the hot zing of metal across her arm. She looked away instinctively and when she looked back, Sandro was on the floor. Blood pooled around him, his and hers, and she felt rather than saw someone behind her. Whirling around, she confronted the familiar face of Chase.

Her relief enormous, she watched, shock making everything move in slow motion, as Chase bent to Sandro's naked, bloody body. He glanced up, flicking his hair out of his eyes with a jerk of his head. "Grab an arm and let's go!"

Nobody shot at them as they dragged Sandro through the gory mess out of the building. Because nobody was left standing, except Megan herself.

Chapter Fifteen

ಐ

"I can't believe this." Ricardo strode from one end of the hospital room to the other and back again. He raked his fingers through his hair, a gesture that reminded Megan achingly of Sandro. The man lying in the bed might never do that again.

So cold, so still. Sandro lay on his back, attached to pumps and tubes. Monitors beeped at regular intervals. The bullet had struck his heart and now it was a matter of time. No one could save him using conventional methods. All they could do was keep pumping blood into him to replace the blood leaving him and wait until the Cephalox wore off. Then he could heal for himself.

If he wanted to. So far he hadn't regained consciousness.

She sat next to him, watching his chest rise and fall in the machine-aided breathing. Every half hour the doctor tested his blood, and shook his head. "We'll give it another half hour," he said every time and went away again after saying, "Call me if there's any change."

There hadn't been. Ann Reynolds had called, promising to come in later in the day. She was busy facing the press. It was hardly likely the destruction of the hospital sleep lab wouldn't stay out of the news, especially when STORM was involved, so Ann had to give the Talents' side of the story. She was arranging for some of the rooms, now clear of the Talents who'd been tortured in them, opened for media scrutiny. It might help in the upcoming discussion and in Congress, necessary to give Talents the same rights as other people.

Not that Megan cared. Her world had shrunk to watching one chest rise and fall, terrified the next one would be the last. If she stopped watching, he might die. She'd tried pushing her mind into his but he was completely asleep, aided by the drugs the doctors pumped into him.

This wing of the Mount Sinai hospital had been here for years. Privately endowed, believed by the world at large to be a specialist heart unit, it was a vivid example of how Talents had lived until recently. Hiding in plain sight, Ann called it. Now they didn't need to hide. The world was fresh and new.

Except for Sandro. Just as this new phase was starting, he was dying.

Ricardo broke into her thoughts. "He's from a different age, my brother. He thinks chivalry isn't dead." He gave a mirthless laugh. "Well, it's nearly killed him. You mean he didn't even tell you about bonding?"

The machine monitoring Sandro's heart leaped and they both froze, staring at it. After a fraught moment it resumed its regular rhythm.

Megan took a shaky breath. "He told me nothing. He says he's dying and Ann says it's true."

"Fucking knight errant," Ricardo muttered. "Do you want me to tell you what he decided not to about bonding?"

She glanced away at him, then straight back to Sandro's chest. Ricardo was handsome, his face leaner than Sandro's, slighter in build but that wasn't saying much. In the borrowed t-shirt and jeans, he looked super-hot, his dark hair brushing his shoulders, his eyes pools of passion. But not for her. She only wanted one man now and he lay on the bed, unconscious.

"Tell me," she said grimly. "If there's the slightest chance, I want to know."

"Yeah." Ricardo continued his pacing. "I feel like shit telling you because he obviously didn't want you to know but you will find out one day and then you'll feel like shit because he kept it from you." The sound of his footsteps stopped. "That's it. I can't live with myself if I don't tell you. Because you *will* find out and then you'll never know if it would have worked or not. Okay, babe."

He dragged a chair to the other side of the bed and sat where she could see him without taking her attention from the rise and fall of Sandro's chest.

"So here it is."

* * * * *

Sandro opened his eyes. He was staring at a white, featureless ceiling and the smell of antiseptic lay in his nostrils. A hospital, unless Heaven had some kind of waiting room.

No, he was still alive. Disappointment filled him and when he heard her voice he knew what hell felt like.

"Sandro?"

He turned his head and cautiously tried to move one arm. It lifted with no restraints. "Hi." He couldn't smile yet.

"Hi." She didn't smile either. "Why didn't you tell me?" She looked away, fiddled with a carafe and glass. "Would you like some water?"

"Yes and why didn't I tell you what?"

She turned back, the surface of the water in the glass trembling. "I'm sorry, forget I said anything. Just sit up and drink the water."

"I won't forget anything. Where's Ricardo?"

She put the glass down and stood to help him sit. Although parts of him creaked into action—the results of old age rather than his injuries, he suspected—he seemed to have recovered from the shot that had ripped through him with the power of a Jovian bolt of lightning. "Start by bringing me up to speed."

She held the glass to his lips. He took it from her, deliberately gripping the glass at the base so they wouldn't touch. He wasn't ready to add touch to the sensations racing through his brain, at least not touching Megan. A surge of love left him in no doubt, if he'd ever had it, that she was the woman for him. He longed to take her in his arms but was terrified it would lead to more, and things he should have the courage to end. If the operation was over, he had no more excuse to stay. His time was over. He had to face reality and go.

"You've been under for two days. You nearly died, Sandro."

"I know. I wanted to die. It would have been cleaner, Megan."

She swallowed but didn't take her gaze away from his. "I couldn't leave you behind, Sandro. You shouldn't have asked me to."

"I was afraid of that. So you got me out?"

"Chase helped. You were bleeding out and they couldn't shape-shift you, so they did first aid on you, then brought you here and just kept you going until the Cephalox wore off. Then they shape-shifted you and kept you sedated until you healed."

He gave her the glass, empty now, and this time didn't avoid contact. She shivered and turned to put the glass down. "Do you want any more?"

"Not right now. Where's Ricardo?"

"He left when he was sure you were okay. Better, he said, that we talk together first." She wouldn't look at him.

"So are you getting on with him?"

She smiled, shaky but he was glad to see it. "Yes. We think we were able to communicate because we can both hear dog whistles."

He blinked. "Say that again."

"We can both hear very high-pitched sounds. Simple as that. He tried using a channel at the highest end of his capacity and the lab was blocking telepathy using a sonic field."

"Not silver."

"No. You were right about the crate, that had silver inhibitors built in to it but not the lab."

He purposely kept the discussion on the impersonal. She was close to breaking. He didn't try to enter her mind. He didn't need to. He saw her tension in every shaking digit, every nervous movement of her head, looking around at nothing, then back at him, or rather, at a spot just below his chin. Besides, a suspicion was forming in his mind, something he didn't want to think about right now and he needed the time himself to decide what he'd say to her. "So not soul mates."

She smiled and glanced up at him, a hot, sweet instant of eye contact. "No. Friends. I like him a lot, Sandro. But I think that's because he reminds me of you."

"Give it a chance." He badly wanted to call her "sweetheart" or "darling" but not now. He had to back off, give Ricardo the chance he needed to charm her or he'd have to leave her alone with no one to console her or care for her.

"We talked about it, Sandro. Neither of us thinks there's more than friendship between us." Then she did lift her eyes to his face and he gasped at the intensity of her gaze. Still he didn't enter her mind, though every part of him screamed at him to do it. "Sandro, I love you. That's not going to change and I can't make it. I don't want to. You've given me everything I need. If you walk away now, you'll kill me."

"Baby, I have to." Not wanting to resist anymore, he took her hand and felt the sweetness of body contact. The endearment, the one he hadn't deliberately blocked himself from using, slipped out too naturally. As always, he found her touch intoxicating, and he wanted more, things he couldn't have. It had to end now. "There's nothing left for us, however much we want it."

"There's a chance. Ricardo explained to me about bonding."

He gritted his teeth. The last thing he'd do before leaving America would be to strangle his brother. "The risk's too high, Megan. I won't risk you by trying to bond."

"Why didn't you tell me?"

"I didn't want to put you in that situation." Partly right but he also wanted to protect her, cherish her, as all his instincts screamed at him to do.

"You have no right, Sandro." He opened his mouth to protest but she was still talking. He let her talk. "I'm a dragon now, thanks to you, part of the community, as Ann made clear to me while you were asleep. I'm subject to the same rights and under the same threats as everyone else. So how long do you think it would be after your death before I heard about bonding? And how do you imagine I'd feel then?"

He swallowed. Things had moved so fast recently he hadn't thought that one out. She'd been a shape-shifter for so short a time—before that she would have left the shape-shifter world behind, an outsider again, and there'd have been a good chance she never heard about it but now—

She was right. She would have heard about bonding and she might have hated him for not telling her. "I'm sorry," he said. "I know that's inadequate—"

"Yeah," she said and cleared her throat. "Sure but never mind that." She gripped his hand tighter. "Sandro, I've been thinking."

"I was afraid of that. You tend to turn everything on its head when you think."

She smiled. "I do, don't I? Well, I'm not about to change now. I want to bond with you, Sandro."

He had a feeling she was going to say that. "No. No, sweetheart. The risk's too great."

"Let me see if I got this right." She frowned and he longed to kiss it away but that might not be wise under the circumstances. Not when he was planning to disappear from her life. "The chances are good. When a couple bonds, it's more often the longer life they adopt."

"We don't get the choice, sweetheart. You could end up with my lifespan, what there is left of it."

"Even less now." She glanced away, down at their linked hands and he knew she was about to tell him something bad. "Apparently, some of the drugs they managed to get into you before we got to you aren't good for someone in your condition. They've accelerated the process."

"How long?" he managed in a voice suddenly gone dry.

"Six months, they said, maybe a few more. Not a year."

It took courage to tell him that, so much courage. He didn't realize how much until she lifted her head. The expression in her eyes tore him apart. If he ever doubted her love, he'd be convinced of it now. This wasn't a short-term, half-assed thing, an obsession with something glamorous and different. He'd had that before, plenty of times. Megan saw right through to the man underneath all the shapes, all the training, all the lives, and that was what she loved.

He loved her the same way.

And because he loved her, he couldn't let her do this. "Put yourself in my place." He fought hard to keep his voice steady, refusing to give in to all the urges to pull her into his arms, take her now, while he still could, one more time before he walked away. "I've had a good life, one—two loves, many lovers and I'm happy to go. How do you think I'll feel if I take you with me? You've only just started, Megan, there is so much for you to do, to see. I know the statistics too. In seventy percent of cases, when a couple bonds, they take the lifespan of the youngest person. But that means in thirty percent of cases, they take on the older lifespan. That's me, in case you were in any doubt. And you just told me I have less than a year left. Nuh-uh, no way. You also know that to bond, both participants have to consent. Well I don't."

Tears shone in her eyes, tears she didn't try to hide or wipe away. "Sandro, I love you. I loved Paul too and he was taken from me on the brink of happiness. We held ourselves back, did the right thing, so we could love, free and clear. When I was finally no longer his student, no longer had any reason to keep us apart, he upped and died on me. I don't want that to happen again. I *know* how it feels for that to happen, and long life or not, that's something I'll never get over. Not twice. I managed it the first time but I moved countries, got professional help and effectively cut myself off from intimacy and love. Jack and I are friends, we always knew that, so by sticking with him, letting others think what they wanted to, I deliberately stopped anyone else getting close to me. Until you erupted into my life. And you gave me no choice, Sandro. From that first dragon ride until now I've been hopelessly in love with you. I won't let you die, knowing I could have done something to stop it, knowing the alternative was to spend months with you before we both died. That's what I want, Sandro. What I really want."

His grip loosened on her hand but only so he could link his fingers between hers and draw her close. There was no stopping their kiss now.

He took her mouth, refusing to admit anything else into his mind, living the moment, before he pulled away. "Open your mind," he whispered, his breath coming hotly back at him, reflected off her lips. "Let me see if this is real." He kissed her again, short and sweet. "If there's a scintilla of doubt or of charity in there, I'll get out of this bed now and go where you won't find me. Understand?"

"Yes." She smiled up at him. "It's all yours, Sandro. I'm all yours."

"And no trying to hide anything. I could open all your doors, learn all your secrets if I wanted."

"I have no secrets from you. Not anymore."

She didn't. Awed, he entered her mind with his, now blessedly freed from the chemical restraints of Cephalox. She'd thrown every door open, all her secrets there for him to read. He saw her fears, the ones she kept locked down, the ones she hid from herself, her hopes, her loves. What he didn't see was doubt or the sense that she was doing this for him, not for her. She wanted to bond with him because her life would be over without him. He saw her suffering after Paul's death and felt guilty that Paul had died and he, Sandro, was the recipient of this wonderful bounty. He spared a moment of prayer for the man who'd behaved honorably but still lost everything in the end. He understood.

He stroked her cheek, savoring the soft texture under his fingers. It was selfish of him to think of himself, that he'd die and she'd have to go on without him. She didn't want that. "If you watch another lover die, it'll break you."

"Yes."

It would prove too much for her to bear. She'd have a half-life, maybe spent in and out of psychiatrists' offices and hospitals. Not whole, not complete, as the time with him was. If he made her suffer that, he deserved to die. Not in six months but now.

He took a breath, dizzy at the step they were about to take. "All right. I'll bond with you."

* * * * *

Once he'd made the decision, he felt lighter as if a burden had gone. Even if they ended up with his lifespan, they'd live it to the full and they'd grow old together, she wouldn't have to watch him age and die. That made it better, somehow. But what made his decision right was her. He wouldn't allow her the kind of suffering that his death would cause her, couldn't bear to think about it.

He felt a chime in his mind and he withdrew from hers. "Ricardo wants to know what we decided. Shall we tell him?"

"Yes please." He tugged her hand and she took the short distance between her chair and the bed, the space that took her into his arms where, after all, she belonged.

The door opened and Ricardo came in, followed by Ann. Ricardo strode to the bed and gave them both a hug, enclosing them in his arms for a brief, comradely embrace. Then he kissed Megan's cheek. "I'm glad," he said simply. "You can never be sure how long you'll live. I'm hundreds of years younger than you, Sandro, but you could have attended my funeral if things had turned out differently."

"True." Sandro could grin now, joy slowly filling his heart. How could he feel like this when he had so little ahead of him?

Or so much, she reminded him. She was still in his head, just not as deeply as before. *We can live a lifetime in six months. Or five hundred years.*

He laughed and Ann stared at him as if he'd gone crazy. Perhaps he had. "Would someone mind telling me what is going on here?" she demanded in her best I-am-the-commander tones.

Ricardo straightened up and turned to face her. "Megan and Sandro have agreed to bond."

Ann stared at them uncomprehendingly for a few seconds. That was an eternity for the quick-witted leader of STORM. "No. Oh no. You told her your bad news, Sandro?"

"She's known since just before we were captured," he said, holding Megan close. "I didn't want her thinking she needed to rescue me."

"As it happened, she did," Ann said. "Rescue you, that is." She took a step toward the bed and stood there, immaculate in charcoal-gray and white, her suit a masterpiece of the designer's art. If he liked to design in the military style. "But her decision was rational. You were near the doors, with one unknown shooter left standing. It was a fair risk."

"Yes," Megan said and because he rested in her mind, he saw it too. "We'd taken the guards down. Who shot at us? Who shot Sandro?" He hugged her closer when he felt her distress.

Ann sighed heavily and lifted her hand to her eyes in a gesture of weariness. "Bennett. The bastard got away too. He designed that secret lab, so he built in an escape route. It took him to a different part of the campus, where he mingled with the students long enough to get away. We tried to lock the campus down but there were ways in and out we didn't know about."

"Students always have their own ways in and out," observed Megan. "As does the staff. That university wasn't built with security in mind. They built new bits on to the old bits as they needed them and access was equally haphazard."

"We have an alert out on him. Not only with our people but with the FBI too." Ann shrugged. "The offenses he committed covered more than experimentations with shape-shifters and other Talents."

"So it's out of our hands?"

"Out of yours, certainly." She paused. "Not necessarily mine."

"Did we get the computer hardware?"

"Some of it. Don't worry about that, you're off all cases for now. On sick leave." Her steady look didn't waver as she met his eyes straightly. "Nobody outside this room knows about your problem. When you leave it or when you've done what you plan, let me know the result and what you want to do."

Good of her. "Nobody knows except Chase and Johann and Ca—" No. Carilla was dead. His heart plummeted and despite holding the body of the woman he loved, he remembered the laughing, sassy presence of his teammate and friend. He turned to Megan. "How's Jack?"

"Coping." Her mouth tightened and he didn't need to look at her to see she was near tears.

"We have him and we'll monitor him until he decides what to do," Ann said. Sandro could have sworn he heard a sheen of emotion in her voice, although not many people would detect it. "He won't go back to the university."

"I imagine it's more like a circus at the moment," Megan commented.

"You haven't watched the TV news?" Ann seemed surprised, her carefully plucked brows rising to an elegant arch.

"I've been busy," was all Megan said, with admirable restraint.

"Hmm. You might have found time. I would have done." Sandro would vouch for that. Ann's breast cancer operation five years ago hadn't stopped her insisting on having the news and internet connection in her room. She'd run STORM, then a covert organization, from her hospital room. "To answer your question, yes, it's a circus. We took what we wanted out of it and then let the media in. We let them see the bodies. Oh yes, did you think they would just get rid of Talents once they'd killed them? And the dissection lab, with preserved parts."

No more. Megan's agonized voice in his mind made him interrupt Ann's dispassionate account. He knew Ann wasn't uncaring—she was doing her job, recording, assessing, using the terrible experiences there to help Talents improve their positions. Even more important now. They'd seen these places, closed them down before. He let his mind go back to the first laboratory he'd ever seen. An old shape-shifter even then, the sight had shocked him with its impersonal torture, emotionless and sterile. Megan must feel like that. "So you're busy making TV appearances?"

"And talking to Congress. I've been asked to address it next month." Ann paused once more, gathering her thoughts. "When you know what you're going to do, Sandro, I'd appreciate you telling me. I could use your help in this new situation."

"I'm a bust as a team leader now." He might be a bust as everything except Megan's lover for whatever time they had left. Strange how, once he made the decision, he felt at peace, ready to accept her decision and face whatever was to come together.

"That's not what I need right now. But that will keep. I need to formulate new plans."

He could see her mind veering off, planning, thinking, ticking over with ideas and problems to overcome. That went a long way to explain why a mortal ran STORM and not a Talent. Ann had one of the best mental shields he'd ever come across but he didn't need to read her telepathically. They'd been friends for a long time.

"Go, Ann. I'll keep in touch, I promise."

She surprised the hell out of him by turning back when she reached the door and saying, "Take care. Both of you."

* * * * *

It seemed years since they'd been together in the apartment, not days. So much had happened. But they had to do this now and they agreed they wanted to do it in private. Megan still had no idea what she should do or what he expected of her. Most of the novels she'd read had a kind of ritual, so she supposed they'd recite something to each other. She stood ready, in the middle of the airy living room, chin up, feet together. Just like school. She felt young and untutored, unsure of what exactly she'd agreed to. Bonding involved sharing her life force. A bonded couple would take on one lifespan, would die at the same time. That was why she wanted it but more than that she didn't know.

"Sandro, does this mean we have to live together, that we can never live apart?"

"Do you want to live apart?" He crossed the room to her, a glass of juice in each hand. He gave her one and she took it, sipping the refreshing liquid.

"No but I meant *have* to. For instance, if we have to spend time apart for any reason, will it hurt?"

"Are you having second thoughts?"

She looked up into his dear face. "No." He had to believe her. He remained in her mind now, there for all time.

"It means we open our minds and bodies and join our life forces. One life, one body, one soul."

It sounded perfect.

He smiled. "Finish your drink, then we'll go for it. I know how it's done but it's a first for me too."

"Yeah, right." She finished the drink before she wondered, "Has this anything to do with the ceremony?"

He frowned. "Ceremony? Oh, you mean like marriage or something? That comes later, sweetheart, and you have to let me ask you first. I'm old-fashioned, as you've no doubt noticed."

"I meant bonding."

"No." He gave her a one-sided smile and took her empty glass. "And the drink was because I was thirsty and I thought you'd like one too."

Now she felt stupid.

"No, you're not. Just as nervous as me." He paused on his way back to the kitchen and glanced back at her. "I said a prayer while you were in the shower. I hope you don't mind."

She wasn't particularly religious. "I might have joined you."

He was smiling when he returned to her but she felt his nervousness. They remained open, ready for whatever came next. He took her hand and led her upstairs to the bed. There it lay before them, its plain blue cover a kind of altar cloth in her imagination. This was where they would do the deed then.

His hands on her shoulders, he turned her to him and undid the sash of the pale blue toweling robe she'd donned after her shower. She undid his for him at the same time. They allowed the robes to slide away, leaving them both totally naked. He put his hands over hers as she lifted them, holding them loosely between his in the age-old gesture of prayer. "You don't have to do this. Even now, you can say no."

"We've been through this, Sandro. Decision time came and went." Her resolve remained firm. She knew she'd made the right decision. This was so right.

He clasped her hands and drew them apart, holding them wide while he perused her body. "You are so beautiful, Megan."

"I'm glad you think so. I think you're beautiful too."

Smiling warmly, he pulled her hands, drawing her close until her breasts grazed his chest. "I love you, Megan."

"I love you, Sandro."

He kissed her. Wondering if call and response was somehow part of the ritual, she gave herself up to his kiss. He released her hands, and she curled them around him, feeling the hard muscles of his back under her palms. He held her reverently, as if she were some kind of precious object and his kiss paid homage to her. Touching his tongue to hers in greeting, he stroked it softly and withdrew. When he smiled, he broke her heart.

Without words, he guided her to sit on the bed, then lifted her legs so she lay on the soft cover. He joined her and curved his arm around her shoulders, his other arm loosely around her waist. Face to face, they smiled at each other, calm and relaxed.

"There are no words, *carissima*, no ritual words," he said. She felt his voice through her body, echoing in her mind. "We make love and leave our minds open and willing. Put the desire to bond in the forefront, keep it there. And we'll see what happens. Our marks will heat, we might partially shift. Don't freak, love, I'm here and you're here."

"I'm not afraid. I welcome it, because it will be what I want with all my heart."

The warmth in his dark eyes seared her with its intensity. "It's what I want too."

He rolled them both so he lay on top of her, his upper body weight on his elbows. He lifted and his cock slid between her thighs as she opened to him. It slid inside her, lay just inside her opening.

He stopped moving. "You're a little tight. I don't want to hurt you."

"You won't. You can't hurt me now, Sandro."

He pushed but stopped again. "We have all night. I want to love you, Megan. All night long. Whatever happens, we have tonight."

"And tomorrow," she reminded him as she skimmed her hands across the broad expanse of his back. "One day at a time. It's all we can ever have. Who knows what will come after that?"

"Yes." He slid in a little more. "Today. Here. Now. You're right." For the first time since his capture, he laughed, really laughed out of sheer happiness. She shifted and he gained another couple of inches. "It happened to us so fast, we never really had time to assimilate it. Come away with me?"

"Anywhere."

With a rush, moisture flooded from her and he pushed in all the way.

Her reaction was instantaneous. Pushing her shoulders against the bed, she lifted her hips to join him, closing her eyes to experience the sensation more intensely. Remembering what he said, she put her consent to the bonding firmly at the front of her mind, visualizing a sticky note, a blue one, with her consent and signature and pasting it there. It sounded weird but it worked.

When she opened her eyes again, he was gazing down at her and moving gently inside her. When she tightened her hold on him, he took them into the whirlwind.

No intermediate but right there, into the world of sensation that belonged to them alone. There he was, with her, making the magic and part of it. "This is the only magic we need," he whispered, taking her lips in a ravishing kiss.

Their tongues met as their bodies meshed, he in her, their minds fully open, fully aware. Warmth spiraled into heat, escalated into unbearable tingling and she exploded into orgasm, only dimly aware of Sandro's cry as he joined her.

As if walking through a gauzy veil, which flowed behind them both as they went further into their world, sight became clear and instead of him and her they became *us, one, me.*

At the same time she felt her claws extend. She hadn't intended for that to happen but he'd said be aware, let it happen, so she did but lifted her fingertips away from his back so she wouldn't score him at the height of passion.

They had gone beyond orgasm to a new world made up of color and sensation. Sight, hearing, scent, all was him, bound up with him, part of him. When she felt a warm, scaly surface slide along her body and around her waist she knew it was his tail and he'd responded as she had just done, partially shape-shifting. She saw and felt his wonderment, a kind of greenish-blue in color, clear and fresh. Hers sparkled alongside his and the glow of love surrounded them.

Her thigh heated, and she felt every line of the little dragon inscribed there come to life, burning but without pain. Nothing could touch them here, nothing could hurt them.

Then something appeared, or rather, formed. She seemed to blend with his form, like separate rivulets meeting and forming into a river, flowing toward the ocean, many miles away. They flowed together now and she left Megan behind, becoming one, becoming something new. It felt good, right. True.

* * * * *

She opened her eyes. Like before, she looked straight into his but this time she effortlessly slipped into his mind. No barriers lay between them now. None ever would. They were bound, and when they went on, they would do it together.

They lay still, Sandro still over her, his body in hers, still hard, or perhaps hardened again. She had no way of knowing how long they'd been in their own world and when she looked past the circle of light from the bedside lamp, she realized it had grown dark. "How long?"

He licked his lips. "I have no idea. We got back here around six, so maybe an hour, an hour and a half?" Gazing into her eyes, his smile warmed his face and her heart. "Who cares? It's done, my love. We are one."

"That's what it really means, isn't it? We're one. Together. Different."

"Different," he agreed, lowering his head to kiss her gently. "But the same." He opened his mouth over hers in a more passionate kiss and began to thrust. Their linking was their natural state. Megan wondered if they'd sleep every night like this, and looked forward to it.

There was no tomorrow. Only today.

Epilogue

"I love it here. Can we stay here forever?"

Sandro's hand closed over hers across the small table set between their chairs. "As long as you like, *carissima*."

She smiled warmly at him. "As long as *we* like."

"Yes. More wine?"

She watched the setting sun as he went to the kitchen to fetch another bottle of chianti. Maybe they should have ordered a barrel. She loved the wine of this area, rich and fruity. Tuscany was incredibly beautiful and this house, not the *palazzo* of her imagination but an unassuming farmhouse, set on a rolling hill in the countryside outside Florence, was perfect for a honeymoon.

When she lifted her hand to pick up her glass, the diamond in her ring caught the last rays of the setting sun and glowed warmly in the golden light. Sandro had insisted on formalizing their bonding by a wedding before they left for this place. They'd done it on short notice, just enough time for her family to fly across to watch their daughter marry this beautiful Italian.

Lover, husband and friend. And bonded mate. Could she stay this happy for the rest of her life?

"You will if I can make it so." She hadn't heard him return although his intrusion into her thoughts no longer startled her. Rather, it seemed like the natural way of things and she'd be surprised if he didn't pick up on them. They spoke in a mixture of thoughts and speech when they were alone together, sometimes unaware which method they were using.

"All five hundred years?"

"Probably nearer to four hundred, nine hundred and ninety-nine now." For they'd been lucky. After the hospital examined them and told him the ageing process had now halted, they were sure. Until then they hadn't known whose lifespan they'd taken but it didn't seem as important as it once had. Live for today was their new motto. Each day lasted a lifetime now, savored and enjoyed to the full.

He refilled their glasses and sat down again, stretching out his hand to take hers.

Then they heard the growl of a car. A car with a powerful engine. "I thought we had the only Ferrari in the village?" he said, recognizing the sound.

"Not now, it seems," she said, happy to remain with him and wait to see who else owned a Ferrari. The village was about five miles away but a road curled around the hill. When the sound paused, then resumed, the pitch of the engine telling them the car had changed gear to take in the gentle gradient of the hill, they realized the car was coming to them. They had the only house at the end of this narrow road.

The car negotiated the bend and then they saw it. A red dot, getting ever closer. They waited to see who it was. "Should I get another glass?" she asked.

"Not until we find out who it is. We might not want to offer them hospitality."

Only then did she pick up the prickle of tension in his mind. "Should we be on alert?"

He glanced at her. "I hope those jeans aren't favorites because if this car brings danger, you'll have to shape-shift."

"We both will."

"Yes."

The car drew to a halt before the front entrance of the house. They watched and waited. Footsteps sounding like the tap of heels came around the side of the building toward them.

Sandro relaxed. "I only know one person who would drive a Ferrari up a hill and then walk around the country in high heels." He got to his feet. "I'll get that glass."

He strolled across the grass and Megan watched him give Ann Reynolds a swift hug before indicating their seats and walking on to the house. Ann joined them.

As usual, Megan could tell nothing from her demeanor. She'd learned that Ann kept her emotions locked away, as she did her formidable mind, behind unbreakable mental shields and immaculate makeup. Her short, gray hair lay in a precise bob and her clothes, while more relaxed than the city, were creaseless and stainless. An A-line skirt in pale blue topped by a short-sleeved top in the same color made Ann look immaculate and crisp. Not like Megan's own jeans and soft t-shirt, which she'd worn all day. No stains but plenty of creases. And no bra, she remembered, as she hugged Ann and encountered the hard line of structured underwear.

"You look well, Ann."

"So do you. Rested. Do you feel rested?"

"Why?"

Sandro walked back to them, taking the space between them in effortless strides. He saw Ann seated before he sat on the chair Megan had occupied and pulled Megan down to sit on his lap. "Yes, why, Ann? Not that we're not delighted to see you but what brings you out here? You must be busy from what we've been seeing on the news reports."

Ann picked up her glass and swirled the red liquid around the crystal clear goblet before inhaling the bouquet and sipping. She closed her eyes for a moment of enjoyment and for once she smiled. A small, closed-mouth smile but a smile nonetheless. "You must send me some of this at home, Sandro."

"It's only the local chianti," he said, amusement coloring his deep voice.

"It's fresh and it tastes of Italy. It will probably taste of nothing special in New York. I'd like to bottle all of this." Her usually controlled tones broke a little on the last word. She took another sip before she looked back at them. "I'm sorry. Yes, it's been busy. And frantic."

Sandro curled his arm around Megan tightly as if he knew something was coming. She felt his apprehension and knew their lives were about to change again. Perhaps they wouldn't spend the next four hundred or so years here after all. But they'd always have this time and this place.

"Sandro, I need your help," Ann said abruptly. "And yours, of course, Megan." She finished her wine and put the glass down with a determined click. "Have you ever thought of going into politics?"

Also by Lynne Connolly

eBooks:
Cougar Challenge: Beauty of Sunset
Cougar Challenge: Syechelles Sunset
Cougar Challenge: Sunshine on Chrome
Ecstasy in Red 1: Red Alert
Ecstasy in Red 2: Red Heat
Ecstasy in Red 3: Red Shadow
Ecstasy in Red 4: Red Inferno
Emotion in Motion
Pure Wildfire 1: Sunfire
Pure Wildfire 2: Icefire
Pure Wildfire 3: Moonfire
Pure Wildfire 4: Thunderfire

Print Books:
Pure Wildfire 1: Sunfire
Tempt the Cougar *(anthology)*

About the Author

Lynne Connolly writes for a number of online publishers. She writes paranormal romance, contemporary romance and historical romance. She is the winner of two Eppies (now retitled the EPIC ebook awards) and a goodly number of Recommended Reads etc from review sites.

While these are very gratifying, that isn't why she writes. She wants to bring the stories in her head to life and share them with others, in the hope that they might give her some peace.

She lives in the UK with her family, cat and doll's houses. Creating worlds on paper or in miniature seems to be her specialty!

Lynne welcomes comments from readers. You can find her website and email address on her author bio page at www.ellorascave.com.

Tell Us What You Think

We appreciate hearing reader opinions about our books. You can email us at Comments@EllorasCave.com.

Why an electronic book?

We live in the Information Age—an exciting time in the history of human civilization, in which technology rules supreme and continues to progress in leaps and bounds every minute of every day. For a multitude of reasons, more and more avid literary fans are opting to purchase e-books instead of paper books. The question from those not yet initiated into the world of electronic reading is simply: *Why?*

1. *Price.* An electronic title at Ellora's Cave Publishing and Cerridwen Press runs anywhere from 40% to 75% less than the cover price of the exact same title in paperback format. Why? Basic mathematics and cost. It is less expensive to publish an e-book (no paper and printing, no warehousing and shipping) than it is to publish a paperback, so the savings are passed along to the consumer.

2. *Space.* Running out of room in your house for your books? That is one worry you will never have with electronic books. For a low one-time cost, you can purchase a handheld device specifically designed for e-reading. Many e-readers have large, convenient screens for viewing. Better yet, hundreds of titles can be stored within your new library—on a single microchip. There are a variety of e-readers from different manufacturers. You can also read e-books on your PC or laptop computer. (Please note that Ellora's Cave does not endorse any specific brands.

You can check our websites at www.ellorascave.com or www.cerridwenpress.com for information we make available to new consumers.)

3. *Mobility.* Because your new e-library consists of only a microchip within a small, easily transportable e-reader, your entire cache of books can be taken with you wherever you go.

4. *Personal Viewing Preferences.* Are the words you are currently reading too small? Too large? Too… ANNOYING? Paperback books cannot be modified according to personal preferences, but e-books can.

5. *Instant Gratification.* Is it the middle of the night and all the bookstores near you are closed? Are you tired of waiting days, sometimes weeks, for bookstores to ship the novels you bought? Ellora's Cave Publishing sells instantaneous downloads twenty-four hours a day, seven days a week, every day of the year. Our webstore is never closed. Our e-book delivery system is 100% automated, meaning your order is filled as soon as you pay for it.

Those are a few of the top reasons why electronic books are replacing paperbacks for many avid readers.

As always, Ellora's Cave and Cerridwen Press welcome your questions and comments. We invite you to email us at Comments@ellorascave.com or write to us directly at Ellora's Cave Publishing Inc., 1056 Home Avenue, Akron, OH 44310-3502.

MAKE EACH DAY MORE *EXCITING* WITH OUR

Ellora's Cavemen Calendar

☥ www.EllorasCave.com ☥

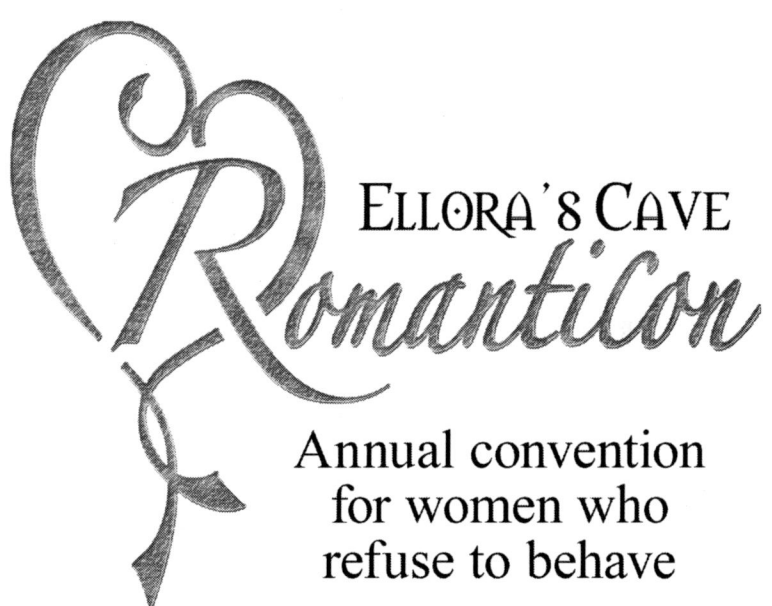

Discover for yourself why readers can't get enough of the multiple award-winning publisher Ellora's Cave.

Whether you prefer e-books or paperbacks, be sure to visit EC on the web at www.ellorascave.com

for an erotic reading experience that will leave you breathless.

LaVergne, TN USA
19 February 2011
217095LV00002B/8/P